Physical Magic

Other books by William C. Tracy

The Dissolutionverse:
Novellas and Novelettes:
The Five Hive Plateau
Tuning the Symphony
Merchants and Maji
The Society of Two Houses
Journey to the Top of the Nether

The Dissolution Cycle:
The Seeds of Dissolution (Book I)
Facets of the Nether (Book II)
Fall of the Imperium (Book III)

Other Books:
Epic Fantasy:
Fruits of the Gods

Anthologies:
Distant Gardens
Farther Reefs
Lofty Mountains
Fiery Deeps
The World of Juno

Science Fiction
The Biomass Conflux
Of Mycelium and Men
Down Among the Mushrooms
To a Fungus Unknown
The Spores of Wrath

Physical Magic

BOOK 1 OF THE SHIFTING LANDS

William C. Tracy

Space Wizard Science Fantasy
Raleigh, NC
www.spacewizardsciencefantasy.com

Cover art by Serene Chia
Lettering by Audrey Logsdon
Editing by Heather Tracy
Book Layout © 2015 BookDesignTemplates.com

Physical Magic/William C. Tracy.— 1st ed.
ISBN 978-1-960247-30-8

Author's website: www.spacewizardsciencefantasy.com

Dedicated to all those years of getting the moves *just* right in Wado Ryu karate, so that I could then figure out *why* I did them.

CONTENTS

CHAPTER ONE

Skulking

Silluka skulked through the alleys of the Huaca, looking for a pocket to pick in the early morning haze. She existed in a tenuous position. Not an undesirable—yet—but also not a full citizen with all the rights accompanying it. She would have to test for that, and if she did, the elders would take one look at her, and at her arm, and fail her. So, she skulked.

Except she only had two days until her eighteenth birthday. It was the last chance for her to test. The last chance to become a citizen, or to get left behind when the Huaca moved inland again. Her people had lived in this Huaca—this place of shelter in the tumultuous earth—since before she was born and before her parents had been born, ever since the coast had fractured and fallen beneath the sea. Now a new coast was slowly rising into a mountain range, heralding the coming of a new island, drawing nearer from out in the boiling ocean.

But none of that mattered, as Silluka was on her own to secure her next meal. Anything to keep from going back to the miserable farm where her brother Ichu barely scraped by, now their parents were gone.

There was a line of old people—easy targets—in the village center, performing the morning ritual, taking the chayu slower than the younger Huaca. The wall of storms hiding the boiling ocean from view made everything damp. The line of rain and thunder surrounded the coast, and this morning, she could barely see the forms of the storm warriors zipping in and out of the wall of water and mist. The extra fog would give her a little cover.

In the village center, the practitioners' hands opened from fists, one finger at a time in *The Wing Grows*. That morphed into open hands moving across the body in *The*

Wind in The Leaves, which became *Raven Spreads Her Wings*, where the arms opened full, then came back together and pushed forward in *Giving Water*. The ritual took five minutes moving quickly, but it could be stretched out to thirty minutes or more when performed slowly, then it could be performed again. And again. Perfection was the goal, placing the body in the exact position to call down the power of the gods. The last move, *Pray*, was always omitted in the morning ritual, to keep that very thing from happening. The Uncles, Aunts and Entles did not look favorably on people trying to steal their power, so it was said.

Silluka rubbed the stump end of her right arm, just past her elbow. There was a nub on one end that might have been a thumb, in a better life, and it was serviceable to hold light things. But it would never perform the graceful finger curls and stretches bodycasting required of a citizen.

Which meant she had no guilt about relieving some of these old slowpokes from their bags of spokes while they did what she could not. What use was keeping money when the whole village would have to move inland again soon? They were penned in, with the desert to the west, the wall of storms to the east and north, and the volcanoes to the south. The desert would become arable in a few more years, their geologists said, as the mountains continued growing from the coast and water began tricking inland from the wall of storms.

Silluka crept forward until she was just behind the last line of elderly Huaca. She set her feet in Basic stance, gripping the ground. She was marginally better at chayus requiring only her feet, but she had never produced the ampuka, the glow from the gods that accompanied the correct performance of a chayu. The sign of a citizen.

They were nearly to *Mossy Rock Leaps the Bank*, the first forward flip in the morning ritual, and Silluka took the time to position her feet and her arms—as much as she could with the right—in the higher position required, not for the morning ritual, but for *Quirra Hides His Nuts*, the perfect chayu to remove things people didn't want removed.

It was best performed in Dexterity or Reflex stance, but Silluka wasn't very good at those. She didn't see the need to practice like the rest of the Huaca, when she would never pass the test. She brought her arms closer, mimicking a quirra's. The chayu wouldn't work for her, not fully, but the motions at least were the right ones to snatch an object in front and bring it in close, hiding it. An old man's spoke purse was right in front of her, and he was tucking his hips under, ready for the forward flip, which put his purse right within reach.

Her left hand, with its quick fingers, shot out...and missed. The old man had moved out of the way, lithe as a grass snake, and glared at her. She saw his eyes flick to her stump and then back, the invariable pity warring with anger in his face.

"Don't make me call the patrol, girl," he whispered. "Just go back to the undesirables, where you belong."

She wasn't an undesirable. Not yet. By all the gods, her brother was the best bodycaster in the Huaca. Stung, Silluka stepped back, her feet reaching for the darkness of the alley, away from the overcast sky.

Yet her eyes lingered on the figures flitting about the wall of storms, barely visible from here. They were the guard of Tiyu Pacha, Uncle Sky, gods unto themselves. They kept the Huaca safe from the worst storms. There was no sense worrying when the next tsunami or tidal wave would come, because the storm warriors would shield them from the worst, or the people of the Huaca would call out with their bodies to Tiyu Pacha and he would protect them. The citizens would.

It was the way of the world. Those who were not in the protection of the Huaca died. In the Huaca, the strong survived. Where did that leave her?

"I wasn't...I was just..." The excuses fell from her as an older woman, with none of the man's pity, pointed.

"Thief!"

The shout made heads turn across the town center, including a group of young bodycasters, led by a familiar figure, who immediately headed her direction.

Hufi. He'd received his citizen chit two years ago. His parents had been friends with hers, when they were both young. Before her parents had been crushed in an earthquake. The last time he'd talked to her, he'd asked when she was planning to test for her citizenship, as if it was something he thought she could ever pass.

Silluka ran, her mind scrambling through every chayu she half-knew. None were good for running and she wasn't good at any of them anyway. The patrol behind her were fit and strong. She was short for her age and thin, without the benefit of regular meals. No wonder she looked like an undesirable.

Fortunately, she knew the alleys of the town, and swung left, slipping in the mud from the ever-present drizzle. The sun came out rarely, this close to the wall of storms.

The patrol was closing already, faster than her. She turned another left, then a right, into a closer alley between two houses. It had exits from both ends, and the houses had low roofs. Plenty of places to escape.

Silluka planted her feet in Basic stance, her whole left arm in front, her stump behind it in a guard. The end was sensitive, but she could give a surprising punch with it.

The patrol panted around the corner, skidding to a stop in front of her. Five of them against a small girl with one hand. Hufi grinned, in the lead, his feet planted in a perfect Dexterity stance, hands already rolling through the matched motions of *Jakua's Claws*, each finger flexing precisely. It was adroitness Silluka couldn't hope to match, and her nose wrinkled in distaste. Hufi had been a pain in her backside when they were little kids, too.

"Stealing again, Silluka?" he said. Talking gave him a chance to finish the chayu. It was a tactic he'd used before.

"Why don't you stay with the old people, Hufi?" she answered. "Maybe they can teach you a few things about speed."

Silluka struck first.

Her punch went wide as his hips shifted him out of the way, but it interrupted his chayu just as the glow of the ampuka was starting to build.

He barely seemed to notice, as one hand, still in a claw, caught her punch and pulled her across his body and toward his cohorts.

Silluka moved with the momentum, trying to slip between a tall, pretty girl and a meaty boy, making sure her stump was up front and in their face. No reaction from the girl, but the boy blanched and fell back, just enough for her to slip through.

She reoriented, scanning the group. The others had rearranged as she turned, and Hufi was halfway through *Jakua's Claws* again. One of the last two, a girl even shorter than her, was performing what looked like *Tortoise's Heavy Foot* from Strength stance. Any strike she made would be amplified with strength given from Tiyu Tiksimuyu—Uncle Earth. The longer this fight lasted, the more the odds were not in her favor. But if she ran now, they would chase her down again, and she would be more tired from the chase.

Instead, she slipped back into the fray, throwing her stump into Meaty Boy's face. She'd pegged him as the most skittish from the beginning. She sidestepped the strong, but slow, blow from the short girl, and reached for the low roof on the right. Just a handsbreadth away.

Hufi's hand grabbed her right bicep, *Jakua's Claws* giving him unnatural gripping strength, fingers digging into her flesh. Silluka gritted her teeth and strained to climb on the roof, but it was like climbing with her arm tied to an iron spike driven into the ground. She glared over her shoulder.

Hufi was surrounded by the ampuka.

His whole body glowed with light from the gods. To have performed a full chayu so quickly, so precisely, spoke of skill far above her own, even barring her stump.

While she strained, Tall Girl and Meaty Boy caught her shoulders and other arm, pulling her away from the roof.

"Don't you have a birthday coming up, Silluka?" Hufi said as he handed her off to his team. "Another few days and you won't be able to test. Then what happens when the village moves inland? The undesirables get left behind, you know."

"I know. I have plenty of time," Silluka said. "Two whole days. I was planning on wowing the elders with something like *Foam Tossed in the Waves* tomorrow."

"Doesn't that require lots of finger movements?" Meaty Boy said. Both Silluka and Hufi stared at him until he looked away, embarrassed.

"Not the brightest patrol they stuck you with, is it?"

"It doesn't take smarts to do a chayu," Hufi said. "Just lots of practice. And two hands. Let's see what the elders do with you."

Silluka sniffed. Hufi had been a brat when he was tugging at his mother's heels, and he was a brat now.

They let her walk to the town center, where the elders' building was, and didn't try to carry her. She wasn't concerned about being brought up for stealing. It had happened before. She would be assigned some community work—which she would do halfheartedly—then everyone would pretend to forget they didn't provide for those less fortunate in the Huaca.

No, the issue, as she and Hufi both knew, was that her eighteenth birthday was in two days. Once they realized who she was, they wouldn't care if she was stealing, or even if she was feeding the old people to the jakuas. The elders were getting ready for the next migration, which meant they were sorting the Huaca into who would go and who would stay. Who was a citizen, and who was not. They'd be forcing every young person in the town to test.

Which was why Silluka didn't struggle as at least two of the patrol kept hold of her shoulders or upper arms at all times. She didn't let herself even contemplate escape. Better to let them think she was defeated.

"Why steal, Silluka?" Hufi asked while they walked, almost companionably. As if his group of barely tamed jakuas hadn't run her down in an alley. "You could be practicing, preparing for your test. You could help the Huaca instead of hurting. Work with the older folks or something. It's close to migration time again. The coast is barely habitable. I'm sure your parents' farm isn't doing great either."

"My *brother's* farm," Silluka corrected. "And if our parents hadn't died in the last big earthquake—one the Huaca didn't *help* them survive, I might add—they might be able to support me. Ichu does what he can, but he might as well try to hoard nuts in a rock."

Hufi looked abashed for a moment, then straightened. Silluka completely ignored his four cronies. "I'm sorry about that, Silluka," he said. "The whole town suffered. My parents had to build a new house."

"Did they." Silluka let the obvious implications—that he still *had* parents—sink in. She waved her stump for emphasis, showing off how it ended just beyond her right elbow. "I'm not so good with a hammer and nails. Glad the Huaca decided to support you in your hour of need, like they do for all *citizens*." Her parents had both been citizens. "You know what the elders will make me do when we get there. You're forcing me to be left behind when the migration starts."

It wasn't quite true—she could have practiced more. She'd put off the test, attempting to gather supplies on her own because she subconsciously knew what the result of testing would be. She could have asked Ichu to help her— but her words had the desired effect. Hufi stopped trying to talk to her after that, and they marched in silence. By the time they reached the town center, the pretty tall girl and Meaty Boy had begun to relax their grip, just a little. *Jakua's Claws* had faded away, and Hufi didn't have the ampuka around him any longer.

Silluka waited until they were at the three steps to the raised hall where the elders sat to make her break.

She ducked low, twisting, her stump slipping easily out of Tall Girl's grasp. Meaty Boy held her fast, though, and she didn't have enough momentum to pull him, not in such close quarters. Instead, she dropped her knees, getting her center far underneath his, though he must weigh nearly twice what she did. She pushed him on his rear and surged past him, straight into the smaller girls' arms. She had a grip like iron and Silluka's mouth pursed in distaste. The members of the patrol were all well-toned and well-fed, taken care of by the elders. She could have been hoarding food for her own personal migration by now, if she'd just gotten some spokes.

Hufi, the tall girl, and the last member, a thinner boy with a swoop of dark hair, were moving their hands rhythmically in Strength stance. Silluka squirmed, but couldn't get free. They were performing a group chayu, but one she didn't recognize. There were hundreds of chayus and no one could remember all of them—or at least she couldn't.

Hufi and the two others began to glow with a shared light as Meaty Boy got to his feet and helped the short girl hold her. Then Hufi stepped forward, the other two flanking him, and grasped her shoulder with one hand. Silluka gasped at the firmness. It wasn't painful, but it was like his fingers had wrapped all the way around and *through* her shoulder.

"*Root Grows Around the Rock*," Hufi said. The other two stayed close, obviously concentrating. "Keeps people from getting away so easily. It's something they teach us when we start going on patrols, as citizens. It's time for you to try to be one. The elders won't care about you stealing, you know, but they will want you to test."

He stepped forward and Silluka moved with him. She couldn't not. It was the inevitable force of tree roots growing through soil, pushing her to her confrontation with the elders. Whether she wanted to or not, she would find out if she had the skill to become a citizen, or forever be cast out as an undesirable.

Test

Hufi propelled her down the short hall of the elders' building, the walls lined with benches where people would wait to see the ones who led the Huaca and could judge those who failed their testing.

He was still trying to reassure her, as if it would matter. "They've been here every day, these last few months, preparing for the migration, and testing anyone who wants."

They were also, Silluka was sure, handling the business of the Huaca and answering questions and requests. It must take hours every day. Her stomach fluttered in anticipation of seeing them. She didn't care about a citizen chit. She didn't.

"Great," she replied, trying to see Hufi over her shoulder. *Root Grows Around the Rock* kept her facing mostly forward. "I just have to show off a chayu, which I probably don't know, and the ampuka, which I've never done, to elders who will see me as a drain on the Huaca. Easy."

Hufi was silent, but kept pushing her toward the elders' building. All she had to do was make a connection with the Tiyus, Tiyas, and Tiyes, and the ampuka would come. Could that really happen? Maybe they'd be lenient. The strong survived in the Huaca, but the elders needed as many strong people as they could to help in the migration. Anyone without a chit—and that number was larger than those who had them—would be left to travel on their own, without any support from the elders. Some would surely make it to the next Huaca, inland. Maybe some would find a suitable home. There were undesirables on little farms along the coast, though they didn't have the protection from the gods the Huaca did. Not many of them survived for long.

"Let me tidy my hair at least," she said, before the big stone doors. They weren't old. Nothing in the town was. The Huaca had moved here from nearer the coast around seventy years ago. The last Huaca was now part of a mountain range, or underwater, or something.

"Make it quick," Tall Girl said, and gave Silluka a wink. If she hadn't been restrained and about to meet the elders who had doomed her parents, she might have winked back.

"You'd be much prettier if you didn't frown so much," Silluka said instead. She fluffed her shoulder-length hair, then dragged her hand through it. It probably looked like a quirra had nested in it. A pair of grimy men, large and dirty, had chased her out of the last house she'd squatted in.

"Ready?" Hufi asked. He was being pretty decent about dragging her in front of the elders. Likely a way to get her out from under his feet for good. She'd never been good at tests.

"Wish me luck," she said, to silence, and pushed through the doors. *Root Grows Around the Rock* fell away as she left the patrol behind, not that there was anywhere to run in front of the elders.

Silluka then realized Hufi's one last kindness. He and his patrol hadn't escorted her into the audience chamber. She wasn't coming before the elders as a thief, but solely as a testing candidate.

Seven of the elders were here. Every citizen past the age of bodycasting in the town was technically an elder, but these were the ones who made the decisions for the Huaca this day. Four women and three men. None of them under sixty-five. The woman in the center looked like she might have been near eighty.

Silluka didn't know their names, except for Papaki, a retiring older man who had come to check on her and Ichu after their parents died. If she had been a citizen, or really, anyone who had a future in the Huaca, she might have paid attention to the others, but she'd been born with her stump, and it had been apparent her whole life she'd never be a citizen.

Except.

Except she was here now, and they were going to test her, and *if* she passed, they would give her a citizen chit.

And they were all staring at her stump, out on display.

"You have come to test for citizenship?" the old woman in the middle asked. A correction, then. This woman wasn't staring at her stump. She was staring Silluka directly in the eyes.

"Yes, Elder." Her voice was soft, subservient. Silluka cleared her throat. She'd either leave a citizen or an undesirable. "Yes. I have come to test for my citizen chit." Louder. That was better. A few of the other elders smiled condescendingly. Not the one in the middle.

"Please." The woman gestured to the stone-rimmed circle in the middle of the floor. All chayus were to be performed in the circle, and stepping out of it was an instant disqualification. "Can you give us *Foam Tossed in the Waves*?"

Silluka's jaw nearly dropped. For all her joking, that was one of the most difficult chayus to test on. It came from Dexterity stance, and used the legs and arms moving in different directions at the same time. Just the finger manipulations caused most to miss the ampuka.

"Perhaps something simpler for the girl in light of her situation and our need for more citizens, Elder Quilqi?" Elder Papaki suggested. "How about *Tree in the Wind* instead?"

Elder Quilqi shrugged, as if the difference was not something noticeable. "Acceptable. *Tree in the Wind*, then."

Silluka blinked at the whiplash. If *Foam Tossed in the Waves* was one of the hardest chayus to summon the ampuka with, *Tree in the Wind* was one of the easiest. It started in Basic stance, and was used to strengthen the legs and stave off tiredness. It only used the shoulders, and the arms and hands didn't even do anything. It was perhaps the only chayu she might be able to complete without her right forearm.

She could be a citizen.

Silluka stepped into the stone circle, planting her feet in Basic stance.

"*Tree in the Wind*, elders," she said, and began.

She had performed the chayu before, but never actually committed to it. The few times she'd practiced it, she had stopped before the end, certain the ampuka wouldn't show. Today she could not be so blasé.

She swayed to one side, her arm and stump coming up only by movement of her shoulders, circling around in the front. The rest used her legs.

Each movement was deceptively simple, merely as if she were shifting her weight, but the precise tension of muscles was important. Her shoulders and hips had to be in the correct alignment all the time to make this chayu effective.

Silluka let her body recall where it was supposed to be. She hadn't really practiced any chayu in days—maybe a week. She was rusty, but couldn't show it. Her left foot slowly rose up, then set directly in front of the right. The slowness of the chayu was only offset by the length. This chayu lasted several minutes—longer than average. Nearly as long as the morning ritual.

Her right foot lifted to touch her left calf, where it would remain as she shifted her weight and pivoted.

That was when the earthquake struck.

Earthquakes were a common occurrence as the earth rose and shifted. With the approaching island—the reason the coast was turning into mountains—rumbles beneath the ground had become more prevalent over the last several years. Fortunately, the volcanoes were only to the south. This area was folding up like an accordion as the new island ground over theirs. Soon, the two landmasses would merge, with a range of mountains in between and—so their geologists predicted—water cycling down through the desert to the west, turning it fertile.

Most earthquakes were small, tamped down by Tiyu Tiksimuyu. Silluka tried not to wobble, tensing her calf muscles in rhythm with the rolling of the floor. The earthquake would pass in a moment. It was no effort to maintain her balance. Even the undesirables of the Huaca could keep upright when the earth shuddered beneath them.

Silluka's right foot came down, her left lifting now to touch her right leg. The floor heaved and tilted toward the elders. She gritted her teeth and relaxed just slightly, moving with the floor. This was exactly the time to perform *Tree in the Wind*. This was what it was designed for. She would not fail.

"Tiyu Tiksimuyu, Uncle Earth, give us peace from the rolling land," Elder Papaki called out. He rose from his seat enough to make the sign of the earth, a movement using arms and legs, the emblem of Tiyu Tiksimuyu, and call on the god.

The shape made by the passage of his limbs glowed brown in the air, like polished wood, and the quake lessened, then stilled. Silluka paced through the next move, always smooth, always careful. A bead of sweat rolled into her left eye, but she refused even to blink. Each muscle tensed only as much as needed to take her weight, then relaxed when not in use. She used only the minimal effort to capture the beauty of the chayu and connect with the ampuka.

Was that a gathering of energy within her? She only had six more moves, and the chayu was complete. She was almost there.

The next one was a step-step, right foot then left, the only quick movement in the chayu.

As her right foot was in the air, the ground roared and buckled, and the center of the stone center split with a *crack*. A block fell from the ceiling to her right, smashing into the floor with a puff of dust.

"Tiyu Tiksimuyu save us!" several elders cried out at once.

Silluka stumbled, coming down heavily on her right foot, grimacing as it twisted painfully against the earth. The gathering feeling of the ampuka fled.

The trembling continued at a low pace and Silluka made a mockery of the remaining moves, barely finishing the chayu. She swallowed and looked up at the elders, coming back to rest in her Basic stance. Her eyes burned with the pain in her right foot and the shame of defeat, but she held her head high.

The others cast worried glances upward as the earth continued to rock in a low tremor, but Elder Quilqi stared dispassionately down at Silluka.

"I see no ampuka," she said.

"Perhaps the girl might test again, because of the extenuating circumstances," Elder Papaki suggested.

"One test per year. That is the rule," Elder Quilqi said. "How old are you, girl?"

Silluka swallowed. "Sev-seventeen, elder." Her voice trembled like a quirra in a jakua's paws.

Elder Papaki squinted forward, waving a cloud of dust away. "But not for long, if I remember correctly. When is your birthday?"

"In two days." Now her voice was merely a whisper.

The elder looked almost pained. "I fear I have bent the rules as much as I can for you."

"Then it is done," Elder Quilqi said, as if bored by the proceedings. "You will be too old to test again, according to the Huaca's rules. We must get back to planning the migration. As many citizens as possible must be saved."

Silluka stared back, refusing to bend or shed tears before the elder. She wouldn't have taken the test again even if they had let her, migration or not. Chayus required a whole body, every muscle exactly placed. She'd known that when she started, but Hufi and her own delusions had given her false hope. The earthquake was an excuse. She'd known she would never show the ampuka. She would never be a citizen, and when the Huaca fled this place as the growing mountains ripped it to shreds, she would be left behind with the others to make her own path.

"Thank you for the opportunity, elders," she said, and limped out of the half-destroyed audience chamber before they could catch the glint of a tear. The only way she would get away from the approaching island was through her own smarts.

CHAPTER THREE

Picking Pockets

Silluka fled past Hufi and the others of his patrol, righting benches and sweeping away dirt. They must have stayed long enough to be caught in the earthquake and now were helping to clean up.

"Did you pass?" Meaty Boy asked, and Silluka barely saw Hufi raise a hand to quiet him as she hobbled out the front doors of the elders' building on her aching ankle. She didn't dare turn to see Tall Girl's pitying stare. So much for Hufi's kindness. She'd have been better off letting the elders give her community work for stealing. Maybe the elders would have thought she was useful and given her a place in the migration.

When she was outside, she turned left, and ran down the alley separating the elders' building from other government buildings of the Huaca. Her ankle was already feeling better. It hadn't been a strain, thank Tiya Qhalikay. Only enough to derail her chayu. She stopped at a little nook where the buildings didn't line up, cramming herself into the tight space.

Only then did she let herself go, shaking with tears. The imagined faces of Hufi's patrol stared at her, judging. She had *almost* been there! She'd felt the ampuka building within her. She could have been a citizen.

Silluka dashed the tears away. Stupid. And stupid of her to think it. She'd kept those thoughts away for almost eighteen years, refusing to let her mind go to the obvious answer. She would *never* be a citizen. Being a citizen required a person to be whole of body, or at least able to do a few chayus correctly.

Being a citizen didn't require smarts, or thinking, or planning. That wasn't highly regarded in the Huaca. Citizens didn't need smarts to do a chayu. Citizens didn't need smarts to show the ampuka and connect with the gods. They just required practice, and muscle memory. Put every finger, every muscle in exactly the right place, and the ampuka would show.

She knew highly regarded citizens who were dumber than a bag of acorns.

There were many more undesirables than citizens in the Huaca and surrounding it. The ones who were injured, or sick, or didn't like to practice every day, or were too out of shape. The Huaca was strong, and dedicated, and *stupid*.

Silluka survived by her smarts, and she'd keep doing it. She sniffed and blinked away the rest of her regrets. She didn't need Hufi, or that pretty tall girl, or Meaty Boy, or the elders with their noses in the air.

She just needed herself.

And she needed Ichu, because he was her brother, but that wasn't going to last.

Sweet, dependable, hard-working Ichu. He still ran the farm their parents had left behind when they died, even though the land was turning to rock and the crops died more often than they produced.

Ichu didn't need *her*, though. He'd been a citizen since he was fourteen, a year before she was born. He was the strongest bodycaster she knew, if not the fastest. *He* wouldn't get left behind when the Huaca left for a new home.

But she would.

Silluka pounded the stone wall of the building she hid behind with her hand.

Ichu would make some desperate attempt to take her with him when they left. She knew he would. She'd argue with him until she ran out of breath, but he'd insist.

She hadn't let herself think about it until now, but that was exactly what he'd do. If she had passed the test today, instead of failing like an...like an *undesirable*, she could have avoided a lot of arguments.

It didn't take smarts to be Huaca, but it might help.

Silluka sat back against the wall looking up into the cloudy sky. She could just see the top of the wall of storms from here. It wasn't raining right now, thankfully. Instead of pining for one of the storm warriors to come down and grant her wishes, what if she took matters into her own hands?

What if she *had* a citizen chit when she went back to Ichu? She'd been picking pockets since she was ten. The chits weren't marked or individual. Citizens sometimes dueled with chayus and took them from each other. She could have tried to take one before now, and failed, but there was always that allure, hanging covered in the back of her mind. She could still take the test. Instead, she'd tried to hoard food or money, thinking that would help her. It had been a half-hearted attempt because she hadn't wanted to consider what was coming. Well, the elders were in a panic. The migration was coming, no matter what anyone wanted. The shifting land cared nothing for its inhabitants. Her parents were proof of that.

Silluka was the only one who could shape her destiny. She imagined the thin, old face of the elder from the test— Elder Quilqi had been her name. Dried up, dusty old crone. She'd stared Silluka down like she was nothing, demanded she do the most complicated chayu a non-citizen could test on!

Old people didn't need citizen chits, and elders certainly didn't. They'd been taking up space in the Huaca for years. Most didn't even try to summon the ampuka. They were too old and shaky to get all the movements exactly right, which was why the patrols were given to the young, while the old sat back and governed. They'd already proven themselves.

Food, money, and even the chayus ultimately meant nothing in the face of the migration. Silluka would steal Elder Quilqi's chit. The old bat probably wouldn't even report it, too scared to say that an undesirable had stolen her citizenship.

Silluka straightened and smiled. This was too easy.

* * *

She hung around the elders' building until the day grew dark, watching people go in and out. People entered to petition, complain, test, and more.

Silluka stood up from her slouch against a wall as one of the elders came out. It was hard to see in the fading light, but she could tell Elder Papaki by the way he walked. The elder was unbowed with age, a model of good posture, but moved slower than younger Huaca. She briefly considered following him, but Elder Papaki had tried to help her. She watched him leave.

A few stars began to poke through the ever-present clouds as candles snuffed out in the back rooms of the building. The last stragglers were finishing up their work for the day and leaving. Still no Elder Quilqi. Did she sleep there?

Silluka was about to give up—about to follow the last elderly Huaca to leave, in hopes of getting anyone's chit— when Quilqi's tall silhouette appeared. Silluka could *sense* it was her. The last one out of the building, she was practically *begging* for Silluka to take her chit.

She slouched along the wall, keeping to the shadows, far enough back so Quilqi wouldn't see her. There were still too many people out, here in the center of the Huaca. Most people lived closer to the edges of the town, and Silluka followed the old woman until no others were around, the houses turning into a hodgepodge of separate dwellings. Little light shone between them.

She started the movements of *Quirra Hides His Nuts* while she walked, moving from Dexterity stance. She was going to do the chayu right this time. It was hard to perform a chayu while moving, and *Quirra Hides His Nuts* certainly had too many hand movements for her to summon the ampuka, but every bit helped.

Elder Quilqi slowed at a corner, seeming to take in the sky and the few stars shining tonight. Like she was just waiting for Silluka to rob her.

Silluka crept, from Dexterity stance to Dexterity stance, like a quirra cautiously approaching a suspicious new plant. Elder Quilqi still stood there, head back, looking up.

This was too easy.

Silluka slowly reached out, the fingers of her left hand brushing the pockets of Quilqi's loose pants, then inside. The elder still didn't move. Her fingers encountered a hexagonal shape and withdrew it.

She had it.

And then she didn't.

Her face was against the wall, her fingers up in the air, and then she was free, blinking around. Where was Elder Quilqi?

"Seas dissolve, child, keep your shoulders back." Fingers like iron weights pulled her shoulders back and down. "And straighten up. You'll never get anywhere with that slouch." The fingers grasped the sides of her head, squeezing and pulling upward, bringing Silluka almost to her toes.

"Just because quirra is hiding his nuts doesn't mean he's lazy about it. Dexterity stance!" A foot touched her ankle, pushing her foot forward slightly, positioning it upward just a touch.

"There. That's better. Now, take these back and we can try again." The hand spun her around until Silluka stared into Elder Quilqi's face, the old woman's sharp eyes roving over Silluka, fingers touching here, there, correcting posture, arms, stance, hips, and legs.

Silluka only realized the touches had stopped when fingers shook a bag in front of her nose.

"Come on now, girl. Take it and let's start again."

"I...what?" Silluka reached out to take the spoke purse—*her* spoke purse—from Elder Quilqi. The chit was nowhere to be seen.

"Good initiative, but poor form. You're never going to connect with the ampuka that way. You could have just asked, you know. You almost had it this afternoon. I'll turn my back and you can try again. Should I look at the stars harder this time?"

"I...you want me to pick your pocket *again?*" Silluka felt like she was sliding down a hole into darkness.

"Again? Windy skies! You hardly tried the first time."

Various facts were flitting around Silluka's head. "Connect with the ampuka? I can't do that."

"And why not? Tiya Aymuray preserve us, child, it's the basic principle of the chayus."

"My stump..." She lifted her right arm in the air.

"What about it?" Elder Quilqi reached out, as if she couldn't help herself, and pushed Silluka's shoulder down. "Relax when you move. You're putting more effort into it than a jakua digging holes to find a stray chipmunk."

"But I need to move every part of my body in exactly the right place to summon the ampuka. How can I do that without a hand?" That was not the question she thought she would be asking right now. Wasn't Elder Quilqi going to call for a patrol or something?

"*Your* body." The elder poked her in the chest with a bony finger. "Is a whole right hand part of *your* body?"

"I...hadn't thought about it that—"

"I can see that. Hmpf. Chasms take us, now, try again." Quilqi spun around. "Aren't those stars interesting? My, is that a storm warrior flying around over there? By Tiye Khuyay, I do hope no one takes advantage of my stargazing to *pick my pocket*. Come on, girl."

Silluka pushed her incredulity down deep into the back of her mind. What had she gotten herself into? She hesitantly planted back into Dexterity stance, helped along by Elder Quilqi rotating two fingers in the air for her to get on with it.

"Arms too," the elder said. "Give me a good form *Quirra Hides His Nuts*."

Silluka raised her arms, placing them where they would go for the beginning of the chayu. Hands—if she had two hands—would go *here*, looping around to form the catching paws, then out and in, snatching and back. She did the movement with both arms, as much as she had of them, trying to ignore the obvious—that she could never make it work.

Elder Quilqi dropped her pretense, eagle eyes roving over Silluka's form. "Shoulders down, elbows in. Curl those fingers."

"But I don't have—"

"*Imagine*, and focus, child. Use your intent. Coasts collide! What do they teach you these days?"

Silluka frowned, but dropped her shoulders and brought her elbows closer to her center. It would put her nonexistent right hand *there* if she did so.

A core of power brushed her center, just for an instant, as if a thread connected her through the ground, to the center of the island.

Silluka gasped, and trembled, and the thread of power dropped away.

"Good!" Elder Quilqi grabbed Silluka's upper arms and shook them out, the tension flowing away like water. She stared into Silluka's eyes for just a moment, as if looking for something. "I knew I was out here for a good reason. You failed much less that time."

"But I still failed."

Quilqi blew out her breath in a rude noise. "And will that stop you?"

"What about all the undesirables? People with frailties and disabilities can't do chayus. They can't connect with the ampuka. They're not citizens—ow!"

The elder had poked her in the head with a pointy finger. "Lazy is its own challenge. You failed on your own merits, child. You can succeed on them too."

Silluka was suddenly suspicious. Had Elder Quilqi made sure they would be alone by leaving so late?

No. That was stupid. But what she said was different than what the elders taught. And Silluka had felt that spark, just for a moment.

"Why has no one ever told me this before? Why does *no one* else in the Huaca think this way?" Silluka spread her arms wide. "Should I believe one elder when all the wisdom of the Huaca tells me you're wrong? That I'm an undesirable?"

Elder Quilqi shrugged. "There is more to the world than this little village. More than this island. These villagers don't know everything, and I think you have potential." She stood straight, raising her chin. "Now, will you come with me, child? There are some people I think you should meet."

Silluka blinked. The elder's constant changes in the conversation were giving her whiplash. "Now? It's almost full dark?"

"They don't sleep much, and neither do I," Quilqi said. "I don't give many second chances, either. You've already had one today. You won't get another."

Silluka narrowed her eyes at the elder. She'd said *these villagers*, not *the Huaca*. Like she wasn't a part of them.

"I'll come with you," she said.

CHAPTER FOUR

The Allwiya

Elder Quilqi led Silluka ever farther from the center of the Huaca, toward the very outskirts of the village.

"You're taking me to the Allwiya?" Silluka guessed. "I thought you *didn't* want me to be an undesirable."

"How often have you spoken with one of the Allwiya, child?" Elder Quilqi didn't pause as she walked.

"They can't speak. They're barely better than the trained jakuas." Silluka hadn't crossed paths with the strange little creatures often—mostly they were seen scuttling across rooftops and through garbage piles near the edge of the Huaca, all eight limbs moving at once. It wasn't like any of them could attempt to test for citizenship.

"Rolling earth, child! Just because you don't know another being's language doesn't mean they can't speak," the elder sniffed. "They provide a steady supply of nails, screws, fabricated plates, and mechanical devices to the Huaca. Where do you think our water sills come from? Or the blinds for our windows? Have you ever seen a citizen making something like that? Of course not."

"So, they're good at little trinkets. How does that help me become a citizen?" Silluka stomped along behind the taller elder. She had been hoping for some secret holdout or a hermit-like teacher in a cave who eschewed the elders' teaching, not boneless little creatures.

"Perhaps if you pay attention, you will learn," Quilqi said. "Ah. Here we are. Good behavior, now. We don't want to offend."

She stooped before a tiny door, only up to Silluka's waist, and gave an odd rap with one hand, drumming the backs of her fingers in sequence against the wood. Silluka peered at her form in the near darkness. Was all this worth it? Elder Papaki and the others had to know what they were doing, didn't they? That was what every person in the Huaca aspired to be, one day. The elders were the keepers of the chayus and knew them better than anyone else. But Quilqi behaved less and less like what Silluka thought of the elders—stuffy old bores so pent up with studying geological charts and old chayu descriptions that it might be days before anyone noticed one of them had keeled over.

She was about to speak when the little door opened enough to admit five tentacles, each as long as her forearm, which curled around the frame. Bright light shone from behind them. The tip of one wiggled at the elder, then another at Silluka. Three came off the door with a squelch and crossed in some sort of symbol.

"They say to come in." Elder Quilqi got down on her knees, mud from the earlier rain pressing into the knees of her loose cloth pants, and crawled through the opening door.

Silluka stopped openmouthed at the door, then shrugged. "I guess this day can't get any weirder." She crawled through after the elder, trying to keep the mud off her pants, but failing. Her stump could keep her up, but wasn't as long as her other arm, which meant she was lopsided.

Behind the little door was a workshop. Brilliant light spewed from a candle attached to the wall that hardly flickered at all. What kind of wax did they use to get such a flame? Silluka couldn't even look straight at it, and it bathed the small room in enough light to easily see details.

Elder Quilqi straightened, her hands on her lower back. The ceiling here was high enough for them to stand straight, if barely. Her brother Ichu would have needed to duck, but the top of Elder Quilqi's white hair just brushed the stone above them.

As she blinked her eyes to adjust to the brightness, Silluka saw Quilqi was twisting her fingers with lightning speed at an Allwiya, whose great goggle eyes stared up at her from near the floor. The creature was bright pink, standing on six of its eight tentacled legs, its body balanced in the air, only as high as the elder's knees. The two other tentacles twisted into shapes back at the elder.

"This is Muola," the elder said, still wiggling her fingers. "Say hello."

"Um. Hello," Silluka said. Her eyes kept being drawn to the walls of the little room, where objects of all shapes and sizes hung. Finely detailed metal, lengths of wood, perfectly circular hoops of metal with bulky boxes strapped to one side, and gracefully curving arms with little blobs at the ends.

"Are these all the things you said the Allwiya made?" Silluka asked.

"Mountains erupt, child! Don't interrupt Muola," the elder said, but there was a hint of humor in her tone. Silluka looked back sharply to see Quilqi smiling and the top of Muola's body shivering. It shifted through colors from pink, to green, to blue. A laugh?

The Allwiya raised two more tentacles and made a sequence of complex signs, then their body shivered again. Quilqi snorted a laugh.

"What?" Silluka tried not to sound indignant, but if the elder had dragged her across town just to laugh at her—

"Muola says you're technically correct, that these are things the Allwiya made, but these are just their standard tools. The real inventions are in the other room." Quilqi turned back to Muola, speaking as her fingers danced, this time. "Are they in today, Muola? I have a villager with some potential, I think, and I wanted to connect her with like-minded people. They might work well with each other."

Like minded? Did the elder think she had the mind of a tiny boneless creature that crawled through garbage?

Muola signed something back, and this time Silluka watched closely. The creature had made the same gesture several times and made it again.

"Then they're available? Excellent. Please let them know we'd like to talk with them for a bit." The elder turned to Silluka, crossing her fingers in a loop across her body. "This is 'hello.' You might want to try it out, so you don't sound so ungrateful."

Silluka hesitantly brought her fingers across her body. She couldn't do the full gesture—Quilqi had used both hands—but she used her right stump with the intent of doing the same thing.

"Close enough for our purposes," Quilqi said with the ghost of a smile. "Lead on, Muola."

The small creature leapt nimbly to a countertop, and grabbed a switch, pulling with all their weight. The far wall of the room, covered with the Allwiya's tools, folded up like an accordion, revealing a passage lit by more of the brilliant candles.

"After you." Elder Quilqi gestured Silluka forward.

At the end of the hallway was another hatch like the front door and Quilqi knocked, then got down on her knees and crawled through the opening. She left a trail of mud.

Silluka followed and had to blink back tears as she emerged into a room even brighter than the one before. The dazzling candles lit every wall, with two on the ceiling and one on the floor. Piles of garbage—mostly twisted metal and wood—were everywhere. She rubbed her eyes, trying to see the mysterious people the elder wanted her to meet.

"Say hello. Come on, child, like I taught you." Quilqi's voice was harsh, from the nearby blob of color she occupied. Silluka squinted, hunting for a shape. Something moved among piles of debris, and she faced that direction, making the same hand gesture.

Multiple arms waved back. Silluka blinked again. This Allwiya was a blotchy green and blue, and was *tiny*. Like they could fit in her hand. Or ride on her shoulder. They might have been the smallest one she'd ever seen, not that she'd seen that many.

They continued waving at Silluka, making gestures too fast to follow, then scuttled across the wall, seeming to hang in the air as they did. They picked up pieces of metal, four arms fitting them together as the others propelled them closer.

"Meet Lugopo," Elder Quilqi said. "They and Muola supply most of the contraptions for our village."

The creature—Lugopo—skidded to a halt, hanging an arm's reach from Silluka's face, one tentacle curled around a strip of wire sticking out from the wall like a strange blue flower. They fiddled with the pieces of metal they'd gathered, three tentacles fitting them together with small, quick actions, while the other four kept gesticulating at Silluka. Large yellow eyes stared at her, unblinking.

"What—what are they saying?" she asked. The smell was starting to tickle her brain. It was like a garbage dump covered in seaweed.

"Ah..." The elder cleared her throat. "'Welcome, hello, this is my workshop. I have many devices here to show you. If I can just get this one crammed?' No, fitted? Stars fall! Slow down, Lugopo, I can't keep up!"

Lugopo finally forced the metal wire—like a circlet with dangling curved filaments—down over the top of their body. It hovered a finger's width above the top of their large eyes, and, with one tentacle still holding on to the supporting wire from the wall, another pressed a sequence of switches, while the remaining six frantically gestured.

"'I have worked on this mechanism for the last half-year,'" the elder translated, "'and finally have a chance to show off?'"—a tentacle waggle from Lugopo—"'*demonstrate* this and I hope it works to—'"

Suddenly another, metallic, mechanical voice took over.

"—at last get an opportunity to bloviate! Greetings! So happy to visitors! This is lair of deathtraps!" Lugopo's eyes crossed, staring upward, and they ripped the mechanism off their head and banged it against the wall, then put it back on.

"Excuse! This is my workshop! Translation circlet is rotten kelp." They took it off again. Smack. "Still under torture." Smack. "Construction."

The voice was tinny and small, like someone had given a chipmunk a cone to speak through and told to call an unfamiliar chayu.

"Ah. Greetings," Silluka said, again making the gesture the elder had showed her.

"My parent does what with crabs?" Lugopo's eyes bulged, then landed on Silluka's stump. "Ah, your tentacle has been chewed off—" Smack. "Is missing. I can extrapolate the insult. Meaning. Greetings to you too."

"Um." Silluka grasped for something to say. She was tired and overwhelmed from the events of day. This morning she'd been trying to pick an old man's pocket, and here she was, after failing the citizen's test she never thought she'd take, taken under the wing of an elder unlike any elder, and talking to an Allwiya with actual piles of trash in their tiny room.

"Elder Quilqi wanted me to meet you?" she finally managed.

"And it has been accomplished! What other social conditions, no, compunctions must be met?" Lugopo swung closer on the metal jutting from the wall, and Silluka's eyes crossed as the tiny Allwiya touched her nose with a smooth tentacle. "The old biddy"—smack—"the elder is an excellent judge of secret shame. Character. I welcome any student of hers to my lair. Workshop."

"The elder says I can be a citizen, even with this." Silluka raised her right arm.

Lugopo dropped from the metal wire to Silluka's stump, and she tensed, holding back a scream, not daring to move. The Allwiya's skin was cold and smooth, and their limbs wrapped around her biceps and triceps like she had a floppy ball attached to her stump. They changed color to match her ochre skin, blending in seamlessly except for the metal circlet above their eyes.

"What are you doing?" Her voice didn't quite come out in a yell.

"Islands crumble, child, don't be so jumpy," Elder Quilqi said. "Lugopo has a hobby of recording chayus."

Several tentacles squelched off Silluka's stump to wave around. "Is plotting of mine. Habit. Fascination. Huaca

Aunts, Uncles, and Entles are source of power. Not like the Allwiya."

"Recording Chayus? Like the elders' records? What does that have to do with my stump?" Lugopo's mechanical words caught up to her. "And where do the Allwiya get their power, then?"

"From own gods, naturally. Whirling Abyss. Crawling Dark of Squirming. Manylegs of Reaching." Lugopo reached up with three tentacles and pressed buttons on their circlet. "Like Aunts, Uncles, and Entles...but different."

"And your...gods...do what?"

"Fiery depths, child, they help the Allwiya invent, of course." Elder Quilqi shook her head, signing at the same time. "What do they teach you these days? The Allwiya are not from our island. They came from the last landmass that arrived on this coast, several hundred years ago. Surely you know that?"

"I may have heard that somewhere," Silluka said. She hadn't ever really thought about it. The lands far up north, across a steep mountain range, were said to be the Allwiya's home.

She flexed her arm just a bit when Lugopo tapped on her biceps, then her triceps. She was getting used to the strange feeling. The little Allwiya's body wasn't actually that cold, just colder than hers. The tentacles were strangely gentle, like having a massage from lots of tiny fingers.

"Just like the Huaca have Tiye Kwirpuyay, who gave us and the rest of their siblings our chayus at the beginning, the gods of the Allwiya inspire them to create and discover." Elder Quilqi watched Lugopo's movements with interest, as if she could see something Silluka couldn't.

"Make many implements of destruction!" Lugopo smacked the circlet. "Creation!"

"That still doesn't tell me how Lugopo's going to help my chayu," Silluka said. "Unless they're going to build me a better arm."

Five of Lugopo's arms popped off Silluka's arm, reaching for the ceiling. "Merely specify requirements! Would you like spikes? Flames? Hydraulic—"

"None of that, now," Elder Quilqi broke in. "I think Silluka might benefit from your other inventions, though."

"Other inventions! Then it is the fated time to apply measurements of chayus to world domination?"—smack—"to increase ability?"

"Let's start a little smaller," the elder said. "Just to let her keep up with the caravans when they leave. I won't have any apprentice of mine falling behind."

Apprentice? That was new. Silluka tried to respond that she didn't need help keeping up with the caravans, but even with the excitement and bright lights, her jaw cracked in a yawn.

"Good denture," Lugopo's translator chirped.

"Ah yes, you young folk need sleep, don't you. Cold moon! It must be after midnight. Lugopo, show her to your spare room and you and I can talk." The elder's fingers kept wiggling for a few seconds after she finished speaking, and Silluka regarded her suspiciously. What was she trying to do?

"Certainly! Right here." Lugopo leapt off Silluka's stump and sprang across the wall, pulling levers. Another section unfolded into a human-sized nook, complete with a sleeping mat. How big was the inside of this building? It had seemed like just a shack when they approached, though it had been dark. "Used for visitors. Will provide wake attack—" Smack. "Wake-up call in the morning."

Silluka yawned again, picking her way through the piles of garbage. "I probably won't be able to sleep with you two yapping away," she said, and laid down on the mattress. She'd been kicked out of the last several nooks and crannies in the Huaca she'd found. It was nice to have a soft bed and a roof over her head.

She watched Elder Quilqi and Lugopo trade signs, their fingers and tentacles a blur. She tried to pay attention to repeated symbols, but before she could get very far, she was asleep.

CHAPTER FIVE

The Visitor

Ichu rolled over in the dawn light. It was sunny today, which meant he could bring in crops. He blinked sleep from his eyes and rose, his mind already whirling through in what order he'd need to do things. Eat, then get the tools from the shed, bring in the maize first so it would have a chance to dry out, then the squash, what there was of them...

He'd have to keep an eye on the skies and move quickly. Lately, blue skies only meant a big storm was moving in fast. If he was lucky, he'd get enough to keep him fed and have a little to sell at the market.

"Come back to bed, Ichy," Kuillay said from a nest of blankets. His strong hand gripped Ichu's wrist. "It's too early."

"I have a farm to run, and it's a bright day, Kuillay." Ichu pulled his hand free. Kuillay was the latest in a line of men and women from the Huaca who shared his bed after he won the bodycasting tournament the year previous. None had stayed long. Kuillay had been with him two months so far.

"Can't you pick that stuff later? At least do the morning ritual with me." Kuillay peeked imploring eyes from under a pile of jakua-fur layers. He'd brought the expensive blankets with him when he moved in, claiming he couldn't sleep without them.

The last at least gave Ichu pause. He rarely missed the morning ritual. He could feel his shoulders tightening just thinking about skipping it.

"For me and my lovely eyes, Ichy," Kuillay implored. "You always say that's my best feature."

"Quickly, then," Ichu threw on loose linen pants and a shirt with an open neck. He skipped starting a fire in favor of a protein-rich breakfast of nuts, grains, and berries that would give him the energy to work in the fields most of the day. When he checked on Kuillay, the man was still tucked under the covers, staring at the ceiling.

"Did you bring me breakfast?" he asked, blinking long eyelashes.

"I...no, Kuillay, I really need to get out in the fields today. You know how important it is to get the crops in when I can."

"You wouldn't mind just a little bite for me, would you? Maybe some scrambled eggs and a little fruit?"

And so it went. Ichu wrangled, and Kuillay asked for more. By the time he got the man out of bed, served him breakfast, and went through a rushed version of the morning ritual, dark clouds were marching from the wall of storms toward the mountainous coast.

Ichu lugged baskets, a hoe, and a rake from storage while Kuillay cheered him on from a seat on the porch. The clouds had turned slate gray and were moving faster than any he'd seen in a while. A hurricane? Were the gods fighting again? No, it didn't have the right look to it. Just a big storm then? His thoughts briefly turned to his sister, hoping Silluka had found food and shelter in town. If it got too bad, he'd have to bring her back here. She'd gotten sick before, trying to live on her own in the streets.

He'd only found three good ears of corn by the time the rain started.

The darker clouds were fast approaching, and a glance to Kuillay showed him staring off into the distance. Ichu bit the inside of his cheek to keep from yelling. After today, the man was gone, no matter how lovely his eyes were. He didn't know how Kuillay had gotten his citizenship chit, but he probably had a doting grandparent among the elders.

Ichu set the hoe down and placed his feet in Blocking stance, short, and with knees and feet turned in. He began *Caterpillar Weaves His Cocoon* by tensing his core and driving the energy out toward his hands. They curled in, then rose as he dropped his shoulders into an accepting form, each move precise. His knees bent further as the glow of the ampuka grew around him. As it did, the rain lessened on his skin, though it was increasing around him. He paced through the moves of the chayu, the gleam from his already wet skin illuminating the rows of sickly corn around him. The blessing of Tiya Aymuray—Aunt Harvest—kept him dry and warm. In minutes he finished, and the rain beat against a shell of light a finger width from his skin.

The chayu would keep for maybe an hour. He was strong—one of the strongest in the Huaca—even though he could tell his ability was slipping. He was into his thirties, and bodycasting, especially the more physical chayus, took a toll on the body. Exact placement was required to bring the ampuka out, to be accepted by the gods. It was why the elders studied, refining the movements for the next generation. The elders who ran the Huaca, like Papaki and Sinchi, had reached the height of their talent, just like he had, but as their bodies aged, they'd turned to study. It was what lay in store for him. Maybe one of the elders would find a way to stave off aging one day, but that hadn't happened yet. It was already too late for him.

He paced quickly through the corn, placing the ears in a basket he held close to him, under the protection of his arms and the cocoon of the chayu. The stalks had taken in far too much water this season already, and many of the ears showed signs of crazy-top, with long tassels and underdeveloped kernels. They wouldn't taste good nor have a lot of nutrients, but they were what he could grow here near the coast and the wall of storms.

He could tell the squash were too far gone before he got there. They were moldy and smelly. It had rained every day for nearly a month. He had wasted much of that time with Kuillay. If Silluka had been around, she could have helped. Where *was* that girl? She had been missing for over a week this time, trying to prove she could live on her own, stealing in the village. It was an affront to the education their parents had provided for her.

Ichu stomped to the porch and dropped the meager basket of corn in Kuillay's lap, who grunted.

"You got mud on my pants!"

"That's not all you'll get," Ichu growled.

"But Ichy..."

"*Don't* call me Ichy! Take your innumerable hair products and your jakua covers and go back to the Huaca. Today."

Kuillay pushed the basket off his lap, pouting. He flounced inside. "Fine. I'll start getting my things together. Don't expect me to tell any tales of your prowess in the village."

Ichu rolled his eyes and picked up the spilled corn. The rain was only getting harder. He needed to pull in the rest of the crops. There were two more fields, farther out. If Kuillay hadn't delayed him so much, he would have gotten to them already.

Silluka. He needed her back here. They'd have to pull up all the plants and restructure the fields for even more drainage. With the mountain rising under him, the drainage never stayed level from month to month. It was a good thing there were several growing seasons a year. He thought he could get in one last crop before the caravans left, if he had her help. He'd heard tales from their parents, who had heard from their parents, that the crops had been much better nearer the coast, before the Huaca moved inland as the mountains rose.

He got the corn laid out inside so it would dry as much as it could then went to the main room of the house, an open area suitable for bodycasting. It was time to bring Silluka back home. Time was short, and her eighteenth birthday was tomorrow. Maybe he could get her to practice with him once or twice at least. If he went with her before the elders, and asked for their leniency with an easy chayu, it was possible she could be a full citizen by the time they left. If Kuillay could do it, Silluka could. Then they could grow a few more ears of corn to add to the town's stores and ensure their place in the migration.

Caterpillar Weaves His Cocoon had worn off and Ichu started from Dexterity stance this time, feet light on the ground, as his arms opened up and outward, like great wings. This chayu was difficult, even for him, and he ignored Kuillay's childish stomping and banging. Elder Papaki taught him it not three years ago—one of the most demanding chayus the elders knew. It was a good sign they would recruit him as an elder before long.

Head up, feet moving like skimming over the treetops. His fingers opened wide as they came around, scooping air as if he were gathering all the signs and portents around him. The ampuka grew around him again as *Eagle Watches from on High* took form, a shape described in the air by his body. It was that of a great bird, wings gathering air currents, eyes sharp enough to see through stone. His feet made questing movements this way and that, covering a surprising amount of ground.

Several minutes later, he pulled his arms close, tucked in, though his head was held high in perfect posture. He focused on his little sister, her habits, her movements, how she acted and what she wished for. His connection with Tiye Kwirpuyay—Entle Magic—granted him the means to track her down.

"I want you gone by the time I get back!" he called as he opened the door of the old farmhouse. Kuillay grunted something angry in the other room.

He would have been concerned the passionate man might break or steal something on his way out, except there was nothing to steal and the house was near to falling down. They would migrate to a new, better Huaca soon. Ichu just needed to last until then.

Eagle Watches from on High gave him the signs he needed to track his sister. She was obviously in town, and Ichu ran the thirty minutes it took to get there, unencumbered by harvest or baggage and even getting a bit ahead of the rain. It seemed to be centralized right around the farm. Often the storms were worse nearer the coast.

Once in the village, the eagle's signs grew, standing out with a glow whenever he crossed where she had stood or walked. He brushed aside Huaca who wanted to talk to him, or tell him about the preparations for the migration. None of them had news of Silluka.

He found three nests in abandoned buildings, though one had two undesirables—old men—living there now. All seemed a few days old. Had something happened to her recently?

Silluka. She thought she was lesser because she couldn't bodycast like the others in the Huaca. Ichu knew she was smart, and tenacious when she put her mind to something. She had simply dismissed ever working with the rest of the Huaca because she saw how they treated undesirables. And it was a fair assessment, but Ichu had offered to help her train many times. Even if she couldn't summon the ampuka, she could still help the rest of the village. Many houses had undesirable members, sheltered by the citizens in the family, who led normal lives. Undesirable, then citizen, then elder. The hierarchy worked, and people who dedicated themselves to the chayu could progress from one to another.

Ichu found more recent tracks near the center of the village, hasty steps standing out in yesterday's mud, many covered over by passing villagers. The glow of Silluka's trail. If he'd gotten here after the rain, they likely would have been completely washed away, even to eagle's eyes.

His sister's footsteps were confused, moving back and forth across the town, as if she'd been chased. He passed older citizens performing chayus in the late morning in the town center. What had Silluka been doing here? Then the footprints led, slow and dragging, toward the elders' building. Had she finally been caught stealing? He should have been here for her, but the farm took far too much of his time as it was.

He rolled his shoulders, mentally getting ready for a fight with the elders over her, thinking of reasons to explain why she should test, and *pass* her test, to be a contributing member of the Huaca. Except in front of the elders' building, his eagle's eyes found her footsteps leading *away* again. She'd gone inside, then left.

Had she actually tried to test out for her citizen chit? Alone? Impossible.

Whatever the events, he rushed after the last set of footprints, leading across the Huaca to the outskirts, following someone, then past a strange shuffle as if she'd danced with them for a moment, then following them closer into the Allwiya quarters. Huaca didn't know much about the strange little beings. He traded with them sometimes for farm implements, but they always seemed disappointed he didn't want more from them. What, he couldn't imagine. He had everything he needed with his chayus.

He knocked at a small door where Silluka and the other person's footprints ended. The second set led away again, only an hour or so old, but his sister hadn't exited. One of the Allwiya answered, signing fast at him. He had a few words, but not enough to make sense of what they were saying.

"My sister?" he tried. "I'm looking for her. Her tracks led me here."

Several tentacles waved at him, but he didn't catch the meaning past the term for "tool," or "implement."

"She's about this high?" He gestured to his chest. "Missing part of her right arm?"

The tentacles seemed exasperated and waved him inside. Ichu stared at the entrance. He wasn't sure his shoulders would even fit through.

"I think I'm too big for your little house—" he started but the tentacles cut him off again, cycling through yellow and orange. Were those good colors? Bad?

There was a grinding noise and Ichu stepped back. The entire wall was moving up, opening with hidden hinges into a passage nearly as tall as he was.

"Oh. Thank you," he said, and ducked into the little room filled with the knick-knacks of the Allwiya hanging on the walls. They loved having little bits of metal and wood around them, as if the mere presence was comforting. They seemed to create them from the trash they sorted through.

From in here, he could hear voices, one of them definitely Silluka and the other a strange, high voice. They were behind the walls somewhere and he looked down at the Allwiya, shorter than his knees.

"You know where she is, don't you. Can you take me to her?"

The wave this time seemed more like a "calm down" gesture, and Ichu frowned as the creature leisurely walked across the room on many tentacles and pulled a series of other levers. The far wall, covered in the Allwiya's ornaments, slid aside, revealing a short hallway and a room covered in piles of garbage. There, Silluka stood with a second Allwiya, no bigger than his hand, draping wires across his sister's good arm like they were trying to turn her into another of their ornaments.

"...you can position it in exactly the right place for the chayu?" Silluka was saying. She still hadn't noticed him. "And I'll be able to use it even with my arm?"

"Yes, but measurements are essential. Limbs must break in right places." Was that high voice coming from that Allwiya? Ichu was about to rush forward at the mention of breaking limbs when the little creature smacked their head. "Bend. Joints with bones are so strange. Oh. Greetings."

The Allwiya's eyes had turned to Ichu, and he cleared his throat. Silluka's head popped up and her eyes hooded, as if he'd found her doing something wrong. He wasn't sure what he had found, in fact.

"What are you doing here?" she asked. She didn't drop her arm, where the Allwiya was still scuttling around, wrapping and unwrapping bits of wood and metal.

"Hello to you too. Those are the first words after you don't come home for a week? Your birthday is tomorrow."

"I figured you wouldn't want me to be around with Kuillay and his lovely eyes."

Ichu bit his tongue. He'd deserved that. "He's gone. I told him to get out by the time I came back."

"Was it the jakua sheets?" Silluka asked. Her face was carefully blank.

Ichu tried to hold in his smile, but he finally gave in to his smirk. "A bit, yeah. That and the names."

"But why would that bother you, *Iiiichy?*" Now Silluka grinned and Ichu let himself laugh in response. The Allwiya was looking from him to his sister with their little bug eyes.

"Alright, I'm sorry. But will you come home? I need to get the harvest in. And I should help you practice, for tomorrow."

Silluka's smile slipped, and she looked to the Allwiya. "I've finally found...something," she said. "I don't know what it is. But I think Lugopo might be able to help me."

"Help you with what?" Ichu watched the Allwiya, who waved at their name. Lugopo, evidently.

"With contorting body." They smacked the metal circlet. "With bodycasting. Only a first try. Need much time to scheme. To craft."

"But you can't..." Ichu trailed off, but he'd already seen the change in his sister's face. "I'm sorry. I shouldn't—"

"You're just like the rest of them," Silluka blurted. "Some people don't think I need a citizen chit just to travel with everyone else. If I had only succeeded at..." she clamped her lips closed.

Ichu cocked his head. Surely she couldn't have. "Did you...? Did you test with the elders for a citizen chit? Without practicing?" Silluka's face darkened. "And you failed." It might have been the residue of *Eagle Watches from on High*—it had faded once he wasn't concentrating on it—or it might have just been his intuition about his little sister. "Why didn't you come home? This is exactly what we've talked about before. I could have helped you. I can still help you now. I'll go with you, beg them to give you one more chance."

Silluka's frown dragged her lips down into a pout. "They already told me I can't test again."

Ichu knew he should stop but the words rolled from him. He'd *told* her. "Then it's done. You only had *one* last chance to test before your birthday. With the migration, they won't let you stay with the main caravan. They won't let you stay with *me*. You've got to come home, now, and help me get in the harvest. At least if I have something to sell, I can raise a few more spokes so you can trade with people on your way. You'll have to stay behind the Huaca, but maybe I can—"

"*Ichu*!" Silluka cut him off. "I'm not going back. I'm not helping you bring in the harvest. It's not worth it." She lifted her arm with Lugopo curled around it. The Allwiya huddled in like they didn't want to be the focus of the conversation. "The Allwiya have helped me more in one night than you have in two years since our parents died. I'm staying here with them."

"*No*." Stubborn girl. Ichu set his feet in Strength stance. *Tortoise Shoulders His Load* was so familiar, he could feel the ampuka connecting with the very first foot stamp. His back rounded as he braced his legs, letting the connection to Tiyu Tiksimuyu—Uncle Earth—form.

"Let her go, Lugopo," he growled. "Silluka is coming with me."

"Fascinating," the Allwiya chirped. "Would you mind me stealing—measuring—as you perform the chayu?" They leapt from Silluka's arm, bits of wire dangling from their tentacles, and began holding them up near Ichu's calves.

"I'm not a baby anymore, Ichu," Silluka said. She looked like she would bolt, but Ichu literally filled the only exit. He rushed through the chayu, sloppy, but finished it in seconds while he stared his sister down.

"Last chance. Are you coming back to the farm with me, or am I carrying you?"

"I won't go back there." Silluka crossed her arms.

"I can make you."

Silluka raised her chin. "Will that prove anything?"

Ichu stepped around the little Allwiya, who gave a chirp of disappointment at not finishing whatever they were doing to his ankles. The glow of the ampuka surrounded him, making things he carried light as feathers. He reached for Silluka, his hands wide.

She raised her arms as if to ward him away, but he enfolded her in a hug.

"I'm sorry I wasn't there," he mumbled into her shoulder. "I've been an ass, with Kuillay around. Please come back. Just help me for a few days. We'll figure something out, both for the farm and for you."

Silluka's shoulders relaxed.

"Ok. Give me a moment." She pushed away, then spoke intently with Lugopo for a few moments.

"Will you *let* me carry you?" he asked, and this time she nodded.

He hoisted Silluka up, carrying her in his arms like he had when she was little, and barreled out of the little hut. Once outside, he slung her up to his shoulders. He'd done this hundreds of times when she was little, carrying her faster than she could ever go herself. He started the run back to the farm. She'd agreed to come back under protest, but it was for her own good. He could feel her cold annoyance.

Silluka eventually relaxed as they got closer, riding his shoulders in her usual position with her left arm crossed over her stump like it had been her idea.

As they entered the rainstorm surrounding the farm—a strange, centralized storm then—Ichu picked up his pace and tried to plan for the quickest way to harvest the rest of the farm. With Silluka there...

"He's still here?" It was the first thing she'd said in many minutes. Ichu glanced up to see a pile of blankets and hair products on the front porch of the house, Kuillay standing behind them with his arms crossed.

"Uncles curse that man," Ichu grumbled. He set Silluka down, finally. "He probably just doesn't want to get wet. How about if you help me kick him out?"

"That might even be worth the ride here," Silluka said, still scowling. She knew how much the farm meant to him. He'd get an earful later, but she'd likely help, for a time. She'd sneak back to those Allwiya later but at least he'd get a few days' work from her, and maybe he could get her to practice the chayus a little.

Ichu had only taken one step forward when what looked like a ball of spiky metal shot out of the dark clouds. It blasted down in a trail of fire, exploding into the roof of the house. The entire structure crashed down like a pile of sticks, burying Kuillay and his blankets and hair products, and the ball rolled from the wreckage into the cornfield, smashing the plants to pulp and digging a gash in the wet mud.

CHAPTER SIX

Turtle

"Aunts, Uncles, and Entles! What was that?"

Ichu shook his head at his sister's shock. He didn't know either, but it had ploughed through his house and his farm like they were dry grass. This wasn't a random hailstone. It had spikes.

"Go check on Kuillay. I'll investigate," Ichu said in a low voice. Silluka picked up on his tone and nodded. There was a time for arguing and division, and there was a time for action. Everyone in the Huaca, undesirable or not, knew it. When a tsunami crashed into the shore, or a hurricane blew through, it was no longer time to quibble. Living in the Huaca meant being strong in adversity. He'd lost his parents, his farm was dying, and now his house was gone too. He was used to rebuilding.

Silluka ran to the pile of wood and stone that used to be the house, picking carefully through the wreckage. Ichu paced across the yard, chayus running through his head as he tried to assess what had happened. Had the storm picked up a rock from offshore, melded by the two islands approaching each other? Was it something from the wall of storms? From beyond? Why had the gods not protected him? Ichu looked up, but the entire sky out over the sea was covered by dark—no, *black*—clouds. He couldn't see the wall of storms at all.

The gash in the ground ran straight from the house and out through the main field. Corn stalks were everywhere. At least he had picked this field this morning, but nothing else would be coming from it anytime soon. And the corn had been stored in the house, he realized. Well. Maybe there wasn't time to rebuild the farm once more before the migration.

He walked along the trench. At the bottom of it, the earth was smooth and slick, like it had been melted. Ichu put a hand out and the heat coming off it made him pull back quickly.

Stalks obscured the end of the groove, and Ichu threw them aside as he walked, the last vestiges of *Tortoise Shoulders His Load* lending him strength to lift. The effect from chayus could work together, but the effect of the first decreased when the practitioner concentrated on the second. If he was quick, he could add to his boosted strength with another useful chayu like *Quirra Hibernates in the Winter* to keep the heat from touching him.

He was most of the way across the field, picking through the torn earth and plants, when Silluka panted up behind him. She was clutching the end of her right arm with her left hand, picking at it like she did when she was nervous.

"I'm...I'm sorry, Ichu," she said. "He must have been right under the thing that crashed into the house."

The stab of pain was less than Ichu would have thought. Kuillay had been a beautiful pest, but there had been a reason Ichu had let him stay for months when he'd turned out previous suitors in days or weeks. It was nice to have someone to care for. Still, the man had been useless at all but the most basic activities. He'd never have amounted to anything in the Huaca.

"The strong survive in the Huaca," he murmured. It was what people said when natural disasters took loved ones from them. The stronger the Huaca, the more people would live. He jabbed his chin forward. "Let's see what this thing is, and then I guess we'll go back to the village. There's nothing left, here."

Silluka opened her mouth to say something, but as he took one more step, the ground ahead erupted, dirt and stalks flying to all sides. Ichu shielded his eyes, throwing his other arm in front of his sister. When he looked again, a shape was rising from the destruction.

It wasn't a ball. Facing them was what looked like a shell of rock, jagged edges forming sharp points. A limb lifted to one side, then disappeared in front of the shell, and Ichu realized its back was to them. But the back of what?

"Get away!" he told Silluka and set his feet in Dexterity stance. He began the finger curls and wrist strikes that made up *Jakua's Claws*, ready for whatever this foreign creature might be.

It turned before he was done, fast as a striking snake, and he only caught a flash of red eyes before it was on him, rocky fists pummeling his raised arms.

Jakua's Claws curled around the incoming strikes, catching and redirecting them, while Ichu stomped his feet out into Immovable stance, legs flexing and rocking in *Roots in Fitted Stone*. The Chayu would make him nigh unmovable, at the expense of quick movement. He could feel the last vestiges of *Tortoise Shoulders His Load* leaving him, his strength decreasing and the strikes bruising his arms. One could only realistically keep two or maybe three chayus active at once, with at most a fourth fading away.

Then Silluka was there to the side, whipping a hoe with her one arm into the creature's side, distracting it.

"I said get back!" Ichu cried, and Silluka ignored him as usual, but she'd given him an instant to see the creature in full.

It was taller than him, and he was tall for one of the Huaca. The face was similar to a man's, but hard, like it was made of chipped stone, the skin slate gray. Red eyes—no, eyes *glowing* red—stared murder at him above an elongated and smoothed nose and mouth, more like an eagle's beak than a man's mouth.

It had two arms, two legs, all wrapped in coarse fiber, like bark or wood beaten to flexibility. There was an insignia on the chest plate, a carving of a beast with a long snout and overhanging teeth.

Ichu's body was already moving through *Tortoise's Heavy Foot*, which would make his strikes powerful enough to break stone. He couldn't stray from the chayu while he did so, and despite the momentary distraction from Silluka, the creature kept pummeling him.

Ichu finished the third chayu in quick succession, each one only a few moves long. His body glowed with the ampuka, browns and purples with the blessing from the gods, enough to cast shadows against the creature. He'd feel this strain tomorrow. He caught the next strike, trying to throw his attacker off his stance, but the stonelike creature barely moved.

His eyes widened as the fist pulled back and sent him flying.

Ichu landed with a crash among dirt, rocks, and corn stalks, *Roots in Fitted Stone* keeping anything from breaking his skin. He rolled over in time to see the beast run at him like a tree falling, quick, but with no grace.

He rolled, pushed off from one arm, and spun to a standing position, twisting to throw a foot out in a snap kick directly into its path as it ran into him.

There was a sound like thunder as his foot contacted the bark-like armor. *Roots in Fitted Stone* and *Tortoise's Heavy Foot* made his strike something that could kick through rock. But the creature only stopped, swaying, then raised a vial of thick, red liquid to its beak and drank, quicker than Ichu could recover and grab for the vial. The glow spread from its eyes to cover its upper body, like the glow of the ampuka, but dark and deadly.

The beak twisted into a grin, more flexible than he thought.

Then it punched him.

Ichu blinked back to consciousness twenty paces away, the churned dirt conforming to his body. His chayus were dissipating. He'd done them quickly and without precision, so their effects hadn't lasted. The more perfect they were, the more powerful.

Then Silluka was beside him again, pulling with her hand and trying to pry him up with her stump.

"It's coming! Get up! Get up!"

She pulled him to his feet, stronger than he remembered, and he turned just in time to cross his arms for another blow. He twisted to redirect the attack, and surprisingly, it worked. The creature flew past and Silluka tugged him the other way. So, strong, but not very flexible.

"Tiya Qhalikay, Aunt Healing, keep him from injury!" Silluka called as they both ran back toward the house.

"It's gaining." Ichu spared a look back to see the creature—as if a turtle had decided to be a man—down another vial of red liquid. Even from here, he could see its thick neck tense, like new strength coursed down its body. It started running. Fast.

Strong. Fast. Not as reactive.

Ichu pushed Silluka to one side and dove the other way as it shot past. It hadn't expected them to be that nimble. Its charge took the creature far into the distance, nearly past the limits of the farm before it slowed.

"It's looping around," Silluka said.

"Do you know *Flock of Starlings?*"

She grimaced. "I've maybe seen it once? It isn't that common."

He didn't have time to say she would have known more if she'd ever practiced.

"Follow my lead." Ichu went into Dexterity stance. They had seconds to start. *Flock of Starlings* was a group chayu. As long as the overall form was close, mistakes, or physical limitations, melded into the whole. Even if his sister couldn't do all the hand movements, he could be more precise in his to make up for her. He began, using only his eyes to signal her to start with him. Ahead, the creature was coming around in a wide arc. It seemed not to be able to turn quickly with whatever was in the last vial it had drunk.

"Now arms," he said. "Good. Fingers—well, what you can do. Keep the legs light." He had urged Silluka to practice with him for years. He hadn't dreamed he'd have to teach her while an alien turtleman raced toward them.

Almost there. Ichu picked up his foot, expanding the muscles on just the outside of his leg to lengthen it and curve inward. Exact muscle manipulation took years to master, and his sister didn't have it. Still, the chayu around them began to glow, more around him, but the ampuka spread to Silluka.

"I'm doing it!" she called. "Elder Quilqi was right!"

Who? But Ichu didn't have time to question. The last move of the chayu fell into place and he felt the wind rising under him, his speed linked to Silluka's and bound to Tiyu Pacha—Uncle Sky.

"Run!"

They both took off toward the village as the turtleman sped through where they'd been standing with a screech like grinding earth, leaving a gash in the rock where its claws had passed. It shot off to their left as they ran back to the Huaca, lifted as if on wings.

"What *was* that?" Silluka asked as they ran, the glow of the ampuka surrounding them. "Have you ever seen something like that before?"

"A storm came up fast this morning, directly from the wall of storms," Ichu answered.

"Then you think it was a storm warrior?"

He laughed. "A god wouldn't deign to come down to earth." Then he sobered. All the signs pointed to the new island, approaching theirs like the Allwiya's had, hundreds of years ago. The elder geologists said the ground near the coast would keep turning into jagged mountains until that island impacted theirs. Maybe it was happening sooner than they thought? Did islands change speed as they raced across the boiling ocean?

"Then what if something got *through* the wall of storms?" Silluka said what he was thinking.

"If it was strong enough to do that, it's stronger than any of the Huaca," Ichu said. "It's going to follow us. We have to warn the village."

CHAPTER SEVEN

Rats Guard Their Nest

The Huaca approached faster than Silluka had ever experienced. She was connected to the ampuka! Power from the realm of the gods and goddesses flowed through her, lending her strength. She would have laughed for joy, but the turtle-like monstrosity was still following them—catching up with them.

Silluka was falling behind. Ichu was already lending her so much strength. Was this what it felt like to be him instead of her, with her small frame and weak muscles?

"We can still make it to the Huaca before it catches up," Ichu called to her. Silluka risked another look back and saw it raise another of those strange glowing vials to its beaky mouth. It ran faster.

"I'm not sure we can," she shouted back. Ichu followed her gaze, then put his head down, legs churning even harder. Silluka felt his speed bleed into her, *Flock of Starlings* not only giving them enhanced speed, but equalizing it between them.

Then Ichu began doing *another* chayu while they ran, all arm, hand, and...head movements? She had never appreciated how powerful her brother was, to hold so much of the Aunts', Uncles', and Entles' energy. How close was he to becoming one of the elders? She didn't recognize this chayu either.

When he was done, the ampuka glowed fiercer around Ichu's throat and he raised his head and *howled*.

It echoed off the trees, bushes, and rocks. Silluka could practically see the wind of it rushing ahead of them to the Huaca. There were words in it, of foes and fighting, but she could barely make it out. The added glow around his throat was extinguished with the one cry.

"Coyote's Howl," Ichu explained when he saw her looking. "The others will be ready."

Silluka couldn't help but look back. The red eyes of the turtleman bored into her. It had covered half again their distance.

"We're not going to make it," she said again.

"We'll make it," Ichu growled. "Just keep running and stop looking back."

Silluka put her head down and ran, legs pumping faster than she thought possible. A shiver went down her spine at the thought of talons reaching for her back.

* * *

They bowled through a line of Huaca, ready as Ichu promised they would be. Silluka stumbled to a halt against a building, panting, and bent over her legs. Someone passed her a flask of water and she saw it was Hufi, already glowing with the ampuka and looking concerned. His patrol was lined up beside him, Meaty Boy—she should really learn his name—nervously glancing between the pretty tall girl and the shorter one, who was busy with a chayu. The boy with the swoop of hair was kneading his hands together as if he would pop his fingers off.

She turned at a call like granite being broken. The turtleman was standing twenty paces away, beaky head inclined, shouting at them. It was issuing a challenge, that was obvious, but what it was, she couldn't tell.

Now she had a moment to observe the turtleman, she saw he—definitely a he, or at least presenting more like the males of the Huaca—was taller than any from the village, arms thick with ropy muscle, and back curved. He didn't have a shell as such, but what looked like spiny plates grew from the back of his neck and upper arms, all the way down to below his waist. They grated almost as loud as his speech, rubbing together as he shifted and gestured. That was why he'd looked like a spiky seed when he landed. He must have curled into a ball and the plates protected his descent. Was that how he got through the wall of storms? What about the storm warriors? Had he defeated them?

"What does he want?" Hufi asked her.

Silluka shrugged. "To fight. He already beat Ichu. We had to run all the way here."

"He beat Ichu?" Hufi paled and looked back to the elders, arranged behind them. As usual, when facing a threat, the younger, stronger bodycaster citizens were in front as a first line of defense, while the older, more experienced Huaca stood in back, planning and crafting longer chayus.

Where was her brother? She glanced around, seeing him talking to several other bodycasters of his generation—friends he knew in the village. He winced as she watched him, one hand going to his ribs. He hid injury well, but even with his connection to the gods, the turtleman had blasted through his defenses quickly. Too quickly. This was a powerful foe.

Another shout made her whip back around to the turtleman. He had stepped forward, craggy arm raised, bellowing toward the gathered villagers. His eyes glowed an unearthly red, and he raised another vial of liquid, downing it with a flourish, then staring defiantly, brandishing the empty vial as if to make sure none missed it. There was a gasp from the crowd as the glow intensified and shifted to a dark, bruised purple. He grinned savagely at the response, then made an obvious "come here" gesture.

Murmurs grew as the villagers spoke amongst themselves, wondering who would accept the challenge.

"We'll take you on!" came a shout next to her, and Silluka saw Hufi step forward, his patrol flanking him on both sides. Meaty Boy looked uncertain, but the others were just as stoic as Hufi. She could almost admire them, though they had cost her a chance at being a citizen.

No. Be fair. That was all her fault. She stood straighter. "Good luck," she said to Hufi's back. He acknowledged with a wave, as his patrol ran forward. Maybe five could overpower him where one wasn't enough. If she had any skill at all with bodycasting, she would have helped, but she was nothing, not even a citizen. An undesirable.

The turtleman roared in triumph, stamping his armored feet, eyes blazing. He squatted, lowering his center of mass, and rolling his shoulders forward. The plates on his back clattered together, sticking up over his shoulders. He met the rushing bodycasters with a growl, instantly throwing the shorter girl and the boy with the swoop of hair off to the sides. They slid and rolled, far out of the action. Tall Girl, Meaty Boy, and Hufi were all glowing with the ampuka. When had they had time to perform a chayu? Silluka *would* learn to summon that feeling. Now she had felt it, first under Elder Quilqi's tutelage and again, running with Ichu, she kicked herself for not trying harder, even with her stump.

If anyone had told her missing an arm was not an impediment to connecting with the ampuka, she would have poured herself into application. But all her life, she'd expected to be an undesirable. Only those at the peak of physical strength, with fine muscular control, could be bodycasters. If that wasn't so, what else were the village elders wrong about?

Hufi and the other two grappled the turtleman, who looked momentarily uncertain, muscles on his arms straining. Why wasn't he moving like he had when fighting Ichu?

Ah, she saw now. They must have performed *Root Grows Around the Rock* and constrained him already. Silluka remembered how the chayu kept her from moving, tying her to her captors.

But the turtleman growled, eyeing the fourth and fifth members of Hufi's patrol, who were up again and running back toward the group. The purple of his eyes spilled over, leaking strange light down his chiseled cheekbones, and the turtleman threw his arms wide with a scream.

Hufi and the other two fell back. Meaty Boy was holding his wrist, shoulders curled forward around it. What had happened? Around her, bodycasters discussed the fight like it was a regular tournament in the arena. Didn't they understand how powerful the turtleman was?

Silluka was distracted by a shout from the elders. The older bodycasters were all in Dexterity stance, bent low, arms moving almost too fast to see. Elder Papaki led them, though Elder Quilqi was not around, and Ichu watched from one side, not participating. They began to interweave their steps, crossing over and around each other so Silluka could hardly tell how many of them there were. At the same moment, she felt the ampuka for the third time in her life. Nothing for over seventeen years, then three times in less than a full day. What had she been doing with her life until now? Did it take catastrophe to the Huaca to get her to act?

A shout of pain divided her attention yet again. The turtleman held Tall Girl by the throat and she clawed at his thick skin to no effect. Silluka had taken three steps forward before she realized what she was doing. She'd have no chance against that thing. She wouldn't have even done that two days ago. What was she thinking?

The turtleman threw Tall Girl even farther than he'd punched Ichu and she landed on the ground with a sickening thud, laying still. Silluka was two steps into running to help, but faster than she thought possible, the turtleman grabbed Hufi, still glowing with the ampuka, and raised him above his head.

"No!" Ichu had one hand forward, even as the other held his ribs, obviously injured. He had seen what Silluka hadn't, or not soon enough. The turtleman brought Hufi down like a falling rock, raising his knee at the same time, and it was only then Silluka saw the bony spikes emerging from his legs.

Hufi jerked and gurgled as the spikes penetrated his back with a sickening crunch. The turtleman threw him away like a leg of meat, gnawed to the marrow. Silluka cried out despite herself, her hand reaching as if to stop what was happening. She'd known Hufi since they were children, playing the gutters. Before her parents died. Before Hufi became a citizen.

The strong survived in the Huaca. The looming threat was even more important than mourning Hufi.

Power erupted through Silluka, and she could barely think, let alone mourn. She could *feel* the elders and older bodycasters behind her, weaving together, like a mass of small animals, bristling with teeth and claws, making themselves look bigger.

She could feel where everyone was around her, too, and they all stepped forward as a group, the whole village of one mind, linked together in body and action. It was a powerful chayu tied to Tiye Kwirpuyay—Aunt Magic. She saw now what she should have seen before. Hufi and his patrol had given the elders enough time to perform the chayu. If she had tried to relate to the other villagers before now rather than stealing from them, she might have known how the village's defenses worked. Ichu certainly would have explained it. The strong protected, but only the strongest survived.

The turtleman watched them approach, his eyes dimmed to only a red glow again, head moving between groups of the Huaca. They were all advancing, surrounding the invader. Silluka was ready to crawl over the turtleman, doing what little she could to take him down. By herself, she was weak, but with the others, she was one bucket of water in a wave of grasping fingers, bared teeth, and strong legs.

They surrounded the turtleman, grabbing at his limbs. He tried to get another vial to his lips, but three villagers held onto his wrist. Another ten fell to the ground, tangling his ankles so he couldn't move. Silluka found herself by his other side and grabbed the thick fiber straps wrapping his body. She tangled her stump around his arm, tying him in place. Ichu was in here somewhere, finding another handhold to slow the monster down.

As the Huaca surrounded him in a sea of people, the turtleman roared, head raised to the sky. He thrashed from side to side, throwing people off as fast as they could scurry back to him. Silluka bucked and jerked, but her hold on his wrap near the center of his mass meant his movements could not toss her away.

But he was still winning. One foot was free, and he used it to knee a villager with the spike, throwing her to the ground, clutching a gash in her stomach.

They wouldn't win. The turtleman would kill them all. Were there more of this monster? Even one was too much for them. What gods did the turtleman have, who were so strong? It was something to do with those vials, Silluka was certain.

Then a cry broke through the scene, like a hawk diving on its prey. Silluka looked back just in time to see Elder Quilqi, white hair streaming behind her, glowing like the morning sun with a bright yellow ampuka. She ran like the wind and leapt the last distance, entire body lined up horizontal behind one fist, the top knuckle extended. Silluka got only a glimpse of wide turtle eyes before the elder's knuckle connected with his forehead with a crack like the sea battering a cliff. Dark, thick blood exploded from the wound and Elder Quilqi landed in a crouch on top of the invader's chest, villagers knocked aside like leaves fallen from a tree.

Silluka shakily released her death grip on the coarse fibers. She had traveled twenty paces with the elder, the turtleman, and a few villagers. The turtleman's body had dug a trench into the rocky earth, his forehead cracked and leaking blood and gore like a ravine opened by an earthquake.

He was dead, eyes glazed, and Elder Quilqi stood over him triumphant. Silluka stared up at the woman who had started her on this journey. She had not been with the others. She was not like any elder Silluka had met before. How long had she been in the Huaca? She must have been around since before Silluka had been born, but she couldn't remember seeing the elder before yesterday. She didn't know many elders, but they were not that strong. They didn't fight, they directed. Their bodies were no longer powerful enough to take the stresses of martial chayus.

"Crashing seas, girl, don't just sit there with your mouth open," Elder Quilqi said. "Haven't you ever seen *Eagle's Tearing Beak*? What do they teach kids these days? Help me get this body back to the village for study. We need to see what this invader is made of."

CHAPTER EIGHT

Examining the Enemy

Silluka wanted to go to Hufi's body, to help out. Her hand shook, and she clasped it over the end of her stump, holding both arms close to her. She had spoken with him minutes ago. It didn't seem real. Several other villagers—ones she didn't know—were dead, and there were more with broken bones, cuts, and scrapes. Their village had weathered hurricanes and tidal waves, ash from volcanoes and violent winds. But just one of the turtlemen had decimated their most powerful bodycasters.

But Elder Quilqi kept a grip on her arm while she peered at the dead invader.

"You're coming with me, girl," she said. "And I want your brother there too. The Allwiya can fix him up."

The other elders seemed to defer to her, not surprising given her show of power. Elder Papaki helped her draft several of the less-injured Huaca to drag the deceased turtleman back to the village, to the Allwiya's section. Several performed *Tortoise Shoulders His Load* to help carry the body. Ichu did not, his hand pressed to his side. She wondered how many of his ribs the turtleman had broken.

Silluka walked next to her brother, both helping to pull the corpse, though they didn't add much to the effort. Ichu winced in pain, and Silluka only had one hand to drag with. There was no good place to grasp part of the turtleman. He seemed to be made of spikes, rough fibers, and coarse skin.

"I'm sorry about Hufi," Ichu said to her as they trudged with the others, heaving the body behind them. "I know you played with him as children."

"He was a spoiled brat," Silluka sniffed, then relented. "But I didn't want to see him go that way."

"The strong survive in the Huaca," Ichu said.

"But do they have to?" Silluka asked. Her brother stared back for a moment, as if uncomprehending.

"Why must only the strong survive?" Silluka asked. "Shouldn't the strong protect the weak? Isn't that what they're there for?" There had been no undesirables besides her in this fight. They were likely hiding in their houses and where they could find shelter. They would have been mowed down like dry grass.

Ichu considered this for a moment. "You'll have to ask the elders," he finally said. "Philosophy is their purview. I'll stick with bodycasting."

At least until he became one of them. She suspected it would happen soon. "That's another thing." If he wouldn't answer that question, she had others. "How long has Elder Quilqi been here? I don't know as many in the Huaca as you do, but I feel like I would have remembered her from when I was a kid. I remember Elder Papaki and what's-her-name, who's good with medicine? Elder Sinchi."

Ichu shook his head. "She arrived a few years ago from a neighboring village in the south, she said. It had been decimated by a volcano, and she traveled north to find someone to take her in. I don't remember her having such a high position with the elders before."

"Not just a high position—she was at the forefront of the elders judging the citizens' test." Silluka played back the memory in her head. Had the others *deferred* to the old woman?

"Only because they know competence when they see it." Silluka and Ichu both jumped in surprise. How had Elder Quilqi moved so silently? "Come on. I'll tell you more at Lugopo's workshop."

* * *

Elder Quilqi shooed the other Huaca away after the turtleman lay in a heap outside the building where Silluka first met Lugopo. That seemed more than just a day ago, now.

"You two stay with me," she directed. "I need someone with a good head on their shoulders to bounce ideas off of. I'm worried about this beast." She kicked the turtleman's leg with a *thock* like dense heartwood.

Once the others were gone, Elder Quilqi knocked at the door to Lugopo's workshop. The little Allwiya scuttled out with Muola, ranging around the corpse in wonder. Both let their tentacles roam on the body, as if their limbs had minds of their own.

"Such joy for this find! Dissection will lead to many new revelations. We will dance around the dead and rejoice!" Lugopo tapped the circlet around their head. "Will study this specimen for new information. Apologies. I am still working on the translation circlet."

"But what *is* he?" Silluka asked.

"You saw him first," Elder Quilqi shot back.

"He came from beyond the wall of storms," Ichu murmured. "He must be one who lives on the island approaching us. If this is the first sign of their power, we are in much danger."

Lugopo, tiny as they were, dragged out several lengths of rope, chain, and strange flat pieces that had a similar consistency to their tentacles. They directed the others— tapping on their translator here and there when it spit out the wrong word—to wrap up the corpse. Once that was done, Muola turned yellow, scampered inside, and pulled a lever. There was a loud whirring noise, and the body was dragged into the workshop.

"We'll leave them to their work," Elder Quilqi said. "Now, you had questions for me. Or about me, as it were." Her eyes were deep, dark, and intent on them.

Ichu was in front of her, Silluka realized. Was he trying to protect her? Could he? How strong was the Elder, to kill the turtleman in one strike?

"Where are you from?" Ichu asked. "You're new to the Huaca." Silluka noticed he didn't mention her power.

"Yes, I'm not from here, but that isn't the right question." The elder put her hands on her hips.

"How are you so influential among the elders already?"

"*That's* the right question." Elder Quilqi pointed at Silluka, then darted an annoyed glare at Ichu. "Thundering clouds, boy, you don't need to act like a mother jakua guarding her young. I think I've demonstrated I have the good of your Huaca as my interest."

"And you also didn't answer my question," Silluka reminded her.

"You're right. I didn't. But my expertise will be invaluable while we deal with what's coming. The elders are spooked. They're already speaking of moving up the trek inland. The turtleman was powerful, but this little out-of-the-way village will soon encounter others nearly as strong."

"But this is *the* Huaca," Ichu protested. "We're the people blessed by the gods. Who else could be more powerful?"

Silluka noticed the elder still hadn't answered them, but her misdirection was too tempting not to follow up on.

"You know more about bodycasting than the rest of the elders, too," Silluka accused.

The elder nodded her head to both points. "I do, and there are *plenty* who are more powerful. Stars and rain, boy, what about the storm warriors? You've seen them with your own eyes. Do you aspire only to the middling heights of your elders?"

Ichu stared back as if he'd never considered the concept. Silluka looked up over his head, where clouds spilled away from the wall of storms, out past the cliffs of the coast. Even from here, she could see the small forms zipping in and out of the constantly falling water. The turtleman had gotten past them.

"Then are they gods, or people?" she asked. Those in the village even had a storm warrior day once a year where they prayed to their protectors.

"What's the difference?" Elder Quilqi shrugged. "If you could fly around a waterspout and keep them from decimating the villages hanging on to life on this coast, would you be considered a god? What is such a feat compared to the power of the Tiyus, Tiyas, and Tiyes?"

But that was different, wasn't it? The chayus didn't come from the storm warriors. They were considered lesser gods to the eight children of Grandfather Death and Grandmother Life. Silluka exchanged a look with her brother and opened her mouth to argue, but Muola scuttled between them at knee-height, waving two tentacles in the air in patterns, skin flashing between green, blue, and white.

"Ah. Looks like Lugopo has found something already," the elder said, and followed the little Allwiya inside.

"I'm sure we can ask her more later," Ichu said, then turned after the two.

Inside, they found Lugopo covered in greenish-black blood, waving three different wicked-looking tools in separate tentacles.

"Such discovery! My skin is burning! Ouch!"

They didn't tap the communication circlet, but promptly dashed on multiple tentacles to a bucket of water and jumped in. They emerged a moment later, glistening and wet. The blood was gone, but there were pockmarks on their bulbous head where the blood must have started corroding.

"Are you well?" Silluka asked, but Lugopo waved the query away with a tentacle.

"Personal safety is less important than new information." They pointed to a chunk of flesh removed from the turtleman's side, dark and slick. "Blunted my scalpel. These tur-tle-men"—the translation circlet choked on the unfamiliar gesture of Lugopo's tentacles—"must be powerful and vicious, waiting to crush their unsuspecting victims with their fearsome strength!"

They reached up and fiddled with the circlet. "That is, their environment must be a harsh one. Their blood is caustic, and they have very tough skin." They held up two empty vials. "Also these. They seem to be the source of the turtle-man's power."

"Was that all you found?" Elder Quilqi leaned forward, by Silluka's side.

Lugopo gestured a negative. "Several more empty vials. Only one still full. I do not know its dark purpose—that is, what it does." They raised another vial, this one with a viscous, purplish fluid in it.

Ichu took it, passing it in front of one of the ever-lit candles in Lugopo's workshop. Silluka saw flecks inside the liquid, drifting languidly.

"I'll take that." Elder Quilqi slipped the vial from Ichu's hands, as smooth as nut oil. Her brother's eyes followed the vial as the elder tucked it away somewhere. "It's likely how these people connect to their gods, just as the Allwiya do with their technology."

"*Their* gods? You mean different from the Tiyus, Tiyas, and Tiyes? How many are there? Why don't they worship the ones we do?" Her questions burbled up suddenly. Silluka wondered how much more Elder Quilqi knew about the world. How much more *was* there? The Storm Warriors weren't the Aunts, Uncles, and Entles, but they were connected...somehow. She wasn't sure how. How much had their village lost, over the years? What else was out there, on their island? Had secrets been lost when her grandparents fled with the rest of the Huaca inland from the coast-turned-mountains?

Surprisingly, Lugopo took up the explanation. "I have mentioned the gods of the Allwiya before. Whirling Abyss. Crawling Dark of Squirming. Manylegs of Reaching. These are not like yours. Would not assume the turtle-man's would be the same either."

"You only have three gods?" Ichu asked. Silluka looked to the elder, who had her arms crossed, mouth quirking in a smile. She must know all this already. Did the elders? Why was it not common knowledge in the Huaca?

Then she understood. It was the same reason she never thought practice was worth it. The Huaca was powerful, but it was not smart. The elders studied their ancient scrolls, but the younger bodycasters only practiced. They had to, to get the intricate gestures of the chayus correct, to summon the ampuka. She'd had more time than most to think about her situation. She didn't practice the chayus all the time. Most undesirables didn't either. They worked around the village, or made repairs, or collected crops from the fields.

Lugopo made an affirmative gesture to Ichu's question. "We have three gods and many. The triplet elders spawn many lesser gods, though we do not revere them. Each of the triplets grants us a specific power. Whirling Abyss makes the mind spin with new connections. Crawling Dark of Squirming gives us the ingenuity to make those ideas reality and know which ones veer too close to the abyss. Finally, Manylegs of Reaching lets us craft like no other, giving us the thrill of creation."

"You know of the Aunts, Uncles, and Entles of the Huaca?" Ichu asked.

Lugopo waved three tentacles, an indeterminate gesture. "I know of your Tiye Kwirpuyay. They are the one who created your chayus, which I study."

Ichu stood straight, hands behind his back, and Silluka barely kept from rolling her eyes. Always the good student.

> "Death and Life begat us all, Death and Life begat the gods.
> Firstborn is Tiye Kwirpuyay, Entle Magic, by which all is done.
> Second is Tiyu Llamkay, Uncle Smith, to fashion our bodies.
> Third is Tiye Khuyay, Entle Love, to join us together.
> Fourth is Tiya Qhalikay, Aunt Healing, to keep us whole.
> Fifth is Tiyu Pacha, Uncle Sky, to keep the stars up.
> Sixth is Tiya Qucha, Aunt Sea, to divide the Sky.
> Seventh is Tiyu Tiksimuyu, Uncle Earth, to hold up our feet.
> Eighth is Tiya Aymuray, Aunt Harvest, to sustain us all.
> Death and Life will welcome us home,
> Death and Life will show us the way."

"The eight siblings keep our land protected, and the Huaca sheltered," Silluka added. "Each one protects us from the calamities of the earth, sea, or sky, keeps our bodies from injury, feeds us, and keeps our magic strong and our community whole." She hadn't heard the children's rhyme in a long time. Perhaps Hufi had been right. She could have been helping the Huaca, rather than leeching off it. She glanced at her stump. She'd made excuses her whole life for what she couldn't do. She could have spent that time learning what the Huaca had lost. Had it kept her from the ampuka? From being a citizen? Maybe it was time to find out what she *could* do.

"Eight! So many barriers against the endless void. But you have ten, yes? More than the eight?" Lugopo reached up on all eight tentacles, standing on the dissection table. They still had to strain backward to meet Silluka's eyes.

Elder Quilqi poked one finger at the gash in the turtleman's side. "Grandfather Death and Grandmother Life no longer grace this world. Even the gods strive to achieve what they have. But that's not what we're discussing here. We're wondering about the gods of this thing." She turned bright eyes to Lugopo. "Your people came here more recently. What do you know of the island you called your home before it impacted the Huaca's land?"

"We have many records," Lugopo gestured. "We are blessed to be the terrors of the boiling ocean"—they tapped the circlet—"that is, we are good seafarers, and traveled all around our island and this larger landmass. Our original island is now a mountain range, far to the northwest, but we have insinuated ourselves all through the villages of the Huaca. From knowledge passed down, your island is several times bigger. It is attracting all the other local landmasses."

Silluka cocked her head. Attracting other islands? Was that why the turtleman's island was coming right for them, hidden behind the wall of storms and raising the coast into mountains?

"By the speed of its approach, I would guess this new island is even smaller than yours," Elder Quilqi cautioned.

"But their warriors are fierce, and powerful." Lugopo prodded the corpse with one of their scalpels. It didn't even cut the skin. "Whoever protects them also gives great power."

"Similar in execution to Uncle Smith, and he's a powerful one," Elder Quilqi muttered. "Which means this village has little chance on its own."

"But where will we go? There are volcanoes to the south, sea to the east and north, and only desert to the west." Ichu was frowning at all of them, hands on hips. He must be as confused as Silluka was, but he hid it well. How ignorant was their village? Did the elders know these things?

"There is far more than desert, boy, but we will need to be strong to cross it. We must make preparations." She turned to Silluka. "You had best come with me. You haven't had much practice with the physical chayus performed here. Perhaps it will be easier to teach you the mental ones, since you have few preconceptions."

"Mental chayus are a myth," Ichu stated.

"Not so."

"*Mental* chayus?" Silluka had never heard of them before, though it seemed her brother had. "Do you mean there are chayus the elders here don't know?"

Quilqi laughed. "Just wait, girl. You'll find out soon enough."

CHAPTER NINE

Preparations

"If you want to start learning chayus, begin with the morning ritual," Ichu told Silluka. She'd shown a new side of herself in the week since the turtleman ploughed through their home. The village elders were in the throes of planning, with Elders Papaki and Sinchi leading the others on how to organize the migration. They'd been alive for the last one, though they'd been children.

Ichu's feet went to Basic stance by instinct, as wide as his hips, legs slightly bent, tension on the outside of his legs to form a circle of strength from the ground to pelvis, and back to ground. His arms rested lightly in front of him, shoulders relaxed and hands open but ready to move.

They were in town, at one of the buildings used for storage near the center. Elder Quilqi had pulled strings with the others to find them a living space, now the farm had been destroyed. There was no point in going back. She hadn't followed up on her talk of the mythical mental chayus, and Ichu was content to let it go, teaching his sister real, practical chayus instead.

Silluka copied him, her right arm placed correctly, had it been made with its full length. He could nearly see where her forearm should have been. Her legs were already in a better stance than the last time he'd made her try the morning ritual with him.

He nodded to her knees. "More tension on the outside of your legs, less on the inside. Create a circle connected to the ground. Let the energy from the gods come up into you, and release back down to the earth."

Silluka frowned, but didn't complain. She pushed her knees out to each side a little more. Ichu gave an accepting nod. It wasn't quite right, but it was better than she had managed before. Chayus had to be nearly perfect in their precision to summon the ampuka. A practitioner could spend their whole life honing a favored chayu, and still have ways to improve. Most bodycasters had a few favorites and stuck to those on a daily basis. Most citizens knew a handful of others. Only the elders had records of *all* the chayus. He had managed to learn and remember more than fifty, during his life. It was a feat no other bodycaster in the village had replicated, securing his place as an elder—the most powerful of bodycasters—when the time came.

"*The Wing Grows* is the first move. Can you show me?"

Silluka crossed her left arm to her right shoulder, and her right elbow came nearly to her center. A good try.

Ichu held a hand to stop her movement, and adjusted her arms, pulling in just a little more so her shoulders dropped forward.

"Feel your shoulder blades open? Now the energy comes all the way from the ground into your arms."

"Arm," Silluka corrected.

"Arm," Ichu conceded, "but you feel how *both* are supposed to move, don't you? Now, again." He did the move himself, completing the motion with both arms crossing back to their side and stretching out, fingers opening like a bird's wing, each finger precise. Even with that one move, he could feel the ampuka growing, his connections to the gods increasing.

"Yes, I feel it," Silluka grumbled as she repeated the move. "I wish someone had told me before how this worked. But I was never taught, as the girl with one arm."

Ichu sighed. "The elders have failed you, and I have failed you as well. I should have taught you myself, but I was busy training and winning competitions in the village. It's my fault." He *had* tried to get her to train with him, but he'd never focused this much on her form. He'd assumed it wouldn't matter. Shouldn't the elders have known this? Papaki had never mentioned it to him.

"No, I should have insisted," Silluka argued. This was new, from her. Before, she had always preferred to think, to watch others, even to read like the elders did. Elder Quilqi had instilled a drive in her to learn. "You wouldn't have gotten so far without practicing like you did."

"And where has that gotten me?" he asked. He hadn't meant to make the remark. It had just popped out.

Silluka stared up at him, abandoning her stance and dropping her arms. "You're the most powerful bodycaster in the Huaca! How can you say that?"

Ichu pursed his lips, debating whether to share his fears. He had kept them inside for so long, taking comfort in men and women awed by his prowess. A sham.

But Silluka was his sister, and the only family he had left, now their parents were gone.

"I'm losing my ability," he forced out. Silluka frowned at him, but it was true. "I'm weaker than I was. My chayus are losing their effectiveness. I'm getting older, Silluka. I'm past my thirty-third year. How many bodycasters do you see my age?"

"I'm sure there are plenty..." Silluka looked upward, obviously counting. "Well, there's...that is..."

"I'm the oldest bodycaster of my ability in the Huaca," Ichu admitted. He kept expecting someone to call him out for this, tell him he had to become an elder, but no one had. It was why he'd pressed himself to win the bodycasting tournament last year. One last time, to prove his worth after their parents had died. There wouldn't be another tournament this year, or likely for some time, until a new Huaca was settled.

"Anyone older is no match for me, or is an elder." He put a hand on his sister's shoulder. Both of them had dropped out of their stances. "So yes, I should have taken the time to teach you better. When I'm an elder, I'll be teaching most of the time. I'm going to start now. Let's do the first move again, but this time *feel* the tension in your arms and legs. Create a circle with the earth and let the gods' power into you."

* * *

Silluka slept well that night, exhausted from Ichu's gentle but persistent corrections to her feet, her arms, her hand, even her head. They hadn't even finished the first five moves of the morning ritual. He said the ampuka wouldn't come unless every muscle was in exactly the right position. Not that the morning ritual was a chayu they completed. Finishing *Pray*, the last move, was said to bring down the power of the gods, a violent, destructive force.

The next morning, she practiced with her brother again, completing another four moves, but there was not nearly as much time for corrections, as a young girl arrived with a summons from Elder Quilqi. She was wanted at the elders' building to learn of certain records. Silluka had been waiting all week to learn more of the mental chayus, but the elder had been caught up with the others in the fallout of the turtleman invader.

"The other elders are like quirras, perched on branches and chittering at the jakua chasing them," Elder Quilqi complained as she strode along a hallway, slightly in front of Silluka. "They were planning for the Huaca to migrate later this year, but now they only see that invaders are coming, and they're pushing up the timetable. We leave in a month. You must learn quickly."

Quilqi gestured Silluka in front of her, into another back corridor of the elders' building. They passed old members of the Huaca, more than she expected, and Silluka got both curious and pitying glances. She refused to hide her stump, letting it hang where all could see.

"In here is the chayu room. A bit sparse, if I'm honest, but it's a good start." The elder pulled Silluka into a chamber covered in cubbies, with charts rolled and stored from floor to ceiling. "Now. Where is that one? I saw it just last year. Well hidden, I see. Dust and dirt! Doesn't anyone clean in here?" She studied a column of scrolls, then pulled one out with a grunt of triumph and gave it to Silluka, who unrolled it.

It was a complex collection of lines, directions, circles, and illustrated body parts. She had only rarely seen a scroll like this. Most of the Huaca couldn't read at all. She was lucky her parents had taught her when she was young, as an alternative to practicing bodycasting. But since they passed, she'd lost access to any scrolls. Ichu didn't put much stock in them.

She didn't recognize this depiction offhand, but she had guesses.

"What is it?" she asked.

Elder Quilqi frowned. "A chayu, girl. I hope you aren't as thick as that, or I've been wasting my time."

The arrows and stops of the Huaca's language did double duty in describing stances and movements. This was certainly a chayu, though a strange one.

"I don't recognize many of the lines," she said.

"That's more like it," the elder said. "If I were to guess, I'd think this chayu has seen little use since before this Huaca moved inland last time." Elder Quilqi's smile widened. "But it still exists, even if the elders no longer teach it, or even understand it. This village has forgotten what makes the chayus special." She pointed to the scroll. "Can you read what the chayu is?"

Silluka felt the weight of the test and concentrated on the scroll. It was an old dialect, not the one her parents had taught her, and she had to make guesses at some of the phonographs.

"With Tiyu Pacha? The air?" Silluka screwed up her nose. She felt the elder staring at her. "And the animal is a quirra, but there's a modifier. Oh! Tiyu Pacha's quirra? What is that?" She looked up to Elder Quilqi despite herself. The old woman had a slight smile, but said nothing. Then it clicked.

"*Flying Quirra* is the name of the chayu, isn't it? But that can't be what it does? Actually flying? Or does it simply make you lighter?"

"So you do have some reasoning ability." The elder looked pleased, despite her words. "You wouldn't have seen what this does because it uses a technique this village has forgotten over the years."

Silluka met the elder's eyes, and almost took a step back. There was *weight* behind them, and power. "And what is that?"

"*Intent*. That's why this doesn't matter." Quilqi motioned toward Silluka's stump. "The connection to the ampuka is forged by the intent behind your moves. The moves merely help direct what you are trying to achieve."

"That seems...too simple. It's completely opposite to everything I've learned. What about body position? Muscle control? That's how Ichu summons the ampuka. It's why I can't. It's what makes a citizen. Elders are the citizens who can do that the best and have survived the longest."

Elder Quilqi tapped the scroll. "Yet these techniques are all here, written down decades before you were born, girl. What do you think your Huaca practiced before it moved here? Do you know how long this little village has existed near the coast?"

Silluka didn't. She assumed there were records somewhere, but the elders didn't speak of where the Huaca originated, save that it was nearer the coast. She tried to gather all the questions buzzing around in her brain and stay on the original topic. There was so much Elder Quilqi wasn't saying.

"But if the ampuka was only a factor of *meaning* to do the chayu, wouldn't I have connected with it before now? What aren't you telling me?"

"Driving rain, girl! If I was to list everything you *don't* know about the chayus, we'd be here until the village packed up and moved. These are the very basic concepts."

"Basic? That the Huaca doesn't practice?" Silluka pressed. "While it does practice a perfection you put no stock in?" She couldn't believe she was defending the very thing that had kept her from becoming a citizen.

The elder's lips twisted in a frustrated grimace. "I believe there has been much lost as your Huaca was forced to move inland, escaping the new island approaching. Perhaps not all by accident. Perfection is a lofty goal, but by its nature, unattainable. You see how long bodycasters last out here, don't you?"

The picture of Elder Quilqi, ablaze with light while killing the turtleman, flashed through her head and Silluka frowned. The elder's body shouldn't have been able to withstand that force, at her age.

"Then tell me what you do differently."

The elder shook her head. "I can't. Not yet. This is why I'm showing you this scroll. You'll learn the whole truth in the migration, but you should have learned this as a child—your whole village should have. I can only lead those who are willing to a different point of view, which starts *here*. Now, look at these marks. What do they tell you?"

Silluka spent the next several hours decoding the chayu under Elder Quilqi's hints and prods. It was...strange. Many of the moves seemed to show more of how to think about the moves than how to perform them. Later, Silluka showed the scroll to Ichu.

"Elder Quilqi let you take this scroll out? Only the elders are supposed to see the chayu scrolls."

"Then maybe that's why our Huaca can't even stand up to one turtleman," Silluka said. She unrolled the chayu and held it out to him. "Can you tell me anything more about what this one says? Please? Have Elder Papaki or Sinchi ever mentioned anything? Elder Quilqi seems to think it's hiding some secret I need to uncover."

Ichu held his hands up. "You're better at that than me. Our parents never trained me to read. That was something they only did for you."

"You...can't read this?" Silluka looked back down at the scroll. While there were unfamiliar elements, the basic pictograms were clear.

"Mother and Father put a lot into your education," Ichu said.

Had she squandered that investment? Silluka resolved to study the chayu scroll until she understood it completely.

* * *

She spent the next week practicing the individual movements of the morning ritual with Ichu and studying the scroll with Elder Quilqi. Lugopo was busy dissecting every part of the turtleman's body, and she got an update every day or two about how it had blunted all their cutting tools, or how the bones were stronger than some types of metal. The little Allwiya had plans for every part of the turtleman's body, in a gruesome, but efficient, series of steps.

The weather got steadily worse, even for their rainy, cloudy village. Every day brought another earthquake, or multiples, and the elders called upon Tiyu Tiksimuyu regularly until they subsided. Silluka was nearly crushed as the side of a home collapsed while she walked from the elders' building to the Allwiya side of the village. Only her quick feet got her out of the way in time. Thank the gods for her extra practice with Ichu.

The next day, the village had to shelter as a hurricane blew along the coast. The elders called upon Tiyu Pacha until the winds lifted from the village. Silluka watched the dome of yellow godly ampuka protecting them from the winds until the main mass of the hurricane passed them by. The Aunts, Uncles, and Entles must have their gaze firmly on the Huaca, as quickly as they were responding to the elders' requests.

The calamities would only get more intense until the new island collided with the coast. The geologists said it had sped up drastically in the last few weeks. It was very near now, and trackers who ran to the coast reported the waters between the islands boiling and sending off incredible gusts of wind. The storm warriors in the wall of storms looked like a cloud of gnats, protecting their charge. Silluka wondered if there were more turtlemen trying to get through.

"Come see! Yes! Cower before the technological prowess of the gods of the deep!" Lugopo pranced around their workshop as Silluka filed in with Ichu and Elder Quilqi. The

Allwiya had sent a hasty note to the elder that morning, scrawled in Huaca pictograms as if they were writing with at least five of their tentacles.

"What is all this, Lugopo?" Elder Quilqi grumped. "I have ten different elders bending my ear about what needs to be packed when for travel. The sleds are only half built and the damage from the hurricane put us even farther behind."

"Crawling Dark of Squirming has blessed me with wild invocations! Come see the terror I have birthed!" They tapped their circlet. "Apologies. Translator is still not perfect. I have crafted a new item from the turtle-man." They slung across the workshop on cleverly placed poles, reaching for a lever with three tentacles. The ever-lit candles flashed as an object dropped from a compartment in the ceiling. Silluka hastily stepped out of the way as it crashed to the ground.

"We are needing sleds to reach the desert, yes? What better conveyance than the bodies of our enemies!"

Elder Quilqi bent over the construct. "These are the plates that grew from the turtleman's back?"

"Held together by sinews from the body. They are far tougher than what I can manufacture here. What incredible bindings and restraints they make!"

Silluka frowned at the little Allwiya, whose wide eyes stared back, then repositioned their circlet with four tentacles.

"Right here, see?" They pointed out straps across the insides of the plates. "Used to stay seated while the sled is moving. For safety."

"You've used the turtleman's body to create tools?" Ichu asked. "That seems like a perversion of what the Huaca call on Uncle Smith for—armoring our bodies from harm. You haven't used bodies of the Huaca, have you?"

Silluka just caught Elder Quilqi's abortive gesture before Lugopo swung to the other side of the workshop.

"Naturally! Manylegs of Reaching provides many blessings." They picked up a long drill which Silluka now saw was fashioned from a femur of one of the Huaca. "And such strong protections!" They placed a curious white dome over their bulbous head. Their eyes peeked out of two naturally formed holes.

"Is that a *skull*?" She thought Ichu's eyes might pop out of his head.

"Well, the original owner isn't using it," Elder Quilqi snapped. "Focus, Lugopo. You're telling us about this new sled."

"I presume the Huaca plan to use the river system to travel when the time comes?" Lugopo swung back down, still wearing the skull, and pointed out the features. "Coarse skin becomes a waterproof barrier between moveable armor plates. Sinew and tendon restraints to keep occupants safe. Steering rig made from arm bones. Brakes from kneecaps and scapulas. And the turtle-man was so big, the sled holds at least ten!" They looked up at their visitors. "Allwiya, that is. Maybe two or three of the Huaca."

Ichu looked sick. "You don't waste anything, do you?"

"Not if possible," Lugopo said. "Whirling Abyss sends so many delightful possibilities."

Silluka peered at the little creature. Was Lugopo glowing? The Allwiya must have something similar to the ampuka.

"But that is not real trap! Bait is here." Lugopo tapped the circlet. "That is, the real reason I called you." They held up the vial Silluka had last seen Elder Quilqi take. She must have given it back later. "I believe this is also how the turtle-men get their power." They shook the little vial. "Contains remnants of other turtle-men. Perhaps more body parts? A way to transfer power? Sacrifice the many to give power to the few?"

They swung across the workshop, above Silluka's head, and picked a tool with a little open circle at one end from the opposite wall. They attached it to the vial and shook it vigorously with three tentacles. The vial glowed a rich, dark red.

"Shows blessing of the gods, yes? Which ones, hard to say."

"Does that work elsewhere?" Ichu asked, suddenly interested.

"Certainly!" Lugopo placed the other end against the skull on their head. A white glow, tinged with sickly-looking dark patches, took form around the bones. "See the blessing of Manylegs of Reaching!"

"And on Huaca? It works on us too?" Ichu was far more insistent than normal. He'd been quieter, more focused, since the farm had been destroyed.

Lugopo swung down to perch on Ichu's shoulder, then placed the tool against his temple, waves of brown, blue, orange, purple, and yellow erupted in an aura around her brother, brilliant to look at.

"Such power to crush your enemies!" Lugopo crowed.

Yet Ichu frowned. "What about my sister?"

"Yes, yes, everything can be measured!" Silluka felt the now-familiar brush of slightly malleable, but firm tentacles on her shoulder, and the coolness of the tool against her head. A faint light shone from her body, mainly yellow, brown, and purple—more than she would have expected.

"Maybe I do have some potential," she said.

"And finally, here." Lugopo swung away from her and to Elder Quilqi.

"No, you don't need—" the elder protested, but Lugopo had already pressed the tool to the old woman's temple.

A radiant blast of light shone forth, so much Silluka had to shade her eyes. How much power did the elder have?

"Ulp," Lugopo squeaked as Elder Quilqi grasped them firmly in one hand and set them down on a table.

"That's quite enough of that. Earthquakes and thunderstorms, doesn't anyone have any privacy any longer?"

CHAPTER TEN

Storm Coming

Ichu stared in silence, blinking at the display of power. This elder was not what she said, though she seemed to favor Silluka for some reason. She had struck the killing blow against the turtleman. She had connected Silluka to the ampuka for the first time. He had to snatch whatever advantage was here, and quickly.

"You must help us train," he told the elder, before he could think about it. She could argue on behalf of his sister. "Silluka still doesn't have a citizen chit. She'll be forced to travel with the undesirables when the village leaves, unless you can vouch for her."

The elder shook her head. "I can bend many rules, but not that one, at least not for now. These elders are resolute in their beliefs. The strong survive in the Huaca." Her lip twisted at the saying.

"Then train us. Share your secrets. I've seen your power against the turtleman. I fought him. I know how powerful he is. Others are coming and someone will need to protect the village as it travels."

Elder Quilqi looked between them for a long moment, from him, to his sister, to the little Allwiya, who was still wearing the gruesome Huaca skull. He didn't know what to make of Lugopo yet, but they seemed eager to please, if a touch morbid. He hadn't spent enough time with Allwiya to know if that was normal, or out of the ordinary.

"What makes you think you have anything to give to this group? If I teach you, you'll have to unlearn most of what you know."

Unlearn? When he was the best bodycaster in the village? Did she rate him lower than the Allwiya? But he bit his lip, keeping a surge of anger in check. For Silluka.

"Then if I have to unlearn, I will." He clenched his fists, and didn't miss the elder's eyes on them.

Quilqi seemed to come to a decision, her face growing serious. She'd been teasing them thus far, showing Silluka bits and pieces as he watched his sister's hope swell. If the elder knew of some way to let her gain strength from the gods like the citizens of the Huaca, he would do anything to make that happen. Perhaps she could even show him how to avoid the slow decline he felt in himself. How had she used such powerful bodycasting, when she had to be past her seventieth year? As much as he'd hounded the elders for their chayus over the years, he could do the same with this woman.

"Fine," the elder finally said. "I was planning to only train the girl, but I can see you're persistent, and I won't get any rest otherwise. Lugopo has his own path to travel." She stood straight, nearly as tall as him. Silluka's eyes were as wide as he thought his were. He had been ready to argue all day. Had the turtleman scared her that much?

"You both know I'm not originally from your Huaca. There are strange traditions here, cut off from the rest of the world. I will show you what I can, but to you two alone! The rest of these little bodycasters have no drive. They only exist. Even your elders study the same chayus again and again. Magma and minerals! They stagnate in their perfection."

Ichu wanted to ask, to find out what she meant and whether that stagnation was related to his own loss of power, but the words stuck in his throat. There would be time later, now she had agreed to teach him. Instead, he turned to Lugopo.

"You can measure our power as bodycasters. Are there other aspects of magic you can record? What about the time the ampuka lasts?"

The little Allwiya hopped from pole to pole until they hung in front of Ichu's nose. "Time! Yes! My machinations are incomplete! Such brilliance from the foremost bodycaster. I have measured only power, but there is a temporal aspect too, until all are cast into the endless void." They swung away, then came back with a metronome like bodycasters would use to time their moves precisely, but this one had the addition of a flat piece of slate connected to it, with a moving arm. They jiggled the metronome with a tentacle and some hidden mechanism moved the slate slightly as the arm made marks in chalk.

"Will record the time of the ampuka. Yes? Shall we begin?"

"Maybe outside?" Ichu suggested. It was very cramped in the Allwiya's workshop, with him, the elder, his sister, the sled made from the turtleman's corpse, and Lugopo. Muola was fortunately somewhere else at the time, as she was at least twice as big as Lugopo.

For the first time since he'd noticed his bodycasting diminishing, Ichu felt a glimmer of hope. Perhaps he would not be consigned to a back room, folded over scrolls he couldn't read.

* * *

Sometime later, Ichu stood with Silluka and Lugopo, the latter dragging a pack full of strange creations. Elder Quilqi paced in front of them. They were in one of the village's bodycasting arenas, deserted as everyone else was busy packing up the village. They had few possessions left to pack. Ichu had performed in this arena many times, beating rivals, winning competitions, and returning triumphant with a new lover. It seemed so insignificant now, with the threat of the new island so close.

"Stances," the elder began, her hands on her hips. "These are the root of the chayu. They are all found in the morning ritual. It connects you to the island beneath you. With no stance, you have no connection to the Tiyus, Tiyas, and Tiyes." She dropped her hands and stood relaxed, feet equally apart, around the width of her hips.

"Basic stance. It is the easiest to perform, but lends no special power." She shifted so her feet turned in, knees pressed out. "Strength stance, to resist attacks." Now she went back on one foot, the other a little out in front. "Reflex stance. For responding to threats."

She shifted through each in turn with a description: Speed, Dexterity, Blocking, and Unmovable. "They all change how a chayu is performed, yes?"

Silluka was nodding along, but Ichu cocked his head. "Surely you mean the other way around? The chayu dictates which stance is used for which moves."

Elder Quilqi looked surprised for a moment, then frowned. "Oh, are we going that far back? What all *have* you lost out here? Fine then. Forget everything you've been taught about how chayus work." She slashed the air with one wrinkled hand. "While some stances are more suited for certain moves, there is no reason one needs to be used instead of another. You might not replace a Dexterity stance with an Unmovable stance when the purpose of that move is to cover ground, but it can be done, and the ampuka will still connect."

"You're saying each chayu could be performed from multiple sets of stances?" Ichu ran through combinations in his mind, his thoughts blossoming with the chayus he knew. "That would lead to..."

"To almost infinite combinations. Yes, boy. Gods and stars! Did you think bodycasting was so rigid?" She shook her head. "Let's try one. *Tortoise Shoulders His Load* should be easy enough. Lugopo, ready with your instruments." She looked to Silluka. "From you, girl, I want to see the ampuka by the end of the day." Then to Ichu. "For you, well, you'll need to unlearn a lot of bad habits."

Ichu felt the ampuka from Tiyu Tiksimuyu flow through him almost immediately. The strength of the earth supported him. He was most familiar with Uncle Earth's chayus anyway, favoring the solid movements and enhancements to strength and balance. Lugopo scampered to him and began to measure obscure angles and auras once he was done, mumbling to themself.

"Hm. Will need a scale. A baseline. How to quantify? One Tortoise? One Ichu. One Tiksimuyu?"

While Ichu waited for the ampuka and its effect to disperse, he helped Silluka with her form, showing where to open and close her shoulder blades, move her elbows in, and provide a path of energy from the ground to her head.

"But no ampuka," she complained.

"Keep trying," Elder Quilqi insisted. "You won't see anything from a single attempt." She hadn't given them any other direction since revealing they could use different stances for the chayus.

"Approximately thirty minutes of benefit from the ampuka," Lugopo stated. Ichu raised his hand to find the brownish glow had dissipated. So short a time? He hadn't been focusing on keeping it active this time, but when he was competing as a bodycaster, he could keep the ampuka from *Tortoise Shoulders His Load* going for over an hour. He really was losing his edge. That had only been last year.

"You see how the chayus work in this simple case, yes?" Quilqi asked. Ichu nodded. It was simple. Silluka was still trying to make the ampuka work, but the chayu required a few finger motions with both hands. She looked frustrated.

"Now try the same one, but in a different stance," the elder instructed. She pointed to Ichu. "For you, in Unmovable stance. For your sister, in Reflex stance."

"Why would that make any difference?" Silluka asked.

"Stormy skies, girl, you want me to teach you or not?"

She hadn't done much teaching so far, but Ichu swallowed his own objections and turned his feet in, knees pointing almost downward, his shoulders hunched into his chest. Unmovable stance was normally only for very static chayus—ones that didn't require the user to move around later. He could see how it might work for *Tortoise Shoulders His Load*, but Reflex stance? That should be totally incompatible.

He moved through the chayu again, paying careful attention to each move as it was subtly different. Halfway through, he felt the ampuka again, but it was deeper, slower, and more powerful. By the end, he was glowing again, the aura darker, like strong honey.

"Very good! More powerful! Is it two Tortoises? One and a half Ichus? Scale must be more precise." Lugopo scampered around him, measuring. Ichu didn't know what such a scale could be used for, but he supposed the Allwiya had a reason.

He turned, wanting to help Silluka, but every move felt like he was underwater. His feet dug grooves in the earth as he stepped, though he felt no extra effort. What was this power?

"You see, now, boy?" Elder Quilqi's words seemed almost too fast. "Chayus can change as needed. The right tool for the right job."

Ichu nodded carefully, watching his sister. Silluka was performing the chayu a second time, her front foot only touching on the ball as she stepped through the motions.

Her eyes widened as the glow began around her feet. "I feel it!" she said. "Why is this so much easier?"

"Because the chayu is focused on the feet and movement now," the elder answered her. "Your hand isn't needed to lift. Instead, you can react with precise timing to evade. Tortoise has many ways of carrying his burden."

"This way depends less on the placement of my stump," Silluka summarized. "I see now."

Then she faltered, and the glow dissipated.

"I had it for a moment!" she said.

"Soon you'll have no problem with any chayu," the elder told her. "Keep practicing. That's one thing your little village has right."

* * *

Over the next week, Elder Quilqi dragged Ichu through every chayu he knew, and a few he was less familiar with. Silluka struggled to get through the basic set every citizen knew. They practiced different stances for each one, and Lugopo muttered strange invocations and calculated percentages on a little board they carried with them always. Ichu supposed it would be helpful for something, but when he tried to talk to the Allwiya about it, all he got were arcane strings of words about energy connection, placement, and temporal residue. Lugopo glowed with a strange white and black light as they spoke.

Despite Elder Quilqi's admonition she would teach only them, they drew the attention of other bodycasters in the village. The first two to arrive were a stocky boy and a tall girl, both about Silluka's age. They introduced themselves as Waskar, the boy, and Tamaya, the girl. Ichu saw Silluka's eyes follow the girl as she introduced herself.

"So, Tamaya?" Silluka said. "I'm...I'm sorry about Hufi. I didn't mean—"

Tamaya shook her head. "The strong survive in the Huaca. He fought the greatest enemy we have faced, and we were able to hold the turtleman off until the elders could call on the gods' power."

"Elder Quilqi is teaching you, even though you failed the test?" Waskar seemed more than a little dense. Ichu raised an eyebrow at the boy.

"Teaching *her*, being the important part," the elder grumbled and the stocky boy paled.

"Apologies, elder. But...can we watch? I've never been taught directly by an elder before."

"Never been... What *does* this village teach?" Elder Quilqi waved a hand. "Fine. Watch. But don't think you can ask me any question that bounces around your quirra brain."

"I can show you some of what I've learned, but I'm not that good," Silluka told Tamaya.

"Anything will be helpful to prepare against more invaders." Tamaya went with Silluka to one side of the arena, where she showed the girl what the elder had taught them. Like Ichu, his sister appreciated all genders for their beauty. He didn't think she had taken a close friend, and he suspected her embarrassment about her missing arm, no matter how well she tried to hide it, was the main cause of that. Maybe this girl would help her with that. He let the boy, Waskar, watch him, but though he was learning many more applications for his chayu, he still felt them decreasing in strength. Lugopo mumbled and hummed about strengths measured in "tortoises" and "Ichus," but he could understand little of what they meant. The scale was different from chayu to chayu, and Ichu couldn't get a straight answer from the Allwiya about what they were measuring or how it was changing.

Several older bodycasters came by as well, but only to shake their heads at the obviously wrong methods they were using. Waskar and Tamaya remained the only ones to practice with them. Silluka talked with them after they practiced, even laughing with them. It was good to see her start to emerge from her shell. She'd taken the death of their parents especially hard, running away from him when he should have kept her close.

Ichu tried to convince several of the older bodycasters of the power of different stances in chayus, but even with his reputation, few tried. When elders Papaki and Sinchi showed up a few days later, they all left—even the two young ones—cowed into preparing the village to evacuate. Only Elder Quilqi kept him and Silluka from being dragged off as well—after a flurry of whispered words with the two other elders.

Silluka still hadn't held on to the ampuka for more than a few minutes, despite the chayus she attempted. Her form was getting better, but she still couldn't generate even a "Tortoise" of energy—Lugopo's new term.

At least Ichu finally had clarity on what Lugopo had been calculating, their circlet squeaking about what "Whirling Abyss" had given them. From the Allwiya's records, most chayus generated between a fourth and one and a half Tortoises. Something simple like *Jakua's Claws* produced about a fourth of a Tortoise, whereas the morning ritual, though it was never completed, Lugopo insisted would generate nearly five Tortoises in power. Changing the stance also modified the number. *Tortoise Shoulders His*

Load in Unmovable stance, for example, generated about one and a third Tortoises. Ichu wasn't sure what all that meant, save that the chayus did what they meant to. If Lugopo was happy with their scale, so was Ichu.

But Ichu wasn't happy about his strength. He could feel his ability lessen day by day. Was this what happened to the elders? But Elder Quilqi was stronger than him. What was different about her? It made little sense, as Ichu's strength was failing, slowly and surely. What had generated a Tortoise and a third last week was only getting him a little over a Tortoise and a quarter this week, at least if Lugopo's figuring was correct.

The weather continued to get worse. It rained almost all the time now, and Ichu resigned himself to staying damp most of the day. At least it was a warm rain, or even hot. The land to the south was beginning to rise, indicating a volcano brewing. They would need to be on their way before it erupted. Even Tiyu Tiksimuyu couldn't protect them from all of its effects. The elders had rounds of Huaca organized at all times to make the symbols of the earth, the sky, the sea, and of healing, to keep the gods focused on them.

* * *

They had been training for a week and a half with Elder Quilqi when the island came through the wall of storms.

Silluka was in the midst of *Quirra Hides His Nuts*, one of her favorite chayus, when she stopped, staring. Ichu followed her gaze. The wall of storms had parted, green dangling plants poking through. They must have been taller than trees for Ichu to see them from this distance.

"It's so tall," Silluka breathed, and Ichu saw she was right. The island cliffs were far above their heads, even above the mountains growing along the coast. The new island would collide with the coast in a few days at this rate, toppling over their village and crushing it.

"It's time to go," he said.

"Past time, I would say." Elder Quilqi eyed the flitting shapes of the storm warriors, parting around the island. "It's moving faster than I expected. Enough practice for today. Gather your things and we'll meet up with the rest of the village. Everyone will have seen what we did."

"I still haven't shown the ampuka for an entire chayu," Silluka said. "The elders won't let me in with the Huaca."

"Then I'll travel with you," Ichu told her. There was no question. He wouldn't abandon his sister.

"Time to figure that out later." The elder shoed them with her hands. "Go, go. Lugopo, gather your tools and help Muola pack the last of the workshop. We need to leave today." The low urgency in the elder's voice put Ichu on edge.

By the time Ichu and Silluka got back to the temporary housing near the elders' building, the whole village was in an uproar. Most of the village supplies had been arranged on four massive sleds over the last week, each as long as a building, with entire teams of jakuas spitting and swiping at the handlers. They'd emptied out the stables and the handlers were performing *Sleeping Beast* as a team to calm them down, but the dark-furred beasts slunk around on padded paws, growling. They felt what was coming as well as the rest of the village.

Ichu could see, after the training from Elder Quilqi, that the chayu might work better in Reflex stance on the sleds rather than the Dexterity stance it was usually performed in. He'd have to mention that to the handlers.

There was a *boom* like the whole island had fallen in on itself and a form streaked through the air toward them like a fireball from a volcano. But it had come from the wall of storms, he was certain of it.

The wall of storms itself was dissolving with the arrival of the island. The storm warriors were in a frenzy, and Ichu thought he spotted more turtlemen fighting them, leaping from the island.

Huaca scattered as the fireball arced closer, like a leaf lazily drifting, it was so high up. Then it grew faster quickly, too quickly. Ichu stared, rooted in place.

Suddenly, Elder Quilqi was in front of him, arms windmilling as she spun through stance after stance. Ichu saw Reflex to Dexterity, to Strength and then Blocking. She went through other stances Ichu didn't have a name for, squatting close to the ground and popping up, arms pressing close, then spinning around her as if she was deflecting an entire flight of arrows fired at her.

The ampuka glowed around her, then grew bigger, enveloping those closest to her and more, until it surrounded the edge of the village closest to the incoming island.

The fireball fell like a meteor and Ichu ducked, certain it would destroy the entire town, but it flashed against Quilqi's shield, guttering out. Something slid down the glowing surface, and the elder spun to a stop, arms coming in, hands together in *Giving Water* from the morning ritual. Ichu had never seen it used in a chayu before. The elder went up on her toes, then spread her hands to the side, the shield dissipating.

The village was silent, staring at the display of power. Several of the other elders had open mouths.

Elder Quilqi ran to what had fallen from the wall of storms, and Ichu saw it was a figure, dressed in glowing armor glittering as if it was fashioned from blue jewels.

"A storm warrior!" Silluka said from his side, and Ichu realized his sister must be right. What had happened? He jogged forward to join the elder, who was cradling the head of the warrior, speaking soft words to them.

As they got closer, he saw the warrior had the appearance of a young woman, though surely a god could appear any age.

Quilqi gently cradled the woman's head to the ground. A helm of glowing blue sapphires was next to her, scorch marks heavy on it. Her face was partially burned, and her eyes were closed.

"She's gone," the elder said. "Her injuries were too severe for me to save her."

"How can a god die?" Ichu protested. "The storm warriors have protected our coast since before my parents were born, keeping the approaching maelstrom between the islands from destroying us."

"And as well you should thank them," the elder shot back. "But the storm warriors are not gods. They are as far below the Tiyus, Tiyas, and Tiyes as you are to the storm warriors. Loma Tika served the storm warriors well for fifteen years. She didn't deserve this fate."

"You know storm warriors?" Silluka asked.

"Hills and valleys, girl. I'm old. I know lots of people."

Ichu stifled a laugh even as he realized the elder had once again not answered a question.

She grunted and pushed to standing, even though he had seen her spin through an incredible array of moves not moments before. "The storms will take this one in a better burial that we can give her as we flee."

"What...about her armor?" Ichu suggested. He didn't want to rob the dead, but the entire village would be traveling into danger.

Elder Quilqi shook her head. "No help there." She tapped the helm with one foot, and it collapsed in on itself. "The armor is sustained by the warrior. It is a part of them, and after death, it dissipates quickly."

Ichu began to head back to the sleds, but Silluka stared at the fallen storm warrior. "They can make armor with the chayus?"

Ichu pulled up short. He hadn't thought of it that way. He didn't know any chayus that created physical objects, but just in the last few minutes, Elder Quilqi had created a barrier, and now, here was the storm warrior's armor. He thought he knew a lot about bodycasting. He was obviously wrong. Unlearning indeed.

He would have asked the elder about it, but that was when the turtlemen appeared through the wall of storms.

CHAPTER ELEVEN

Escape

"Launch the sleds!" Elder Quilqi called, as the four of them, Lugopo on Silluka's shoulder, ran toward the elders' building in the center of town. Lugopo leapt down as they passed the Allwiya district, waving tentacles and their circlet translating a hasty "I shall return victorious!"

Silluka spared glances over her shoulder, watching turtlemen jumping from their island, falling the distance between the wall of storms and the coast like tiny dolls, though she suspected each of them was taller than Ichu. They were out farther than the farm, at the very edge of the land, and would take time to get here. But turtlemen moved fast. She wanted to be away from here, undesirable or not, before any more turtlemen entered the town.

Elder Papaki and another she thought was named Kuchiki were directing the launch of the four great sleds, sending Huaca running this way and that. She spied Tamaya in the crowd but had no chance for even a word. The tall, pretty girl had been receptive while she explained using different stances in the chayus, but when she did them, she complained the ampuka seemed weaker, not stronger. Hufi's crew had been dispersed to other patrols after his death. She wished she could have time to get to know Tamaya better, once they were traveling.

Except she was still an undesirable. She wouldn't be traveling on the sleds no matter how much Ichu pleaded with the elders. He'd tried to keep it secret, but she'd seen him sneak off, cajoling Elder Papaki and the others to include her. But that was one of the base tenets of the Huaca. They fled the shifting land, when needed, searching for their next home. Only the strong survived.

For now, Silluka ran next to her brother. As they reached the sleds, the jakua handlers stopped performing *Sleeping*

Beast and assumed their places at the head of the vehicles, their charges almost as tall at the shoulder as Silluka. The sleek black beasts pawed the ground and hissed, swiping at each other. One of those paws could take her head off. The jakua handlers were all strong bodycasters.

The massive sleds were designed to run on land and water. Jakuas had amazing strength on land and were good swimmers, too. They were the top predator in the jungles, and knew it, even those trained by the handlers from birth. As citizens of the Huaca climbed aboard, the handers began *Running Beast* to get the jakuas ready to pull. The chayu lent them power from Tiyu Tiksimuyu and Tiya Qucha—grace on land and in water. The jakuas would pull the sleds to the closest river, then travel along it until it dried up in the desert.

Huaca citizens ran to take their places on the four giant sleds, but the greater part of the village gathered and watched with their belongings on their backs, gathered around their own means of transport. Undesirables weren't allowed on the larger sleds, nor to use the jakuas. Instead, some families had made their own sleds from hollowed-out trees or even sewn-together leaves. Many were piecemeal affairs and Silluka could see some wouldn't survive past the first day. A line of bodycasters, some she recognized as previous bodycasting tournament champions, stood between the four lead sleds and the undesirables, as if daring them to sneak aboard. None of them did.

Ichu's touch on her arm brought her back to the moment.

"Come with me. I'm not certain if even the citizens will have time to escape, but let me talk to the elders. I can get you a seat with me. We can fight together." He began towing her to one of the jakua-pulled sleds, but Silluka slid out of his grip.

"What about them?" she asked her brother, pointing to the collection of small sleds.

He shook his head. "I can't help all of them. You know that. Let me help you at least."

"And just leave them all to die at the claws of the turtlemen?" She was about to tell her brother how much his elders really cared about their village, but a whistle and clank drew her attention. "No. I've got my own sled."

She ran to a familiar blotchy green and blue form, no bigger than her hand, perched on a contraption rumbling toward them, puffing clouds of steam. Muola and several other Allwiya were perched alongside and hanging off the back. The Allwiya carried no possessions except bags of tools and of dried fish. Lugopo's sled rumbled forward on many tiny, segmented legs, like a centipede.

"There is no room for your immense size here!" Lugopo called out. "But we brought the turtle-sled. It is ready to crush the bones of your enemies!"

The sled made from the turtleman's armor was roped to Lugopo's centipede contraption, and Silluka ran to it. Ichu came up beside her.

"I can travel with you."

"No," she told him. She watched the families of the undesirables. Over half the village was being left behind. The strong survived in the Huaca, but that didn't mean the weak couldn't as well. "Take your place on the jakua sleds. I have another plan."

She kept an eye on the turtlemen, still falling from their island. The storm warriors followed them, leaving the disintegrating wall of storms, and were flying down to the coast to presumably do battle. She hoped they could hold off the attack for a time.

"Who has children and who can't keep up?" she called to the undesirable families. She could see children from toddlers to those six or seven years old. Past that, they would be able to run on their own.

Several families pushed their children forward and she began settling them into the sled, Ichu helping.

"Save a space for yourself," he said.

"I can run as well as any of them," Silluka returned.

"But your..." Ichu trailed off.

"Lacking an arm doesn't have anything to do with running," Silluka said coldly. Her brother had always underestimated her. She had been planning to use the sled herself, but there was no way she was taking that space when most of the village would be slaughtered by the turtlemen. She would be in the same situation if Elder Quilqi hadn't shown her how the elders' traditional ways of using the chayu were complete jakua droppings. She still couldn't hold the ampuka for more than a few moments—only a partial "Tortoise" in Lugopo's terms—but she had more than these people did.

Ichu was still standing there, looking like he would rather dig a hole in the ground and cover himself up. They were wasting time.

"Go! Get to a sled. I can protect myself now." She held up her stump and shook it at Ichu. "This never slowed me down as much as you thought it did. Protect yourself."

Ichu finally nodded, then ran to her and hugged her fiercely. "Be safe," he whispered, and ran to the largest sled, in the front of the procession, where he had a reserved space as the strongest bodycaster in the village. She saw several other bodycasters welcoming him in, patting him on the back, and asking him questions. He would be fine there among his peers.

Silluka turned back to the turtle-sled, where families were busy arranging their young children as safely as possible. There was no fighting, simply solemn discussion between the undesirable families about who would go. It was a sad contrast to the celebration around Ichu.

"Can you take them safely down the river?" she asked Lugopo.

"You wish to keep your conquest secret. I see!" Lugopo clambered around the mechanical centipede, still puffing steam, and pulled at the knots attaching the sled to it. "These young protégés of destruction shall follow your lead and grow to mighty warriors, ready to crush all enemies beneath their might!" Muola gestured a sharp rebuke at them and they absently tapped their translation circlet. "That is, I shall keep the spawn as safe as I would my own."

"Don't Allwiya birth thousands of spawn at once and let them fight until the last few living grow up?" Silluka asked.

"I shall keep them as safe as *your* people's spawn."

That was likely as good as she would get from the strange little creature. She nodded as the main sleds caught her eye again. The jakua—at least a dozen per sled—were churning the ground into mud, muscles under their dark coats rippling as they brought the four sleds into motion. The ground was slick with water, and the land sloped down into a waterway that funneled the constant rain away from the Huaca and farther inland. The rivers had swollen the past weeks, surging their banks and creating a wide, shallow slide of water, perfect for the sleds, but terrible for the banks of irrigating patties terraced next to the river. The Huaca had harvested what crops were ready, much of which was stacked in great piles on the sleds and covered in oiled canvas. The jakuas growled and spit, flicking wetness from their paws as they got the sleds underway.

Silluka turned away from them and back to the undesirable families. "We'll leave all together. We may not have the jakuas, but we can push the sleds ourselves. We'll follow the rest of the village as they blaze a path for us." They'd be able to see the dangers the sleds in front had avoided or defeated. Silluka would turn her placement to an advantage.

Lugopo and the Allwiya led the undesirables, pulling the turtle-sled with the children on it laughing and crying at the adventure. Those families who had crafted sleds came next; their family members who couldn't move as fast loaded on the sleds with their belongings.

Silluka followed on foot with the last of the undesirables. The two homeless men who had pushed her out of her last nest in the village were there, looking hopeless. She nodded in greeting to them, smiling to show there were no hard feelings. That felt like years ago, now.

She kept an eye on the island looming behind them as they followed the sleds, slogging through the mud and water beside the riverbank. The land here sloped down, made even steeper in the last few years. The mountains behind them would eventually collide with the mass of the island, then be ground down into a new mountain range between the Huaca's land and the new island, as the two became one. She had heard a few stories in the village and from the Allwiya about the last time this had happened. It was a time of even worse upheaval, with massive storms and earthquakes. Volcanoes would rise to the south and without the elders continually calling on the Tiyus, Tiyas, and Tiyes to protect them, the disasters would quickly destroy their village. The settlement had served them well while the Huaca lived there, but like anything in this land, it was transitory. Perhaps the new home they found in the desert would last them longer, now the turtleman's island had made contact with theirs. The elders said it had been approaching for a hundred years or more, while the wall of storms shielded them.

But their line of sleds and people were falling behind the rest of the village, as the powerful jakuas found the entrance to waterways. That meant when the turtlemen got here—when, not if—the undesirables would be the first ones attacked. Surely the strong of the Huaca should protect them? Or would the entire village then be decimated? Maybe it was better for the few strong to survive after all, to make certain the Huaca would continue? Silluka gritted her teeth and walked faster.

She wouldn't fall behind. And she would bring the rest of the undesirables with her. If *she* could summon the ampuka, anyone could.

She turned to the two homeless men, who flinched away as if she might beat them.

"Do you know *Flock of Starlings*?" she asked.

"I was never any good at chayus, young mistress," one said. "I was ever clumsy in my movement."

"I thought I was hopeless too." She raised her stump. "But I didn't let that stop me. We're going to fall behind if we don't do something. Get everyone who isn't on a sled close together."

The older men ran off, looking like they would rather be anywhere else, but Silluka and the two rounded up the rest of the undesirables. The village was maybe a thousand people all together, and over half were undesirables. Excluding the ones on the sleds and the children, that left maybe a hundred people fleeing on foot.

Silluka shouted to them as they milled around, obviously wanting to be moving.

"We're going to perform *Flock of Starlings*. Don't worry about getting it right. You don't even all need to use Dexterity stance." There were murmurings through the group, but Silluka raised both arms, her disability clear.

"Hey! Pay attention! I've done this chayu before with my brother *and it worked*. You can do it too."

That quieted most of the complaints.

"Now, who knows Dexterity stance?" About half raised hands. Silluka looked past their heads. There were strange lights coming from the mountains near the coast. Was that the storm warriors fighting the turtlemen? If so, they were approaching fast. She considered the crowd.

"Who knows Dexterity *or* Reflex stance?" More hands went up.

"Speed stance? Basic stance?" Silluka thought those four would be the most helpful for the chayu, based on what she'd learned from Elder Quilqi. *Flock of Starlings* was about movement. Basic stance was the most restrictive of the four, but it at least *allowed* for movement.

Almost everyone had a hand raised by now.

"Good. Follow my movements. Don't worry about being exact. Since this is a group chayu, the placement of your body doesn't need to be as precise as the elders keep telling us. Do the stance you know best out of the four I named. There are so many of us here, the chayu can't help but work!" She hoped her enthusiasm would make up for any lack of ability, but some of the crowd still looked uncertain.

"This won't work!" someone called.

Silluka shook her head. "Don't think like that. It's obvious the elders' teachings haven't worked for you, or you'd be up on those sleds, getting away." She flung her arm out behind her, pointing at the departing vehicles. There was nervous muttering. "I'm showing you a different way—one that *does* work for us undesirables!"

There were fewer sounds of disagreement, and the lights on the mountains were gaining ground fast. She had to start now.

"Arms first, then legs." She demonstrated what she had learned from her brother, finding she could remember the chayu clearly. Practicing so much lately had helped her memory, and she could feel how the chayu was built, what shape it would draw.

"See what I do with my left hand? Do that with both your hands, mirror images." She picked up one leg. But some of the undesirables only had one leg or had crutches.

"Those who can, raise your foot like this." Silluka demonstrated, and that was when the glow began about her, immediately expanding to the nearest undesirables, and growing brighter. There were gasps of amazement from the crowd. Silluka swallowed her own cry of triumph. She hadn't been certain this would work.

"See? Don't stop!" she called. "You can do it! This is what the elders have kept from you. We can keep up with them."

The glow spread as she continued the chayu, and as more joined in. She could feel the power in this chayu. With two it was useful. With one hundred, it was an actual *Flock of Starlings*. A great wave of light rose around them, stronger, more reactive, and faster than when she'd performed it with Ichu. The other stances *added* to the power, instead of taking away—even Basic stance. Like a true group of birds there were many parts. Not all of them had to be perfect.

"Now run!" she said and took off. The others followed, speeding through ankle-deep water, splashing and limping and whooping as they moved faster than they had ever before. They caught up with the sleds and people started pushing them, speeding them along.

Silluka caught up to Lugopo and the other Allwiya, running alongside. Lugopo stared, goggle-eyed, then pulled several levers in an arcane order. The puffs of smoke increased into a belch of steam and the centipede crawled faster, multiple feet stabbing the ground as it pulled itself forward. The children in the sled were all laughing now as it skimmed across the water, leaving spray in its wake.

Ahead, the river branched into three mighty sections, with narrow strips of land between them. The sleds of the Huaca sped along the river, jakuas leaping and pulling to get away from the danger they sensed behind them. But the undesirables were moving faster, buoyed by *Flock of Starlings*, pushing their sleds, or even swimming in some cases. The ampuka glowed around them in the shape of hundreds of birds, all flying in the same direction, shifting and turning as one to avoid dangers and obstacles.

They would make it. The entire village would escape.

And then the earth shook, hard enough to throw sleds twenty paces to one side. Jakuas tumbled and screeched in their harnesses.

A great rent opened up, nearly beneath Silluka's feet, and she threw herself to one side, stump tucked under her to roll to a crouch, facing back toward the undesirables. One of the undesirables' sleds and its people disappeared into the crack in the ground, the river turning into an instant waterfall. Screams and pleas to Tiyu Tiksimuyu filled the air, and the ampuka of many flying birds shattered and dissipated, leaving only undesirables again. The uncle must have had his eye elsewhere, perhaps on the colliding islands, for no divine help came.

Lugopo and Muola came alongside her, the centipede pinging and popping with heat, all the children and Allwiya safe, thanks to the gods.

"Your great conquest continues!" Lugopo chirped, and Silluka nodded, shouting back to be heard over the sudden torrent of water.

"I'm fine. Help the rest of the village!" She stumbled to her feet, weaving as the ground tried to shake her apart, suddenly exhausted from the effort she'd expended. She stared forward. They had almost caught up with the main raft of sleds. She could see people looking back toward them, and even a few climbing down to help, but there was no chance. The earthquake had split the ground across the rivers, creating a great vent that sucked all the flow from the coastal mountains. Not only could Silluka and the undesirables not get to the rest of the Huaca, the main four sleds would be hampered as their river drained off. They had to press forward, or they would be sucked back into the chasm. She could just see the jakuas straining to pull the sleds forward, and she was almost certain Ichu was on the ground, performing a chayu to help out.

She turned back to the undesirables. The sleds that could be saved had been, the people regrouping. But there was no way across. Not without the ampuka.

The ground rattled again, almost knocking her sideways, and Silluka began *Tree in the Wind*, from Strength stance rather than basic, feet lifting and planting. Her arms moved through the starting circle and for once she didn't even think of her stump as anything other than a natural extension of herself.

Intent was what Elder Quilqi told her. That mattered more for a chayu than perfect position and muscle movement. What could you do when the earth heaved and shook? The chayu would never be perfect.

The ampuka rose around her again, her feet gaining stability. The shaking of the earth meant nothing, and her feet gripped the ground as she strode to the undesirables. *This* was what she should have felt during her citizen's test, had the elders truly taught her how to use the chayus.

"We're getting across that chasm!" she shouted to the group. Many had fallen to the ground, and only a few held their feet against the shaking. A few cheered, but most only looked frightened, stealing glances back the way they'd come. They were barely able to walk, but the flashes of light were coming closer, like the aurora during the day. The turtlemen were coming, and the storm warriors weren't holding them back.

There had to be a way to get these people across the chasm. To go around would take time they didn't have, and most could barely walk. Silluka herself would have fallen over except for Elder Quilqi's training. They had to get from here, to there, but the ground itself was against them.

The training. Elder Quilqi had first wanted to teach her the mental chayus, she said. Only later did she explain the basics she didn't know they were missing.

Silluka pulled out the scroll Elder Quilqi had given her from an inner pocket of her tunic. She'd never said exactly what it did, but Silluka had her suspicions. Why would the elders have buried that scroll in the archives unless it was something so inconceivable to them, they thought it wasn't even worth considering?

Something impossible like moving without touching the ground. Like the storm warriors. She read over the first move again, realizing what she had missed before.

Silluka started *Flying Quirra*.

She planted both feet, still stable against the aftershocks with the help of *Tree in the Wind*, then raised her whole, left arm out to the left, hand splayed out as if stretching out a wing. She did as close as she was able with her right arm. She raised her left leg to her right calf, creating a circle of energy as Ichu had taught her. With the practice of the last week, already she felt more confident.

The first real move of the *Flying Quirra* was not a physical one, but settling the mind, a concept that had taken until just now to comprehend. In this moment of chaos, she was the calm in the middle of this storm. Standing like this was not for strength or movement, but for readiness. It was a mental stance.

The ampuka from *Tree in the Wind* intensified, bolstered by her stance. Silluka closed her eyes, envisioning how the energy would cycle through her, marking her *intent* for this chayu. More than any other time in her life, she had a purpose. She had to get across the chasm, and she was taking the undesirables with her.

The only physical moves to the chayu were small changes in her arm position, and switching the stance from left leg on right, to right leg on left, halfway through. The ampuka was like a pressure within her, trying to get out, bubbling up from her center. Silluka eased her breathing to a constant rhythm, even as the heat surging within her felt like she had been laying in the sun for hours.

The last move of the chayu was to drop her arms and *lift* her legs. Both of them.

Silluka opened her eyes as the ground dropped away from beneath her. She was floating. Above the ground. A fierce yellow aura surrounded her, showing the connection with Uncle Sky. She couldn't let her intent go, her *reason*, or the ampuka would leave her. She was tapped directly into a well of energy, and it was burning her up without acting. She stared at the nearest sled, willing herself there, and she floated forward, quick as a swooping bird. The eyes of those on it were wide, fingers pointing at her, but she had no portion of her concentration to devote to responding.

One touch and the sled was weightless, the undesirables on it crying out in fear and joy. She pushed it and it slid, light as a feather, across the chasm. She knew it would make the crossing because she could feel every part of it. It was her whole reason for existing in this moment.

Lugopo and the Allwiya were next. Lugopo's circlet shouted something at her, brandishing some tool, as she made the centipede weightless, but she had no room to process what they said. The children whooped and clung to each other as the turtle-sled slid over the chasm.

She went to another sled and did the same, then another, and another, her vision narrowing to a tube, then a pinprick. Those standing were crowding on to each one, hanging off the sides as they floated away. She could not lose focus.

There was one sled left, and the last few undesirables jumped aboard as she approached, touched it, then grabbed hold herself, directing it over the new waterfall and into open air. She could barely see, her vision narrowing to nothing. Heat was burning her up from the inside. She stared down and saw light and steam, far below. The chasm must reach into the magma under the ground, the water instantly boiling.

The other side of the chasm approached in a haze, people's shouts like ringing in her ears. All her senses were on fire. Her skin was burning. Her mind was being drilled out from the inside.

She collapsed on wet earth, rivulets of water running past her into the jagged gash in the ground. There were people coming for her. Huaca? Elders?

She couldn't tell.

Darkness took her.

CHAPTER TWELVE

Sleds and Rivers

Ichu watched his sister sleep. Elder Quilqi insisted she had gotten to Silluka in time and had performed a complicated chayu consisting only of hand motions over her. He hadn't caught the name of it, except that it had made the yellow light shining from his sister like a full moon wink out. Silluka had been deathly still as all the elders pleaded with Tiye Kwirpuyay—Entle Magic—to keep the ampuka from burning her up. Elder Quilqi hadn't joined with them, instead focusing on Silluka, touching her temple and wrists every so often.

He'd watched her *fly*. What had the elder taught her? While Ichu's body slowly lost its strength, his sister was performing impossible feats like one of the storm warriors. He'd always known she was special, seeing the extra care his parents put into teaching her skills she would need, as she was not suited to performing the chayu. Except now she could do that too. She'd brought the rest of the village, when the elders would have left them behind. Instead of all of them being lost in the earthquake, only one family and their sled had been lost. Others had looked out into the chasm before they resumed their flight, but there was nothing left but bubbling rock, far below. He could only hope the rent in the earth would slow the turtlemen down.

For now, Silluka slept, and Ichu watched. Tamaya and Waskar had come by once to check on her, but then had been sucked into helping the jakua handlers steer. Any able-bodied bodycasters were helping with clearing rocks, fast-growing plants, and other detritus from their path. Others were constantly making the signs of the gods—Entle Love and Aunt Healing to keep them comfortable, Uncle Sky and Uncle Earth to keep the weather clear, Aunt Sea to plead for the river to keep flowing, Aunt Harvest to keep the food stores from spoiling, and Entle Magic to keep their other chayus strong. Not many made the sign of Tiyu Llamkay, Uncle Smith, these days. The Allwiya made all the tools and instruments they needed, and some whispered the Uncle's blessings felt fainter than they had in the past.

The sleds bumped along, pulled by the jakua who growled and snorted with the effort. The big creatures loved the water, diving in when they got too hot. Some would spend part of the time swimming, and the other part walking along the bank. The sleds were big enough to move around on, and even with the teams of animals pulling them, Ichu could jump down and keep pace with them easily. All the possessions and supplies were piled in the middle of each, and people stood or sat around the outside. The jakuas were inconsistent in pulling at best and had to rest often. The handlers had stores of meat and fish to keep them fed, but the jakuas would only serve them for a limited time before they jumped aboard to curl up in their padded boxes. Hopefully they would find a new Huaca by the time the creatures refused to pull any longer, or they were going to have to push the sleds themselves.

The smaller sleds of the undesirables were keeping up or even outpacing them, moving in and around the larger sleds on the river. There was a palpable sense of relief and embarrassment in the air as families that would have been split up spoke with each other, neither side acknowledging how the undesirables had been treated. Elder Quilqi had even pulled Elders Papaki and Sinchi aside in a discussion where voices rose above the slap and splash of the shallow river. Shortly after, the jakua handlers offered to split a few of the prowl off and pull the larger undesirable sleds. Those were beginning to join up with each other, and Ichu guessed soon all the undesirable sleds would be bound together by jungle vines and braided cables, except for the Allwiya conveyance and the turtle-sled. All thanks to Silluka.

Ichu watched the landscape get drier and drier the farther they went inland. He'd been concerned the river itself would dry up, after the earthquake, but even though the water upstream had cut off and the water level had dropped, the river still flowed. Now, though, sediment built in the channel so the jakuas struggled to pull the sleds, half in water and half touching the riverbed.

This was the reason they hadn't moved away from the coast yet, instead waiting until the rising mountains pushed the water inland. Now they had no choice. Fortunately, storms were following them from the coast for now. Many dissipated over the new chasm—likely the heat from the broken earth boiling them away—but it had rained for most of the last day. Ichu guessed they would soon be sliding along sand, however.

On the second day, he finally cornered Elder Quilqi on the side of the lead sled while the other elders were discussing which way to travel. She'd slipped away from him every chance she could, giving him plenty of time to stew over what had happened. But he had to know.

"What did my sister do?" he asked.

"Something very dangerous she's not yet ready for," came the curt answer. A far cry from agreeing to teach them techniques the Huaca had forgotten.

"Elder Quilqi, my sister *flew*. Like the storm warriors do. What did she do?" Ichu stood straight, chest out, as if he would block the elder's path. He still wasn't sure how strong she was.

The elder sighed. "I'm not getting my nap this afternoon, am I? Where do you think the storm warriors get that ability from? It's just a chayu, like the ones you perform. It's simply a different way of thinking about it."

Ichu cocked his head. "A different way? What is there to think about in a chayu? You do it, that's all."

Elder Quilqi waggled a finger in his face. "But you've already learned the stance can be changed for different effects, yes? Dusty deserts, boy, you think you know everything about the chayus? The best bodycaster in a backwater village on the coast?"

"Have you seen the other side of the desert?" Ichu asked, hoping the switch in topic might trip up the old woman. She'd acted as if the Huaca was just a small thing, when it was larger than any other single farm out on the coast. She was far too much a mystery, and almost never gave a straight answer. Where *had* she come from? Certainly not a small farm to the south like she claimed.

"I've seen more of this island, and this world, than you have, that's for certain, boy. You'll soon find the chayus you know are just a drop in the ocean of what's out there."

"And what *is* out there? You won't say."

Now the elder smiled. "That's correct. I'd much rather see your face when you see for yourself." She turned serious. "Did you try to learn *Foam Tossed in the Waves* before you knew all of the morning ritual? No. It would make no sense to you. You know it takes time to perfect what you know. Learning too much now would do you no good, when you already have much to unlearn."

Ichu considered. If she wouldn't answer a question head on, then maybe she would show him. "What *of* my practice? I've seen you bodycast, but the elders of our village stop performing all but the most necessary chayus before they're your age. I'm already feeling the decline in my ability. Can you teach me how to combat that?"

Elder Quilqi only laughed. "My age, hmm? You're not past what, your thirty-fifth year? You've got plenty of time, boy." She held up a hand as he opened his mouth. "I'll show you some things, yes. In time. But stop worrying about that. It only dims your capacity in your mind's eye."

"What about those vials the turtleman used?" he pressed. "They were like concentrated power. How did they work? Lugopo won't say. Do you think they might help me?"

The elder eyes were suddenly sharp on him, like there was a weight of pressure behind them. Ichu resisted the urge to step back. "Do not meddle in what you don't know. I've never seen those vials before, but I get a bad feeling from them. Whirling winds, boy, you want to put an unknown concoction from a different island in your body?

Maybe you're not as smart as I thought. Just as useful to stick an Allwiya tool in your brain. Now leave me to my duties. I have enough elders hanging on my heels." She stomped off, and Ichu was left glowering, with nothing to do but watch the riverbank.

The third day, Silluka still slept, though she drank water when it was put to her mouth. Elder Quilqi checked her every few hours, and performed the chayu of hand motions once more over her when she thought no one was looking. None of the motions were from chayus he knew. They passed the mouth of a connecting river soon after, coming from the north and intersecting their slowing stream, renewing the river and giving them hope the water wouldn't completely dry up. The elders decided to camp for the night there, let the jakuas rest, and see if the villagers could catch any fish in the river.

The next morning, Ichu awoke to cries from other members of the village, pointing up the connecting river. Ichu could just see the sled, though this one had sides turned up more than usual, and rather than being pulled by jakuas, the people in it had long sticks they pressed into the banks to propel them along.

Ichu had never seen people not from the Huaca, except for Elder Quilqi and the Allwiya. There were far-flung farms where undesirables scratched out a living on the harsh land, but none had come to the Huaca in his lifetime. They couldn't have had elders, as they were responsible for finding the Huaca—the sacred places to the gods where they would answer prayers and protect people from the changing weather and earth. They couldn't even have citizens, as that was a title granted by the elders. He pitied anyone not under the Huaca's protection.

The small sled halted near their camp and Ichu could make out the people in it now. There were five people and another three Allwiya. The tentacled beings must have been the ones to alter the sled in such a manner.

As the foremost bodycaster, Ichu went with Elder Quilqi and Elder Papaki to meet the newcomers. An older man, who must have been the patriarch of his family, stood behind a harsh looking girl, even taller than Ichu, who was not short. Her hair seemed almost fixed in place it was so stiff. The planes of her face were like granite, though she was possibly as young as Silluka. Three others, two men and a woman, stood behind them.

"We wish passage with your group, we do," the older man said. "I am Kallpa, and this is my family from our farm." He paused to cough wetly into a piece of cloth, and the large girl patted his back, her eyes dark.

"You come from the north?" Elder Papaki asked. "We were not aware of any, ah, noncitizens that way. Surely the land is too unforgiving to live without the protections of the Uncles, Aunts, and Entles?"

The patriarch tried to speak, then coughed again into the rag, doubling over. Two of the others behind him were coughing as well. The young woman took over. "My father has run our farm for many years, he has, supporting our small family, helpers, and the Allwiya who live with us. We sustain ourselves." Her voice was rough, as if she'd been breathing ash. "A volcano grew up, it did, near the farm when the island came close. Then Eztli Mecatl began to invade. We had to escape, but my father was caught near an eruption and breathed the fumes for too long. Our Allwiya friends made us masks, but they were too late to help him."

"Eztli Mecatl?" Elder Quilqi leaned forward, peering at the young woman. "Is that what the invaders call themselves? How do you know?"

The hard young woman looked surprised for a moment, but her father stood from his coughing fit and gripped her arm. "They are known to us, they are. A few have stealthily landed to the north in the past—enough to learn a bit of their language."

"How did they brave the boiling waters between the islands? They are certain death to enter," Elder Papaki asked.

"The Eztli Mecatl are a strong people," the girl replied, puffing out her chest. "They can survive even the maelstrom between the islands, yes? They have taught us ways of their power to survive with our small farm."

"Peace, Cosquella." Kallpa tucked the rag away and patted her arm. The girl's face went stony for a moment, her dark eyes almost glowing from underneath her brows, then she bowed her head.

"Of course, Father."

"So you see we have knowledge you lack, do you?" Kallpa continued. "We would gladly share the weakness of the Eztli Mecatl in exchange for the protection of your Huaca, food, and medical attention." He paused to cough again, sharp and wet. "I was not the only one caught in the eruption. My nephew was with me at the time, he was." The man and woman behind them were patting the back of the third, younger man, who couldn't seem to catch his breath from coughing.

Elder Papaki looked ready to argue, but Elder Quilqi silenced him with a look. "We'd be happy to have your help. Do you know *Flower Sends Out Pollen*? Elder Sinchi is quite proficient in its use. It may help your lungs. Do you know where you are traveling to?"

"We are escaping the collision between the islands, and the Eztli Mecatl have turned against us," Cosquella blurted. "They killed the rest of our family—"

"Cosquella." Kallpa's voice was sharp, but he collapsed into a coughing fit after. The girl held him up as he hacked into his rag again. The young man behind him had to sit down, the woman holding his arm as he breathed through thick, wet, coughs.

"I've heard enough," Elder Quilqi said. "Papaki, can you alert the other elders as to Kallpa's and his nephew's condition?"

"I'll take the girl the main sled," Ichu volunteered. "The Allwiya will likely want to meet their folk as well." Maybe he could get a little more information from her without her father around.

"A good idea," Elder Quilqi said.

"I must stay with my father," Cosquella objected. "He's sick, and I—"

"Can't do anything but get in the way, girl." Elder Quilqi's face looked as sharp as the girl's. "Flooding rivers, do you want your father to get better or not?"

Cosquella looked shocked into silence. Ichu chuckled and guided her across the bank to where the main sled was tied up, while Elder Papaki took Kallpa and his nephew to another sled. The remainder of the family gathered their possessions, signing to the Allwiya with them.

"The elder will do that to you," he said. "But don't worry. The Huaca has the ear of Tiya Qhalikay, and Aunt Healing can fix any disease. My sister is sick too, but we think the Aunt is guiding her to health."

He stopped Cosquella at the section of the sled where he'd dropped his meager belongings, and where Silluka lay, pale and unmoving.

"This is your sister?" Cosquella asked. Her hard face softened for a moment, looking down. Ichu saw her eyes rest on Silluka's right arm for a moment.

"It is. She...well, she saved over half our village, a few days ago, and she's been asleep since then. She used too much bodycasting."

Ichu still wouldn't have believed that part if he hadn't seen it himself. Silluka, bodycasting *too much*. Bodycasting at all. He was about to ask if Cosquella knew many chayus, when Silluka's eyes fluttered open. They locked on Cosquella's.

"Are you a goddess?" she asked.

CHAPTER THIRTEEN

New Companions

Silluka stared up at the beauty above her. The sun was peeking through clouds for once, and its rays were like a halo around the other girl's head, highlighting her cheekbones.

"Are you a goddess?" The words popped out of her mouth before she could stop them, and she struggled to sit up, then fell back again with a groan, clutching her head, which threatened to explode.

Ichu was next to her, appearing from somewhere out of her vision. "Slow. You've been out for three days. Elder Quilqi says you did too much bodycasting. Your body was breaking down from the strain."

She did bodycasting? Silluka blinked at the memories flooding back. She had performed *Flying Quirra*, but it had been easy once she caught the method behind it. Intent was everything, just like Elder Quilqi said. She could do it again now...

The ampuka drew up into her middle, but it was accompanied by a cramping pain as if it was twisting her insides. Silluka let her concentration go. She wouldn't be able to do any more bodycasting until she had at least gotten some food, and likely not until she had rested for several more days. It might not seem like it took effort, but it obviously took a toll on the body.

She frowned up at the tall, stony woman above her, who had a strange, half-shocked expression on, then felt her cheeks heat as she realized what she'd done.

"Did I just say what I thought I said?" she asked.

The words focused the other woman's attention, and she nodded, a smile playing at her full lips. "Afraid so. Too late to take it back. I'm keeping that compliment." She dropped into a crouch beside Silluka, eyes intent on her. She was wearing rough linen fabric, but was obviously heavily muscled underneath, arms straining against the sleeves, and her chest barely contained in her shirt. "Cosquella. And you are?"

What was her name? Surely, she had one. Maybe she could ask Ichu.

Ah, that was it. "I'm...I'm Silluka. You're not from the Huaca, are you?"

"My father and cousins have a farm north of here, but a volcano came with the new island." She turned, and Silluka saw the ripple of back muscles under her tunic. "See there? You can just make out the glow from the mountain." When she turned back, her eyes reflected the sunlight. They were dark, but not brown. Were they blue? Purple?

"The Huaca are fleeing the approaching island too," Silluka managed. "And the turtlemen who come with it."

Cosquella's face screwed up like she might shout for a moment, then it cleared, and she laughed, a loud, deep sound. "I can see that, I can. Turtlemen indeed. That's a good name for the Eztli Mecatl. Like turtles. Huh."

She chuckled to herself while Ichu helped Silluka sit up.

"I'm going to check on the other newcomers," he said. "You, ah, look like you're ready to welcome Cosquella to our Huaca, so I'll leave you to that." He gave her a sly smile. "I think Lugopo is going to meet the new Allwiya, too."

Silluka couldn't stop the smile she returned to her brother. She'd teased him enough about his conquests over the years. She'd spoken with Tamaya briefly after they practiced together under Elder Quilqi, but the tall pretty girl had been hustled off into helping with packing. She and Waskar, the meaty boy who had been in Hufi's patrol, were surprisingly accepting of her, but Silluka had lost track of them in the confusion. They must have been around the sleds somewhere, but Silluka couldn't take her eyes off this new beauty. She should introduce Cosquella to the others, after all.

"Yes, I can make her welcome," she said.

In fact, it was more like Cosquella was showing her around than the opposite, as the camp was packing up and getting the sleds in position to float once more. Silluka had been unconscious since they started their journey, and Cosquella had made a similar journey from their farm to this join in the river. She was more familiar with how the sleds worked on water. Plus, Cosquella had to practically hold her up. She was still shaky and weak. Not that Silluka was going to complain about the contact. Cosquella's arms were rough, almost scaly, but they were also firm, muscled, and warm.

Cosquella helped lift her from the ground to the lead sled, and Silluka might have let her fingers trail for an extra moment on Cosquella's hands before the larger woman hopped up beside her.

"You should see my father's sled," Cosquella told her, pointing where a small craft was tied to the main Huaca's sled. It had strange, high sides, but seemed to nestle into the river better. "The Allwiya designed it for us just when the volcano began to form. They spent all night attaching the extra planks to the sides."

"It looks like it would work better in the river."

"I think it does," Cosquella said, "but I'm not a sled driver, and we had no jakuas. The Allwiya also came up with the poles to help propel them."

She was interrupted by two figures approaching.

"You're up!" Tamaya bounded over and gave Silluka a hug, then eyed Cosquella up and down. "And you brought a...friend?"

"I'm glad you're alright," Waskar said from behind her. He laid a hand on Tamaya's shoulder and Silluka suddenly realized this might not be as awkward a situation as she thought. He stared at Cosquella's rough skin and strange hair, then shot a curious look at Silluka's arm. Meaty Boy had never been subtle.

"Yes, Cosquella was the first person I saw when I woke," Silluka said. "She and her family are traveling with us, so I'm showing her around."

"These fallen trees aren't going to clear themselves!" someone shouted from the front of the sled, and Tamaya sighed.

"They have us on cleanup duty, trying to keep the sleds going as fast as possible." She pulled on Waskar. "Come on, let's do *Tortoise Shoulders His Load* again. We'll see you soon."

They ran to a group of several other citizens and began their chayu.

"Friends of yours, are they?"

Silluka sighed. "They actually were part of a patrol that forced me to perform chayus in front of the elders before I was ready," she said, and Cosquella's stony face grew harder in confusion. "But you don't have elders where you live, do you? Or tests for citizenship?" Cosquella's continued blank look told volumes. "Well, yes, I guess they're...friends. I feel like everyone is helping out here but me." Then Silluka stumbled as the sled rocked in the water, and Cosquella caught her, fumbling awkwardly with the end of her stump.

"You can hardly stand, you." Her arm was tucked under Silluka's stump, awkwardly, but she was trying not to show it.

"You might be right. Don't worry. It doesn't hurt," Silluka said, referring to her stump. She poked Cosquella in the side with the nub on the end. "See? I can get some use out of it."

She barely kept the surprise off her face. The other girl's side was hard as rock.

"And you've...always been like that, yes?" Cosquella ventured. "I don't mean to cause offense."

"No...no offense taken," Silluka said. "And yes, I was born with it...or without it, you might say. The elders always said I would never be able to bodycast, without a second hand."

"But you have, people say? The others said you saved the poorer members of your village."

Cosquella had a strange, hitching way of talking, like she was more used to speaking another language. Maybe it was simply her family's separation from the Huaca.

"Elder Quilqi has been teaching my brother and I more about bodycasting. She seems to know of different abilities than those taught in my village. I'm starting to realize our elders don't know as much as they think. But I...I don't remember all of what I did. Most of it was in a haze." Silluka could recall performing *Flying Quirra*, but what came after that was disappearing quickly. She couldn't have really *floated* over a chasm, could she? She must just have found a bridge across, moving lightly with *Flying Quirra*.

Cosquella was silent a moment, and Silluka turned the question back to her.

"And you? I noticed your skin is kind of hard. Is that..."

"It's a condition I've had since birth, I have, sort of like yours," Cosquella said. She reached up and ran her free hand over her hair, which didn't move. "My mother died when I was born, and my father said she had the same condition as me, she did, with rough skin like this and thick hair. He tried to teach me a little bodycasting, but I was never able to catch on. I just trained to be the best I could, did I, without relying on the chayus."

"I think it worked," Silluka said, squeezing Cosquella's arm in hers. It was like squeezing a tree limb. They stepped from the sleds to the bank of the river, walking around the camp. "You've got more muscles than my brother, and he's our champion bodycaster." Her mind was screaming at her to stop complimenting this odd girl she'd known for mere minutes, but she couldn't help it. She'd never had any real relationships in the Huaca, unless competing with Hufi when they were younger counted. Tamaya...was a better match for Waskar, if she was honest with herself. She pressed down a lump of sadness at the memory of Hufi. He'd been a pain, but he didn't deserve that death. Yet life was often short in the Huaca, at the whim of the gods and the weather.

"My family teased me about it, they did." Cosquella looked away, and down. Other members of the village preparing the sleds watched them walking, and Silluka tried to lean on Cosquella a little more, as if she still needed the support. "They aren't mean, and I know Papa loves me dearly, but I always knew I was different, was I, like my Mama." She laughed again, that deep loud laugh. "I can't believe I'm telling you this. I barely know you."

"I have the same feeling," Silluka said. She waggled her stump, hooked around Cosquella's arm, and it didn't feel strange at all. There was finally someone else like her. Well, not like her at all, but someone else who was *different*. "Everyone thought I was an undesirable in our village. I'd never amount to anything because I would never be able to bodycast."

"But you did," Cosquella said. "Can you show me?"

Silluka frowned up at the other girl. They'd reached the front of the camp and stepped back on a sled angled across the river to make a bridge. The jakua station was ahead, under a stand of trees, and the big creatures were lolling in the sun and shade, some on their backs, paws in the air. The handlers were nearby as always, ready if one got it into their head to take off. They were trained, but the beast chayus were still the best way to control them.

"You really didn't learn any?" Silluka asked. "But you're so strong. Nothing like me."

Was Cosquella blushing? Her ochre skin had an almost gray undertone—not unhealthy, it simply reminded Silluka of marble. Now that undertone shifted to something like a rose quartz.

"I'm...not very good at being graceful," the big girl admitted. "If you want me to chop down a tree or lug a barrel of water, I can do that, I can, but the small movements are hard to get right sometimes."

Another similarity. Neither of them were good at chayus.

"That doesn't really matter," Silluka said.

"What do you mean it doesn't matter? You have to be exact with how you position your body. We may not have your elders, we don't, but I know that."

Silluka shook her head. "I only have one hand. I *can't* make the forms of the chayus correctly. But I've done several right. I've connected with the ampuka. That's what Elder Quilqi taught me." She motioned with her stump around Cosquella's arm again.

"But that's what my family's always told me too, they did. You don't think they were..." Cosquella looked scared, or maybe angry.

"No. I think they told you what they thought was the truth." Silluka was certain whoever raised this woman was a kind and good person. "I think everyone on this coast thinks that way. I was told the same thing. But Elder Quilqi seems to know something more than them."

"On this coast? But there is only the desert to the west, there is."

"I'm not so certain, any longer." After all, the elder had come from somewhere, hadn't she?

"Show me, please, how to do these chayus," Cosquella said.

Silluka reached across to pat her arm as Lugopo approached, all eight tentacles churning at speed. Several other Allwiya were with them, including the newcomers. Lugopo was the smallest of all of them, by far. "We'll learn together," she promised. Surely the elder had some technique that would help Silluka's new friend.

Lugopo scuttled to Silluka's feet, signaled something to the other Allwiya, then wrapped their tentacles around her linen pants and scurried up her leg. They alighted on her hand, two tentacles holding them up.

"Big news!" the translation circlet chirped. "Many new deathtraps and weapons possible!" Lugopo tapped the thing and Silluka almost thought she detected a bit of chagrin in the new words. "That is, my fellows have showed me innovations they devised. I think it may serve us well."

"Your Allwiya talks?" Cosquella asked. She made a sign to Lugopo, who returned it, then another, with more tentacles. Cosquella laughed.

"Not my Allwiya," Silluka said, "but yes, they designed it themself. I suppose you learned their language on the farm?"

"Lugopo says I have a strange accent, they do. We worked with the Allwiya on our farm. They made all our equipment for us, and even developed fertilizers and new harvest techniques."

"Which they shared with us as well. Such profound knowledge from Crawling Dark of Squirming! Such blessing. But this is why I ambush you here." They held up a wooden ball, which they must have kept under their tentacles while they approached. "This shows heat from far below, the core of the world. It is growing, erupting! The coast where you lived is certainly all destruction now. See here!"

The top of the wooden ball spiraled open, and a tiny metal needle pointed to a squiggle carved into a ring placed around the edge. There were more squiggles all around the circumference of the ring.

"What does this mean?" Silluka asked. She supposed the squiggles were Allwiya writing, but she'd only been interacting with the creatures for a few weeks. She hadn't seen other signs of their language. Whatever it was, it wasn't like the pictures, arrows, and lines of the Huaca.

Lugopo presented the device to Cosquella, who also peered down at it, then shook her head.

"Do you not see the beauty granted by Manylegs of Reaching? This senses the magnetic disruptions caused by the interactions of the tectonic barriers between islands. Yes?" They held up the device again, as if that would make everything clear.

"Lugopo, I have no idea what you're talking about," Silluka said.

"Big boom. The fire under the ground is coming. The sleds must move. Where is the elder?"

"Why didn't you say so?" Silluka said. She pulled Cosquella with her toward the fabric shelters that had been set up on the side of the river. She was feeling much less wobbly after her walk around the sleds. She wasn't quite up to a chayu yet, but maybe later that day.

As if sensing them, Elder Quilqi came from one of the tents as they approached. Her face looked like she'd tried to chew a stone.

"Just the two I was looking for. I've been working with the best bodycasters to help your father, girl." She was staring at Cosquella.

"What's the matter?" Silluka asked. Cosquella hadn't said anything was wrong with her father, just how he raised her.

"Tried to breathe in a volcano, seems like," Elder Quilqi grunted. "He's not in a good way. Collapsed as soon as we got him and his nephew under the care of the best healers."

"But he was only coughing when we got here, he was," Cosquella said. "What did you do to him?" She tensed under Silluka's arm, her skin almost hot to touch.

"Got what dust we could from his lungs, and his nephew's," the elder replied. "I have three good healers who know *Flower Sends Out Pollen*, but it was not an easy task, even when I helped them. We'll have to wait a few days to see what happens to them."

"What happens?" Cosquella said. She disengaged from Silluka's hold, folding her rough arms in front of her. She stood head and shoulders taller than Elder Quilqi, who was not a short woman.

"Island and seas, girl, I can't do miracles. Your father fell over in a faint as soon as we got him to the healers. He'd likely been hanging on while you all escaped from the volcano. If we'd been any later, there wouldn't have been a point to even trying."

"I have to see him," Cosquella cried, pushing past the elder.

"Don't stress him, or your cousin," the elder called after her.

Lugopo tugged at Silluka's arm, still holding the wooden ball. "Most desperate. Death and suffering for all if not addressed!"

The elder glanced at the ball, then at Lugopo. "That close? The islands are coming together." As if she summoned it, another earthquake shook the sleds and set the jakuas snarling. Silluka kept her feet this time, but barely. "We need to get the sleds running now if we don't want the aftershocks following us."

"This is my plea," Lugopo said. They closed the ball and scuttled to Silluka's shoulder.

"So. You're awake." The elder's eyes roamed over Silluka's face. "I see you've found a new friend too. Feeling the aftereffects? You're not powerful enough to control that kind of connection. *Flying Quirra* was a test, not a map. What were you thinking?"

"I was thinking it's the duty of the strong to help those who are weaker," Silluka shot back. "I did what you said. I used my *intent* to perform the chayu, and it worked!"

"It worked, and you almost killed yourself," the elder corrected. She repositioned as another quake shook the sleds. "Good that you've unlocked how your intent works. Now you need to learn control and expand your capabilities. You can't tap into the core like that and expect the power not to overwhelm you. Don't do it again before I give you leave."

"The core?"

"The core of the planet? Where the gods live? Bubbling magma, what do they teach you kids these days?"

"Then that's where the ampuka comes from?"

"Naturally. That's where the gods can affect the world. It's where all their power derives from."

"There is much haste needed," Lugopo put in. They rubbed several of their tentacles together nervously.

Elder Quilqi stood straight, looking toward the coast. "Quite right. This must be a lesson for another time. We need to get the sleds moving quickly. Cosquella's father and cousin will need to be transferred to the second sled, where we can find an open space." Elder Quilqi leaned in close. "Keep an eye on the new girl. There is something strange about her."

"It's just a skin condition," Silluka said. "She already told me about it."

"That's not all there is. But time will tell. Come, help me with—"

There was a *boom* like the world had opened, and a gout of orange light appeared in the distance. The oncoming island was plowing through theirs, spinning up mountains, earthquakes, and volcanoes as it did. Their village was certainly destroyed.

People began running, untying the sleds. The jakua herders began *Waking Beast*.

"Quickly now. The islands are merging and not even the strongest bodycaster can withstand that chaos. We must outrun it. Help me gather the Huaca."

CHAPTER FOURTEEN

Desert

Earthquakes and tremors followed them as Ichu helped guide the sleds. In the last day as they fled the eruptions at the coast, teams cut trees by the river—old growths that were at least twenty years old—and fashioned them into side slats for the sleds like the newcomers had made. It kept the water out, and they found they could fit even more on the sleds before they took on water. The jakuas did not need to pull as hard, and they could use poles to keep the sleds from the riverbanks. It made them go faster, and they needed all the speed they could muster.

His sister had found a similar spirit in Cosquella. The big girl was strange, but polite. Her father and cousin continued to worsen, despite repeated performances of *Flower Sends Out Pollen* to remove the ash from their lungs. Elder Sinchi, who led the healers, said the dust might have caused permanent damage from the length of time inside the body. They could only wait and see what would happen at this point. Even if they didn't worsen, they would likely be weakened the rest of their lives, unable to do any strenuous activity.

The strong survived in the Huaca.

The day after that, the winds came. They could see the eruptions of magma even from here, but now the hot winds brought tiny particles of ash, just like those that had harmed Cosquella's family. Everyone on the sleds wore cloth masks devised by the Allwiya, and the elders prayed to Tiyu Pacha to clear the air.

Uncle Sky must have had his eye on them, because after only three repetitions of the sign of the sky—fingertips touching, hands changing to view the clouds from different configurations—a wind rose in the other direction. Ichu saw a barrier form, the air clearing above them. He hadn't realized the air had been so clouded. It held as they traveled, following with them, flakes of ash collecting on top of the transparent dome. Did so much attention from a god mean the storm warriors from the wall of storms were defeated? Or had they moved to a different place?

"I hope the storms will stop any of the Eztli Mecatl following after us," Ichu told his sister on the next day.

"They are very strong, they are, and resistant to heat," Cosquella warned from Silluka's other side, where she was a constant presence. "They will still follow."

She and Silluka were fast becoming firm friends, and perhaps something more. The two young citizens who had practiced with them in the Huaca, Waskar and Tamaya, sometimes accompanied them, when they were not busy clearing the river of fallen trees and silt. He wished the best for his little sister, now she had found companions. She had not had an easy time in the Huaca, with her missing forearm.

Ichu stared across the four great sleds, holding everyone he had ever known. He'd had relationships with some of the bodycasters here, male and female, but none of them ever lasted. He didn't bear ill-will to any of them, but none still held his interest. A tinge of sadness touched him at Kuillay's fate, when the first turtleman landed, but he brushed it away. He could do nothing for the dead.

There was more to this world than he'd thought, and perhaps the right person for him was out there. He held out his hand, studying the lines etched into his skin. He wasn't so young anymore. What secrets could Elder Quilqi teach him? What did she know, and what had she seen?

The river grew weaker as the last trees disappeared and the ground turned sandy. The elders kept up their prayers day in and day out, and the bubble of clear air stayed around them. They were almost fully into the desert now, and even the water source of the river was not enough to overcome the dryness. In a few more years, this area would be lush with vegetation, but they had been forced to migrate to a new Huaca earlier than expected. The ground continued to shake with the aftereffects of the islands merging, but no new rents opened up, or changed the course of the river, thankfully.

Every day, he practiced the morning ritual, but pondered what Elder Quilqi had taught them. He tried the moves from different stances, and felt the ampuka connecting, but oddly. There were more ways to do even the morning ritual than he'd been taught. All those years of effort. Had they been wasted?

Silluka and Consquella practiced with him, and he marveled at how much his sister had grown in skill in just a few weeks. She used her right arm now, as it was meant to move within the morning ritual, rather than hiding it as she used to. He could see the full motions her arm movements described, though the forearm and hand weren't there. Was this the *intent* behind the chayu Elder Quilqi had taught them? Was his sister besting him in ability? The elder had said he would have to unlearn what he'd learned. Was there enough time for that?

Three days later, as he finished the morning ritual, the air began to clear and the wind against them died down, dissolving the sphere of dust and debris Tiyu Pacha had held back. Ichu said his own silent prayer to the Uncle, then noticed there were still elders at the front of the lead sled, making the sign of the air. Had the god deserted them? The citizen on watch, perched high on the mound of belongings in the middle of the sled, raised a finger, pointing behind them.

Ichu scanned the horizon. There were turtlemen visible in the distance, moving without hurry, confident of their superiority. Uncle Sky must have ceased his protection in case more might was needed against the invaders. He hoped.

There were shouts, and bodycasters began lining the backs of the sleds, ready if the turtlemen tried anything. There were at least ten following them, but as he watched, two split off, disappearing into the low brush to either side of the river. Then another three appeared from different cover. So, there were more than that, but a core party making themselves known. For what reason?

Silluka and Cosquella came up behind him, Lugopo riding Silluka's shoulder. "How did they survive the winds and dust?" his sister asked.

"They are strong warriors," Cosquella said. It was a refrain she had kept up the past few days.

"But you said you knew ones who taught you skills?" Silluka asked her.

He should join the others protecting the sleds. Despite the need to watch the invaders for aggressive movement, Ichu turned to the young woman. If she had information, that might be the difference between holding their own and being overrun.

"We did. The first ones to come, they were desperate enough to cross the boiling sea between the islands. Even these few were much stronger than us, weren't they, bolstered by the harshness of their land. They were teachers and craftsmen from their island, persecuted and chased. I don't remember much of them, I don't, only what they showed us. They left when I was young, taking their chances further into the interior."

"Beginning their conquest early!" Lugopo added. It was a fair point. Would they encounter turtlemen ahead as well as behind?

"Can you tell us more about them? What they might fear? What might defeat them?" Ichu urged. "We must know more, now. I barely held off one of them, but here..." He spread a hand out toward the shapes in the distance. They weren't rushing, but he'd seen how fast they could move. There would be an engagement again, sometime soon.

"I can tell you a little, but my father would know much more. He isn't well, though, not at all," Cosquella said.

"Is it worth asking, so we can defend ourselves?" Silluka suggested gently. "We could help protect him then." *We*, she said, not *they*. His sister already thought better of herself, with just a little practice. He tamped down his smile, but he was proud. Though the lines between undesirable and citizen were blurring. Everyone helped out on the sleds now, no matter if they could use the chayus or not.

"I think it is," Cosquella said. "I need to check on him today in any case, I do. He has not been well the last few days, even with your village's help."

Ichu led the way to the small healing center, near the rear of the second sled. Kallpa and his nephew lay on mats, along with one of the Huaca who had broken his leg falling between two of the sleds.

"Daughter," Kallpa croaked when they entered. Ichu hadn't seen him since the elders had taken him for healing, but he looked much worse now than he had then, his face pale and lips purple. His nephew was sleeping or unconscious, laying behind him.

"Father, how are you feeling?" Cosquella knelt by his side, still up to Ichu's chest even on her knees. She was a very tall girl. "Can I get you anything? Are the healers treating you well, yes?"

She grasped his hand, and Kallpa squeezed back weakly. Even this little exertion was making him pant. "I am tired, Cosquella, I am. I fear even with the healer's efforts, I have little time. I am not the man I was."

"Don't say that, you," Cosquella said.

"It is true. To deny truth is...to ignore the gods." He had to pause for breath, even with that little speech.

"Father, can you tell us of the Eztli Mecatl? There are some following us. I fear we may have to fight them, I do. I don't think these are like the ones we knew."

Kallpa tried to sit up, but fell back to his mat, gasping, purple lips gaping. Ichu clenched his fists, hating they were witness to the older man's weakness. He would squeeze every bit of knowledge from Elder Quilqi, if it would help them live longer, fuller lives. He went to the other side of the mat, and with Cosquella's help, lifted her father slowly until he was resting against a large bolster.

"Thank you," he panted. Silluka crept closer behind Cosquella, resting her hand on the larger woman's shoulder. Lugopo twisted this way and that, their large gleaming eyes seeming to catalog what was in the healing center. Ichu was surprised to see the white and black aura slowly gain strength around them. It was as when the Allwiya had demonstrated the device that showed the ampuka. They leapt from Silluka's shoulder, gathering stray pieces of wood, cloth, and little pieces of metal, breaking small bits from the frame of the tent.

"If the Eztli Mecatl are following...then I must tell you more about...them, I must." Kallpa had to stop with each sentence. "These are not...the ones you knew as a child. These are...the ones they fled from. They are strong as a group...but even stronger by themselves."

Ichu wasn't sure he'd heard correctly. "Wait. You say they are stronger in *fewer* numbers?"

"Yes..." Kallpa had to stop then, coughing. Cosquella held his hand, looking helpless and angry she could not help her father.

Lugopo swung down, a strange funnel of wood, metal and cloth gripped in several tentacles. The white and black glow was even stronger around them, throwing a shadow in the dark tent. "Apologies for intrusion," the circlet chirped. "Have created devious trap—for breathing!" They placed the device in front of Kallpa's mouth. "Mighty words will be aided so color changing reverses."

Kallpa must have been used to the inventions of his own Allwiya because he let Lugopo strap the filter in front of his mouth. He took several breaths, then sat up straighter.

"Many thanks, Allwiya," he said. "Can you craft one for my nephew, yes?"

"With great ease!" Lugopo swung away.

"Can I do anything else for you?" Cosquella asked, but her father held up a hand. He already seemed more animated, his face gaining color.

"Simply listen, you all. This is important." His voice was muffled behind the funnel, but still audible. "You asked of their numbers, you did. What I stated was correct. These Eztli Mecatl will become *stronger* as their numbers reduce, not weaker. This is why the one you fought on his own was so formidable." He paused again to catch his breath, and Ichu leaned in with the others. "They have the power of blood, given to them by their god." Kallpa held up a finger. "Just one, for their home island is tiny, it is. But theirs is a powerful god. I never learned their name, I didn't. The Eztli Mecatl we learned from were heretics, fleeing from the practices of their people, and so they would not say the god's name."

Kallpa rested again, wheezing, which turned into coughing. Cosquella got him a skin of water and Ichu studied her father. He was perhaps younger than he looked, aged from a hard farm life. Maybe Ichu himself would have looked similar in another twenty years. Why would any choose to live away from the protection of the Huaca? Away from the teaching of the elders?

When he finished coughing, and had some water, Kallpa began again.

"Their power fortifies them, makes their bodies nearly invincible, and pervades every part of them. If one falls, another may partake of them, and gain their strength, they can, even while fighting. The ones I spoke to viewed this as a corruption of their original path, though they would not even say what that was. Beware the strongest of their warriors. They can even call metal and earth to them, as armor."

He fell into another coughing fit, one hand pressed to his chest.

"Father, are you alright?" Cosquella leaned toward him. "What can I do for you?"

"This took more of a toll than...I thought," he gasped. "But I have to tell you one more...ahh...thing, I do." He clutched his chest. "Lay me back, you."

Ichu helped Cosquella get him prone again. He groaned.

"We should go. Thank you for your wisdom, Kallpa," Ichu said, but Kallpa held up a weak hand.

"One last thing. Cosquella, closer." Even with Lugopo's funnel, the man's face was deathly pale again. The Allwiya was with his nephew, affixing a second device to his face.

"You don't have to tell me now," Cosquella said. "It's too much."

"If I do not tell you now...I may not get a chance, no." Kallpa's voice was weak.

"Don't say that, Father."

"Hush. Listen. Your mother. I told you...she passed away when you were born." Kallpa's eyelids were fluttering as he struggled to stay conscious. "Don't stop me, you. She was...special, your mother. The Eztli Mecatl, they...they..."

He fell silent.

"What, Father?" Cosquella pressed a hand to his cheek.

Silluka crowded next to her, supporting the older man's arm with her stump and checking for a pulse with her hand.

"I'll get the healers," Ichu said.

"He's still alive, but unconscious," Silluka said as he left. "His pulse is weak."

By the time Ichu got back with Elder Sinchi herself, Kallpa's breathing was shallow. The healer shoed them out as she began the first moves of *Tree Sap Flows*, used to keep the blood moving.

"I'm sure he'll be well soon," Silluka was saying to Cosquella, who was shaking her head. Her strange hair didn't even ruffle in the breeze.

The hot breeze. Ichu blinked, particles stinging his eyes. The air stank of rotten eggs.

Ichu's head whipped around as the river shook, waves slapping against the new boards fixed to the sides of the sled. The wind was coming from the opposite direction. From inland, not from the coast. The shock of the islands clashing had raced ahead of them. They were too late.

He could see the mound forming ahead, pushing the river back toward them in a crest of water. A giant was awakening.

"Volcano!" he called.

CHAPTER FIFTEEN

Volcano

Ichu started the moves of *Tortoise in His Shell* as the jakuas fled to their cages on the first sled. It came from Unmovable stance, but on a whim, he changed it to Strength stance, guessing it would mesh better with the uneven movement of the sleds. As his back rounded and his arms crossed, Silluka and Cosquella came up beside him.

"Follow along!" he shouted. "This is a group chayu and we'll need all the power we can to hold off the blast." The mound of the volcano was building, ahead of them, the peak rounding into a dome that screamed *pressure!*

Silluka watched his movements and fell into Strength stance beside him. The ampuka immediately surged closer. She was much stronger and more competent than the last time they had performed a group chayu together.

"Me too, yes?" Cosquella was hesitant, a strange look on the large girl.

"You too," Ichu said, his arms flowing in a circular arc that described a tortoise's shell.

"Like this. Knees strong, but turned in with the toes," Silluka said. "Hips tucked." She nodded down at her waist, both upper arms moving, and her one hand forming a graceful curve, fingers together and thumb tucked next to them.

Cosquella hesitantly joined in, her movements jerky and ungraceful. As the leader of the group chayu, Ichu could detect a small increase in the ampuka, but not enough. Even Silluka had more than that, before she started training with the elder.

"To me!" he called. "Anyone who knows *Tortoise in His Shell!*"

Several other Huaca ran up, watching for where he was in the process.

"From Strength, not Unmovable," Ichu said. "Trust me on this."

"But that's the wrong stance," someone complained behind his back. He thought it was the stout boy Silluka knew—Waskar.

"Have you done it on a moving sled before?" Silluka grated, and the complainer fell silent. Ichu was both glad his sister had picked up the same reasoning, and that she was confident enough to shut down the objections. He wished he had tried harder to teach her, back when their parents were alive. What a bodycaster she could be now! But they had always let her study and read, to find her own path.

The shell grew around them as more villagers joined in. It surrounded the first sled, a sphere of pink and blue, then grew to cover all four sleds and the undesirables' sled as more Huaca saw and joined in. Nearly everyone who knew the chayu was performing it, including many of the elders. Even a few of the undesirables moved along with them, arms and legs clumsy, but every little bit was needed.

In front of them, the volcano blew its top, fire and death surging toward them faster than a jakua could run.

Twenty seconds later, a sound so deep Ichu could only feel it in his bones washed over them. Rock and fire arced up and away from the new mountain, heading straight for them. He kept performing the chayu, desperately hoping everyone else would as well, because he didn't have time to pray to Tiyu Tiksimuyu. Against the onslaught, the strength of the ampuka increased until it was a blaze of brown and orange light, signaling Aunt Harvest was also lending her protection. The Huaca was strong. His sister was strong.

Several of the elders dropped out and he heard them calling on Tiyu Llamkay, Uncle Smith, to armor their bodies and Uncle Earth to contain the explosion. The ampuka surged again within him in answer to the prayers, like his own source of magma, and his limbs and skin felt stronger. The heat was not nearly so searingly hot.

He braced as the full firestorm engulfed them, now on his fourth repetition of the chayu, nearly a full minute after the first eruption. Debris impacted the forming shell. The sound thrummed through him, blocking out any other noise.

Ichu winced as a piece of rock larger than him impacted the shell, and a tiny crack formed in the swirling colors. Ichu reached the end of *Tortoise in His Shell* again and started a fifth iteration of the chayu.

"Again!" he called. The Huaca around him braced in Strength stance and rounded their backs with the first move.

He watched the crack in the shell. It slowly closed, even as the shell grew thicker. It completely covered the sleds now, mighty against the power of the earth. Only Uncle Smith's hand aiding their bodies was keeping it from collapsing like cloth tossed into a bonfire.

Then the volcano seemed to crimp in on itself as the firm hand of Tiyu Tiksimuyu throttled the effect, fulfilling the elders' prayers, but even the Uncle couldn't completely stop what had started.

Ichu bared his teeth as the glow of lava filtered through the dust in the air. If all went well, it would splash against the shell and form a protective crust around the sleds until the eruption died down. He'd heard from his parents of this exact technique used forty years ago, when one of the southern volcanoes spewed lava all the way to the Huaca. The remaining crust had fertilized crops, once it cooled.

They would need to perform the chayu several more times to make sure the shell—

"Attackers!" came the call through the sleds and Ichu forced his body not to freeze up, to keep moving through the chayu. But he knew instantly what had happened. The turtlemen had been waiting for an opportunity, and the volcano had been the perfect one.

"We can't keep the chayu up and protect ourselves!" Silluka screamed into his ear. He could barely hear over the roar of debris hitting the shell.

"It will have to last," Ichu shouted back, then yelled to the rest of the group, punctuating his words with hand signals so the others might pick up his meaning. "Pick some to stay here and reinforce the shell. Everyone else should defend against the turtlemen." The elders caught his plan and spread the word.

Where was Elder Quilqi?

Cosquella broke away from her chayu with a growl. "I can be more help with defense, I can," she shouted. He could hear her clearly, she was so loud. Her eyes seemed bright, as if they reflected the fire of the volcano. She made fists, her knuckles straining. "You lead the group, Silluka. I'll keep you safe."

Silluka seemed to hesitate, then nodded and settled back into the chayu, a small group of Huaca following her lead. No one said anything about her missing hand now. Those undesirables who couldn't fight grouped with her to bolster the shell as much as they could. The elders were already heading toward the rear sled, ready to come up with strategies to push the turtlemen back.

Ichu ran with them, Cosquella hot on his heels. They joined other warriors already there just as the first turtleman reached the shell surrounding the sleds. At least they would have a few moments to prepare as the protection of Uncle Earth and Aunt Harvest slowed them down.

The lead turtleman placed one hand against the shield of brown and orange light. His beaky mouth frowned, and he pushed harder, then banged on the shell. Hope rose within Ichu. Had they found something to at last stop the turtlemen?

But the invader plucked a vial from his belt and threw it back, swallowing dark red fluid. His eyes met Ichu's and they blazed with inner light. The turtleman's hand made a fist, and plates like those on his back grew over it like gray crystal, spikes jutting out at all angles.

He punched the shell and a crack lanced through it, pieces of orange and brown light falling away. He punched again and made a hole big enough for him to climb through.

Others behind him were doing the same. It was just as Elder Quilqi said, like what Uncle Smith did for the Huaca, but twisted in some way.

"Get ready!" he called.

The first turtleman climbed over the edge of the sled, eyes blazing. Cosquella's fist met its face with a satisfying crunch, and the surprised turtleman fell back over the side, senseless. Ichu felt his eyebrows raise. She had done that much with one punch? The girl *was* strong.

Then more of the creatures were over the sides, twenty or more at once. Kallpa had been right. These were much easier to defeat as a group than individually, though they were still stronger than most citizens. Blows the first Eztli Mecatl he had fought shrugged off took down members here. Cosquella was right beside him as he performed *Jakua's Claws* and broke an attacker's plating with one swipe. Why were they attacking as a group then? Why not attack individually?

Cosquella rained blows on another turtleman, cracking his plates with audible *snaps*, until the creature fell senseless.

Then the glowing vials came out, invaders ducking back through the holes in the shell and gathering around the fallen one, digging bits of flesh from his still form. They placed them in their vials and swigged them quickly, eyes glowing with power.

One of the jakua handlers roused her charges, bringing the sleek, dark beasts forward with *Fighting Beast*. The jakuas pounced on a turtleman, digging great rents in their side.

But like relentless waves of the ocean, each remaining turtleman found the time to take a bit of the fallen one's flesh for their vials. They slipped in and out of the fighting and through holes in the orange and brown shell.

Gradually, the remaining Eztli Mecatl took more hits to fall, then stopped falling, then started pushing the Huaca back, as the fallen became fuel for those who were left. Then there were only five. He and Cosquella fought against one of the five with two other Huaca. When he could spare a glance, he saw five and six apiece against each turtleman, barely keeping them from crossing the sleds.

The one they were fighting growled something in its guttural language as Ichu took a blow on an arm, fortified by *Roots in Fitted Stone*. Cosquella growled something back at it and it laughed, a horrible sound like rocks being ground together.

The entire Huaca was being forced back by only five of the creatures, and they had no place to go. When Ichu snuck another glance behind him, he was greeted by a wall of cooling molten rock, formed into a curve around the sleds, taller than him and still growing. How long had he been fending off the attack? Was Silluka still leading the chayu?

He let Cosquella take the center on the attack. She grinned, all teeth. Her arms, as big around as his, flashed like lightning, barreling punches into their opponent's chest and blocking arms. Where she had been halting and awkward in chayus, she was a natural at hand-to-hand combat. For a moment, the turtleman's attack stalled and Ichu caught a glimpse of Elder Quilqi—finally—in the center of the main sled with the other elders, making the sign for Tiyu Tiksimuyu, calling again on Uncle Earth.

A moment later, the ampuka glowed brightly in three different places on the sleds: one with those performing *Tortoise in His Shell*, another brown aura around the elders calling on the Uncle, and third around the Huaca who fought the five turtlemen. Even with that protection, those fighting with Ichu were being pushed closer to the elders and to the wall of cooling lava.

As Ichu used *Wind from Eagle's Wings* to buffet the turtleman back a step. Elder Quilqi began a new chayu, weaving between the elders, making sharp, concussive moves that reminded Ichu of an earthquake tearing a stretch of land apart. He caught glimpses as he dodged the turtleman's blows. As strong as the invader was now, each strike numbed muscles, though Cosquella was still trading blows, her face a mask of rage. He didn't know what the elder's chayu would do, but they were running out of time.

Tamaya, leading the bodycasters in the group to their left, thrust a dagger deep into her opponent's eye, and the Eztli Mecatl fell back, crashing to the ground. At the same moment the strikes from Ichu's opponent increased to something like hammer blows, and Ichu ground his teeth against them. He could only hold on so long, though Cosquella seemed almost unaffected, leaning into each punch she threw at their opponent. How had she learned that on a farm?

The wall of cooling rock rumbled and Ichu waited for the shell to fail and douse them all in lava. He slid around a strike from the Eztli Mecatl, but the strike grazed his shoulder, almost spinning him around. Could they even finish this fight?

Then the solidifying magma parted like water, and figures in amber armor leapt through it and the shell as if they weren't there, landing heavily on the sleds and running to the fight. There were eight of them, two for each remaining Eztli Mecatl. They wore savage masks, with faces stretched out in rage or passion, and they all glowed with the ampuka, shining bronze like metal buffed by river water.

The Huaca fell back as the new warriors took over, forcing the Eztli Mecatl into a small group, ringing them. Ichu watched in awe as one of the glowing warriors held an arm up, feet stomping in a rhythm. Metal bands around her wrist grew into a sheet of metal that stopped a punch from a turtleman. She followed up with a punch of her own and the turtleman staggered back. Who were these saviors? Ichu snuck a look toward Elder Quilqi, who was watching them, hands on hips, a small smile on her face.

Hesitantly at first, then with excitement, the Huaca aided the glowing warriors, keeping the turtlemen from escaping. As their circle became smaller, they had less room to move, and less room to act.

Finally, the warriors in amber armor raised their fists as one, fingers clenching into fists, and stone pillars punched through the bottom of the sled, capturing the Eztli Mecatl in a cage of stone. Their eyes glowed red and purple from the darkness as they hammered on their prison, breaking pieces off, trying to get free. Then in unison, the warriors gestured again, and another round of pillars grew. With a shout, they clapped their hands and the pillars smashed together with a *thud*. Dark blood leaked from between cracks.

Ichu let out a breath, looking back toward the shell, holding a shoulder bleeding from some wound he couldn't remember. Silluka performed with the others, and Tortoise's Shell still held against the colling lava, but the sleds were stuck here, especially the lead sled, which now had a gaping hole in the bottom. They would have to wait until the volcano died down, sitting targets for any more Eztli Mecatl.

One of the warriors broke off and approached Elder Quilqi, removing his fearsome mask with one hand. It revealed a young man—slightly younger than Ichu, at least by looks. He was strikingly handsome, a light sweat beading on his brow. Ichu wiped blood from his knuckles and brushed his hair back from his face.

"It was good you called us." The man had a deep, resonant voice. "We have been trying to track the Eztli Mecatl movements, but they have a way of disguising themselves from our vision, hiding even from the earth."

"Are you gods?" Ichu was startled to see Silluka nearby. She must have left the group chayu to greet the warriors. Ichu checked the shell held, but it was well reinforced, keeping the lava at bay. Several others kept *Tortoise in His Shell* going, continually reinforcing it. Silluka's eyes were just as drawn to the youthful leader as Ichu's were.

The warrior laughed. "No, little sister. We are mere stone warriors. Surely you have seen the storm warriors, since you hail from the coastal regions. We are like them."

Cosquella drifted to Silluka's side, sweat beaded under her strange, unmoving hair. Silluka checked her over, gently probing bruises for anything broken. Cosquella hissed as Silluka hit a tender rib.

"But we call the storm warriors gods too," another bodycaster said, and several more joined them, covered in ash, dust, and blood. "You saved us from the turtlemen."

"We're no more gods than you are," the stone warrior said, his grin wide and endearing. "We simply know a little more of the way of the world, our chayus more refined. You seem to have a number of physical adepts here, and you have a fine teacher, if you want to learn as we do." He gestured toward Elder Quilqi, who folded her arms. "Is there anything else you need, ancient one?"

The elder seemed to consider for a moment. If the title concerned her, she didn't show it. She glanced to where the wall of lava hid the volcano. "Since you put a hole in these villagers' sled, you could at least lend a hand in repairing it, and getting us going again once the volcano dies down. If you're feeling generous, you could also lead us through the desert, and past any more dangers such as these."

The stone warrior bowed from his hips. "We will do what we can, ancient one. Since the Eztli Mecatl have attacked here once, it's possible they might again." He closed his eyes and held his hands out, fingers spread wide. His brow wrinkled, then his eyes snapped open again. "The tremors are dying away. This eruption has likely released enough of the stress of the new island, at least this far inland. There will be more chaos nearer the coast, but not as much here. As you travel farther inland, you will reach a deep well of solid rock under the desert that will solidify the shifting earth."

"You can tell all that by feel?" Ichu asked. He realized he'd come closer to the stone warrior, taking in the amber armor, decorated with hundreds of small stones against a bronze background. It was similar to the armor of the storm warrior who had died. Was this armor also created from the stone warrior's magic?

The stone warrior seemed to see him for the first time, eyes raking Ichu up and down. He felt as if the man could see all the way through him. The man exuded charisma.

"Caster," the man greeted him. "You seem to have a passable knowledge of the basics and are a strong physical adept. More at least than the rest of the people in your village. You haven't started to feel the elements, then?"

Ichu had never heard of such a thing. "Is this possible? Is it part of the chayus? The ampuka?" He felt as if he was swirled around in a hurricane. First the volcano, then attacking Eztli Mecatl, now he was conversing with gods from legends. Elder Quilqi had been right when she said he had seen little of the world.

"The ampuka's power comes from the core and the Aunts, Uncles, and Entles, as you must know. So does feeling the elements." The storm warrior looked at the assembled Huaca, all of them staring. Even the few still performing *Tortoise in His Shell* had their eyes glued to the stone warrior. "You do *not* know of this? Of how to pass along the ladder of the adepts?"

"We do not," Ichu confirmed. Yet more of the world that had passed by the Huaca. How small was their village, really? "But we're willing to learn."

The stone warrior's stare became more direct. "A good answer. I'm Akamu, leader of this band of stone warriors. If you wish to learn, I'd be happy to show you some techniques." He extended an arm.

"Ichu, strongest bodycaster in the Huaca." Ichu returned a warm smile and grasped the man's arm, thick with ropy muscle. "I'd be honored to learn from you." Bodycasting, and anything else Akamu wanted to show him. He met Akamu's warm brown eyes and the edges of them crinkled in a smile. Oh yes. He could learn much from this man.

"Perhaps we can stay with you a few days, and watch for movement by the Eztli Mecatl," Akamu said, eyes still holding Ichu's as one hand caressed his smooth chin. "What do you say to some guard duty, siblings?"

There was a rousing chorus of shouts from the stone warriors, who all removed their masks, revealing seven more grinning men and women, all except one as young as Akamu. The outlier was a gray-haired woman who was likely old enough to be Ichu's mother. She was still bodycasting at her age? She moved as quickly as the other warriors.

Ichu didn't get a chance to ask before the stone warrior patrol dissipated like steam on a hot day, the seven others going in all directions, to help fortify the shell, to start repairing the hold in the sled, to talk to the elders, and three jumping from the sled to the bank, though cooling lava flowed like honey. They sprang across it like jakua across a stream, their feet not even singed.

Elder Quilqi approached Akamu and him, speaking quietly so only they and Silluka and Cosquella, who were standing nearby, could hear. "You were close, to respond so quickly to my summons."

Akamu nodded, his noble face serious. He—grudgingly, Ichu thought—looked away from him and to the elder. "We were, ancient one. The Eztli Mecatl move swiftly and they are strong. They will overrun this side of the continent if they are not stopped. Chimor needs time to prepare."

Silluka looked as confused as he felt. "Chimor?" Lugopo scampered up his sister's leg, climbing to her shoulder. Their big eyes took in everything, and he couldn't imagine what strange thoughts were going through their head.

Akamu glanced at Silluka, then took another look, eyes narrowing. "Chimor. The capital, past the desert. Are we so far out into the Contisuyu that you don't even know where the Huaca is centered? Does the Allwiya know?"

"I have not heard of this fantastical place! More victims to experiment on!" They tapped the circlet. "That is, more people to meet."

"Well, you have something I have not seen either—a talking Allwiya," Akamu admitted.

"But our village *is* the Huaca," Silluka said. "We find a new Huaca every time we have to move inland."

Akamu looked to Elder Quilqi, who shrugged imperceptibly. Ichu wondered how much wasn't being said. How much had their village lost, being out by itself on the coast?

Akamu blew out a breath. "Well, it seems my patrol does have its work cut out for it." He glanced at Silluka again. "Though perhaps this village is not quite so backward as I thought." He clapped Ichu on the arm. "Come with me and show me what you know."

CHAPTER SIXTEEN

The Stone Warriors

The rest of the stone warriors quickly drafted members of the Huaca to help them with repairs to the sleds. Though the entire village had regarded the far-away storm warriors as gods their entire lives, these stone warriors were easy to talk to. They were obviously no gods, though their abilities were far beyond even the most capable elder—though perhaps not of Elder Quilqi. In no time, the warriors were joking with the Huaca's bodycasters, and no one spared a second glance for their glowing amber armor. How strange, that who they once thought of as gods acted so normal. Ichu noticed how they spoke to an elder was no different to how they addressed an elderly undesirable. There had been many changes over the past few weeks. He was no longer certain what he thought of the elders, undesirables, or even the Huaca as a whole, save that the Uncles, Aunts, and Entles *were* true gods.

Ichu stood across from Akamu on an open spot in the third sled, which had been used for chayu practice while they were traveling. Silluka was nearby, her hand holding on to her partial arm, Lugopo watching everything from her shoulder. Cosquella was hulking nearby, her heavy-lidded eyes watching everything. Ichu assumed she knew as little of the greater world as they did, but the young woman had certainly showed her worth in the fight. If that was without chayus, she would be a titan once she learned. Elder Quilqi stood off to one side, her hands behind her back, chin up. Ichu wondered what other secrets she hid, not that it would be easy to get her to part with them.

"Take me through the sort of chayus you practice," Akamu said, and Ichu fell into Strength stance, beginning *Tortoise Shoulders His Load*, his go-to chayu for anything requiring physical labor. It was relatively quick, and the effects lasted for a good while after the chayu was done—one "Tortoise" of effort, in Lugopo's system.

The ampuka connected after only a few seconds, leaving a glowing brown aura around him after he was finished. Ichu wasn't even breathing heavily. He came to rest before Akamu, wondering what the storm warrior would say. Were there tweaks the other man could give him to increase its prowess?

Instead, Akamu cocked his head to one side. "Impressive. You are connecting to the core by sheer brute force? How much time does it take a physical adept of your village to learn this power? To have such precision is admirable. If you were to use all of your power, you would be a fearful practitioner."

Ichu tried not to show his shock, but some part must have gotten through. He saw Elder Quilqi look down to hide a smile.

"Not...using all my power?" he asked. "This *is* all of it. I'm the strongest bodycaster in the village."

"Is this what Elder Quilqi meant by teaching us intent?" Silluka asked. "People in our village with injuries or missing limbs can't summon the ampuka. Would that technique change how we practice?"

Now Akamu looked confused. "Why would your body type affect your chayu? Being a physical adept is only the first rung of the ladder. Is this why you favor your right arm? Some of the strongest casters I know are old men and women, or those who have been through many battles. Those events leave scars, some larger than others. If what you say was true, none of them would be able to summon the ampuka. Even the freshest mental adept knows the body is only one part of casting. Certain advanced techniques might be hindered, true, but not this."

"More advanced than summoning the ampuka?" Cosquella asked. "That's all my father said was possible, he did, and I can't even do that because of my skin condition."

Akamu shook his head. "With your size and build, I'd be afraid to face you on the battlefield in your full strength."

He broke off and looked from Ichu, to Silluka, to Cosquella, and finally to the elder.

"Ancient one, is there any secret here? Any reason I should not start these three, and whoever wants from the village, on training true casting, beginning with the exercises every physical adept learns?"

Elder Quilqi shook her head. "You may, though be ready for resistance from those they call elders. In my time with them, I've learned this little group has some peculiar ideas about casting. I've found only one real candidate on her way to being a mental adept so far"—she nodded toward Silluka—"but time was short with the Eztli Mecatl invading. By the burning seas, we've been fleeing two islands merging! I've been meaning to teach these three more, but the elders of this little village demand my attention like crows after shiny metal."

"Well then, let me think where to begin." Akamu put his hands behind his back, pacing a few steps right, then left. The sunlight caught his cheekbones, and Ichu admired their structure. Quite a handsome man, and obviously caring of those under his command. His warriors seemed more like a family.

"You all know of the core of the world, yes?" He looked to confused eyes. Ichu had heard the term, but only as a saying, not in practical terms.

"Elder Quilqi said it was where the Aunts, Uncles, and Entles live," Silluka offered.

Akamu nodded. "That's true, but not very useful in a practical sense. The core is how the gods give power to the world through their chayu, and in turn, how the rest of us tap that power to use it."

Lugopo scampered across Silluka's shoulders, tapping their translation circlet. "Not just those gods, but Manylegs, Crawling, and Whirling! All gods are represented, ready to fight for their share of the power."

Akamu raised a finger to acknowledge the point. "Correct, Allwiya. *All* the gods live in the core, not just those of the Huaca. But each set of gods is tied to one tectonic plate, or one island. They influence those native to that island. It's why our chayus are more powerful, the closer to the center of the Huaca."

"But we fled from the Huaca." Silluka looked confused, and Ichu felt the same way. It was like talking with someone using the same words, but speaking a different language.

"You call that the Huaca?" Akamu huffed a quick laugh. "You'll learn more about that soon, I'd wager." He waved the point away. "I'm getting away from the topic, though. The core of the world is how a caster gets his power. The ampuka is the first sign of this, but the core's power makes up all of the world. There are many ways to use it."

"How does that mean I'm not using all my power?" Ichu asked. There was so much he didn't know that he latched on to what was most important for him. Was his fading strength and weakness simply from not tapping the core correctly? Or did his age have something to do with it after all?

Akamu held out both hands, wiggling his fingers rhythmically. First and third fingers, then the second and forth, then each finger dipping in turn. "The very first exercise we learn is *Rattling Leaves*." His fingers began to glow. "This makes a mechanical connection to the ampuka and shows the practitioner what can be done."

Ichu came closer to Akamu. "But the ampuka is only on your fingers. It should cover the whole body. Maybe stronger in some parts, but all over."

Akamu shook his head and gestured to Silluka. "And if one doesn't have part of their body? Should that stop the ampuka from forming?" At Ichu's confused look, he continued. "*Rattling Leaves* is made to let beginners feel the connection and summon it in a safe manner, only around their fingers. It makes the fingers stronger, and more dexterous. The next step is to learn the connection to the core."

"Where the ampuka comes from," Cosquella said. She was listening carefully, frowning, her impressive arms crossed over her chest.

"Yes. Once you feel how the core is connected, you can channel that energy with your intent and the proper chayu." Now Akamu gestured to Lugopo. "That is how it works for those of the Huaca. This is dependent on the god or gods of your birth. The Allwiya channels the same connection through a mental power, hard for us to see, but I have heard that Allwiya can see it between each other."

Silluka turned to the little Allwiya on her shoulder. "You can see what others are thinking?"

"Only when others are making mighty use of Manylegs, Crawling, and Whirling. You cannot see this?" They twisted several tentacles in front of their body. "Most interesting. I will have to study this for tactical advantages." They tapped the circlet. "To see differences between our peoples, that is."

"To get back on track," Ichu broke in, "this intent. It changes how we perform chayus?"

"If the form of the chayu is the practical example of *what* it does, then the intent behind it is *why* you want to do it." Elder Quilqi finally came forward. "This is what I was trying to show you by changing the stances. They open your mind to differences being acceptable. Once you do that, you can use your intent for larger adjustments to the chayus. It's the first step to being a mental adept, rather than just a physical one."

"Larger adjustments? Like what?" Ichu felt his mind reaching for more possibilities. Maybe it was true he was only using part of his power.

"Well, such as storing chayus," Akamu said.

"*Storing* them." Ichu stared back. That would mean...

"Certainly. You don't think the storm warriors and stone warriors can take time to perform full chayus as they respond to threats?"

"But that's why we have shorter chayus, like *Jakua's Claws*," Ichu protested.

"That's merely a segment chayu." Akamu brushed aside the objection.

"A segment of what?" Silluka asked. "I've never heard of that, but then, I haven't heard a lot about chayu theory."

"I haven't heard of it either," Ichu mumbled. There was so much here, glimpses of power he'd never even thought of. Were their elders such worms, scrabbling in the dust when there was ripe fruit just above their heads?

Akamu shook his head. "I am even more impressed. To use chayu so quickly must require a lot of training. But you do the morning ritual, yes?"

"Of course." Ichu was solid at least in that answer. "It's how every bodycaster keeps in form, since it contains movements for every part of the body."

Akamu looked momentarily thoughtful. "I suppose it does, doesn't it. But that's not really the point. Certainly, you see the effect when you finish the chayu?"

"But my father always said he left the last move of the morning ritual off, he did." Cosquella squeezed her fists and glowered. "Was he missing so much knowledge?"

"No, our village doesn't complete the morning ritual either," Silluka answered.

Now Akamu was aghast. "You don't complete the morning ritual? And just leave all the power hanging there? But that's what opens you up to using the core. No wonder you haven't figured out how to break through." He looked at Elder Quilqi. "Were you going to tell them?"

Ichu, his sister, and Cosquella all turned to stare. Lugopo crawled to the top of Silluka's head and curled two tentacles to the sides of his body, approximating hands-on-hips.

The elder threw her hands up. "Scrolls and chayus! I was trying to blend in and not create chaos since I'd only been in that backward village for a few years. I was researching their old records to find where they'd lost their methods. If I told them that, it would mess up my research." She opened a hand to Silluka. "It was only with this girl attempting to reach the core and mental adepthood that I started intervening before she burnt herself to a crisp."

Ichu held up his hands to stop the two from going further. "Wait. Then we *should* complete the morning ritual? We were always taught it would call down the power of the gods."

"What do you think tapping into the core *is*, boy?" Elder Quilqi snapped.

"I think we should back up," Akamu waved his hands. "I begin to see where the disconnect is." All eyes turned back to him, and Elder Quilqi nodded her head for him to continue.

"First"—Akamu held up a finger—"while the morning ritual is not necessary, it opens the practitioner to the core and the full power of the ampuka. It is one of the best ways to train this." He held up another finger. "Second. The morning ritual is an example of a full chayu. Full chayus can be broken down into chayu segments, which will help channel individual abilities, and are quicker to perform." Another finger went up. "Third. Using the full power of the ampuka, full chayus and chayu segments can be stored within the body, to be unleashed with simple commands, thereby banking the actions for quick use." His words sounded almost rote, and Ichu was reminded of a teacher lecturing to his beginning class.

Akamu made a grasping gesture and his amber armor suddenly glowed with an inner light. Silluka and Cosquella drew in breath. Ichu had seen the stone warrior's armor do that during the battle with the turtlemen. He suspected the light acted as extra protection, magnifying the defense power of the amber.

"And you can show us how to do these things?" Silluka almost whispered.

"Some are part of more advanced adepthoods, but overall, these are some of the most basic exercises we learn growing up," Akamu shrugged. "Of course I can show you. The easiest way is to simply complete the morning ritual and see for yourself."

Ichu arranged himself behind Akamu, watching the man's well-toned legs and thighs. Silluka was to one side and Cosquella was to the other. Elder Quilqi had poo-pooed any attempts to get her to join in, but she watched from not far away.

"It won't help me any, and it won't show you what you need to know," she griped. Instead, Lugopo sat on her shoulder, and they communicated in fast sign language.

The chayu was achingly familiar. Ichu had practiced it almost every day of his life. But there was a strange anticipation associated with it now. He had never expected a result from it, save for maybe the very first time his parents had taught it to him, with the warning that he must never finish it lest he be struck down by the gods.

Now he felt it building inside him. Was this because he intended to finish it? Once again, Elder Quilqi's lessons on intent seemed pertinent.

He almost fumbled the last move, *Pray*. He was familiar with it, and it was a simple move, merely pushing the hands together in front of the solar plexus, then pressing straight out and letting the hands open like a leaf.

It was done. Where was...?

The storm of power hit him like a thrown rock. His head snapped back, arms dropping to his side. Akamu, in front of him, simply bowed his head forward.

He could barely move, shocks like lightning strikes coursing through him, but from the corner of his eyes, Ichu could just make out Silluka in the same position as him, shaking, the tip of her partial arm vibrating even faster. On his other side, Cosquella looked simply tense, holding the last position.

"Don't let that power simply leave," Akamu directed in a strained voice. "Push it inward, toward your center, your *sunqu*."

His what?

Ichu closed his eyes, gritting his teeth. He could *feel* the power, more than any ampuka he'd felt before, draining from his fingertips, his head, his toes. Was this the power of the gods? He focused his nascent intent on capturing it and keeping it inside his body somehow.

He thought he might have kept a little, but most vanished into the aura around him. He shared a look with Silluka, who was breathing heavily, shoulders bent in, her hand grasping her stump again as someone else would grasp their opposite elbow.

"Hm. There might be a chance for your village if everyone can pick up on that as fast," Elder Quilqi said from the sidelines. "What do you think, Akamu?"

Ichu regarded the stone warrior, who turned, eyes scraping across the three of them as if they were wayward youths who'd been found feasting on the winter stores. No. He looked closer. There was strain in the warrior's face, a tenseness in his chin and eyes. So, capturing the power in the—what was it? *Sunqu?*—was not an easy task.

Akamu came close to him, his eyes flicking to Ichu's forehead, eyes, and mouth, then with gentle hands he grasped Ichu's fingers, feeling their tips. Finally, after looking to him for approval, he placed his fingers at Ichu's temples, then the center of his forehead. Despite the man's warm fingers and pleasant touch, he drew back from the fingers between his eyes. Akamu nodded and gave him a slight smile.

"That's normal. When the power of the core is stored within you, it's natural to react strongly to others with the same power. Our bodies process it innately, but each does so differently, thus the 'uncomfortable feeling.'" Akamu gave him a different, considering look. "Fortunately, it is only at the body's node points. Other parts may be touched by practitioners whether they hold the power of the core or not."

"I will have to experiment with how that works," Ichu answered. "Perhaps you might have some *other* lessons for me?" He almost kept his face straight, but felt the corner of his lip twitch just slightly.

"That sounds like an...enjoyable task"—Akamu smiled back—"but I must check the others."

He brushed Ichu's fingers with his as he walked to Silluka, whose eyes snapped back to the front as Akamu approached her. She'd been smirking at them, though perhaps he deserved that.

"Impressive," Akamu said, upon performing the same examination on her—though with no lingering touches. "You have stored more of the core's power than your brother."

Ichu kept his mouth closed, though he raised his chin. He was going to practice this new technique every single moment he had.

"You were concerned of your missing hand," Akamu said abruptly. "What do you feel now? Did it affect the morning ritual?"

"I...no, I don't think it did," Silluka finally admitted. Her brow was furrowed, as if she couldn't understand it herself.

"You have a strong intent. That will make up for much and set you on the path to mental adept soon." Akamu was serious now. "I will not lie, missing a limb, or part of a limb, makes it harder to achieve the full effect from chayus, stored, long form, short, or in any other combination. But it is not so much a detriment as there is a benefit from knowing how your body acts. *That* is the most important technique for you to practice. How does your unique body respond to your commands, versus another? Aided by your intent and focus, you could grow to the highest ranks of bodycasters one day."

He gave her a sharp nod and went to Cosquella. Ichu watched his sister for a moment longer. She blinked, obviously trying to take in the storm warrior's advice. Not only did Ichu need to practice this new technique, he needed to practice it with his sister.

Then his head whipped back around at Akamu's grunt of surprise.

"Strange. It is almost as if the core's power does not know where to attach to you."

Cosquella frowned, stiff hair and rough skin a stark contrast to the rest of them. Why did Silluka's difference not matter, but Cosquella's did?

"What do you feel?" Akamu asked her.

"Not much," she admitted. "Did I...do it wrong? I've never been good at bodycasting, ever. My father couldn't even teach me one chayu successfully." She hung her head. "I don't think I'm cut out for this, I'm not. I'll just be one of undesirables they have in Silluka's village."

"Undesirables? There are no such people in Chimor." Akamu stepped back, taking in all of Cosquella. "And I have seen my fair share of beings of all shapes and sizes. There are simply adepts, and those who do not choose that path. We must get to the bottom of how you tap into the core. Remember, its power makes up everything in the world. There is nothing that is not a part of it. Just as Silluka is a special case, so might you be. All it takes is practice."

Akamu traded an unreadable look with Elder Quilqi. "But that can wait until tomorrow."

"We've learned so much already, but there's more, isn't there?" Ichu protested. "You haven't taught us of segment chayus and full chayus, or how to store them—"

"And you won't learn all that today or even in the next week," the elder broke in. "How long did it take for you to learn your first chayu? Really learn it." She raised white eyebrows and Ichu frowned back. He knew what she meant, but he didn't like it.

"Can we not at least learn more of the theory?" Ichu could remember more easily. He was used to learning new chayus now. Surely this was no different.

The elder shook her head. "Compared to the citizens of Chimor you are as children. Even you, Ichu. Stars above! You won't learn what you need in a day and pushing yourself with this kind of power when you barely know how to tap it could burn you to a crisp. These methods take just as much time as your village's method of body control. Don't rush things."

Ichu turned to Akamu. "But you will train us, yes? You will escort us to Chimor and show us the wonders of that city?" And maybe show Ichu a few wonders while he was at it.

Akamu for the first time seemed torn. "I would be honored to take your people all the way to Chimor, but our duties will keep us here for several more months, while the Eztli Mecatl push deeper into this land. My team can take you as far as the edge of the stable desert, past this volcano and through the shaking domain."

Ichu went up to Akamu this time, not trying to hide his attraction, his eyes locked on the other man's. He felt a connection he hadn't in many years. "And will you come to Chimor, eventually? I would be happy to see more of you."

Akamu grinned back. "Oh, we'll be there. *I'll* be there. Chimor is where all of the warriors have their base of operation. Once back, I'll be happy to take you around, and introduce you to the stone warriors, the storm warriors, the sea warriors, and the fire warriors. Maybe you'll even be a fit for one of the teams one day." He took Ichu's proffered hand and squeezed it.

"For now, though, we should go back to the others and get this sled ready to move across the desert. Your village must have all the protection available to pass safely through the lands patrolled by the crazed Allwiya. It's a good thing the ancient one is around to help. You'll need it."

CHAPTER SEVENTEEN

The Shaking Domain

"The crazed Allwiya?" Silluka paused, offering Lugopo an arm to swing off Elder Quilqi's shoulder. "Do you know who they are?"

Lugopo's lidless eyes and lack of face somehow still looked abashed. "We do not share the stories of their conquests. Such terrors of Whirling Abyss, ever reaching for new heights of creation! They do not worship all three gods, only one, and they are not balanced like me!"

Silluka carefully kept her mouth shut, but Lugopo must have sensed something in her demeanor. They tapped the circlet.

"I do not lie! They craft with no head for what will happen. Only what they need at that moment. They are very dangerous!"

"I do not think she doubts your words," Cosquella added. "We had one Allwiya who went to join the crazed ones, they did, just after I was born. Father told the tale—" She stopped and swallowed, and Silluka rested her hand on her shoulder. Riding on her arm, Lugopo reached out with a tentacle and copied the movement. They had left her father in the healing center just before the volcano and the turtlemen's attack. There had not even been time to check on him since.

Cosquella gave a wan smile. "My father told the tale. Wallwa started acting strange—well, stranger, I say—one day, then started building. They didn't stop to rest, their tentacles forming sores and cracks from overuse and lack of water. He came out one day, my father did, and the door to the yard was blocked by a giant contraption that rumbled and quaked the moment he stepped outside. He said he felt it staring at him. It nearly took his leg off. He still has a scar on his thigh, he does."

She shrugged. "But that's about the end of it. Father always makes a big deal of his story, but the other Allwiya performed a ceremony, or some like, and Wallwa fled. We never saw them again."

"They likely joined the others who live between here and the capitol," Akamu put in. Ichu stood close to him. Silluka hoped the storm warrior wouldn't break his heart. He was always more centered when he had someone to take care of. Kuillay had been a mistake from the start, and Ichu had just about gone through the pool of available suitors in the village.

"The crazed Allwiya are completely unpredictable," Akamu continued. "I have seen them ignore parties, ask for a surprisingly reasonable toll, offer to join the travelers or make something for them, or indiscriminately attack them, slaughtering without mercy."

"The drives of Whirling Abyss are unknowable. Unrestricted by Crawling Dark of Squirming and Manylegs of Reaching, such ideas become boundless!" Lugopo reached up with five arms, as if trying to bring the sky to them. Then they brought their tentacles in, clutching themself. "But dangerous. Such conquest may harm the self or friends."

"Yet you will leave our village unprotected while traveling through these lands?" Ichu asked Akamu. "May we not have even one of your number to protect us? I feel we've made a connection. I would enjoy learning more of the next stage of adepthood from you."

Silluka thought her brother was laying it on a bit thick, but Akamu gave him a radiant smile, though he pointed to Elder Quilqi. "The ancient one can protect you more thoroughly than any of my stone warriors could. She can teach you more as well. But your village will not be unprotected. We can keep the Eztli Mecatl occupied behind you. Would you rather have us travel with you, and be on the watch for Allwiya in front *and* Eztli Mecatl sneaking up behind?"

Ichu stepped back, his face worried. "Then we will have to make the most of the days you are with us."

Silluka wasn't certain if Ichu was speaking of the stone warriors as a whole, or of Akamu. Perhaps a little of both.

"Come with me now. I'll introduce you to the others," Akamu said. "Kiqema has already expressed an interest in meeting you." He took her brother away, and Silluka turned back to Cosquella.

"We should prepare too. Don't worry about not tapping into the core today. I'm sure you'll get it next time." She glanced over to Elder Quilqi, who had a pensive look on her old face. "Let's go to your father. He'll want to know you're fine after the attack." Lugopo scampered off to the rest of their kind, muttering about stresses in the sleds.

"Thank you. You're good to an ungainly girl like me, you are. You could be spending time with your other friends."

Silluka gripped Cosquella's rough hand in hers, gesturing with her stump. "'Friends' is a stretch. I know a bit about being different than others. Oh sure, Tamaya is a pretty one, but I'm starting to realize she has the personality of a drowned quirra."

Cosquella laughed her deep loud laugh, and it made something in Silluka's stomach turn to hot jelly.

"And the less said of Waskar, the better."

Cosquella shook her head. "He's not so bad. He should spend more time thinking before he speaks, he should, but not a bad sort. I do worry for my father though."

But when they got to the healing center, Cosquella's father was still unconscious, breathing weakly, gulping for air. Both he and his nephew were wearing the filters Lugopo had created, and Silluka hated to think what their condition would be without the aid.

Elder Sinchi was on duty, as she was most proficient with healing chayus. It was strange to see elders performing so many chayus. It seemed to be taking a toll. She looked tired and shaken, though she moved smoothly through *Tree Sap Flows*, beginning anew every time she finished a repetition. Her eyes asked Silluka for some update.

"The fighting is over, Elder," she said. "The turtlemen are defeated, and stone warriors came to help us, called by Elder Quilqi. We should be moving soon, but my friend wanted to check on the patients."

Cosquella knelt next between the mats holding her father and her cousin, her head bent forward. She grasped each of their still hands in one of hers. Silluka studied her hair, at her chest height even though Cosquella was kneeling. It was like a wave of ebony, slicked back from her brow. Could she cut it? Did it grow? But even though they'd traded stories about their arm and skin, Silluka still found it odd to ask.

"Has there been any change in them?" Cosquella asked Elder Sinchi, who paused at the end of a repetition of *Tree Sap Flows*.

"None, I'm sorry to say. If we are preparing to travel again, it will be rougher for them, once the sleds are moving. I will speak to the other elders—and these stone warriors."

"The strong survive in the Huaca," Cosquella said, and Silluka cocked her head. They had that same saying at her farm? It seemed it was a popular refrain on the coast.

She knelt down next to Cosquella, propping her stump on a mat and putting her hand on Cosquella's back. "Others survive too. We'll visit them every day. Maybe when we get to Chimor, the people there will be able to heal them. Who knows what other abilities they have?"

She met the healer's eyes, begging her not to contradict her words. They all knew the two would likely not make it that long.

* * *

Silluka and Cosquella pitched in with the villagers, the two others from Cosquella's farm, the Allwiya, and the stone warriors. There was much to be done. The volcano quieted over the next day, though it still pumped oozing magma from several vents. The Allwiya made filters for everyone to protect from the dust in the air, and the stone warriors took on the brunt of cleaning up the ash and cooling volcanic stone. They each made gestures, their feet gaining the same amber glow as their armor, before walking barefoot on lava.

The river itself was gone—completely evaporated by the heat of the volcano and covered by a cooling crust of magma. The jakua completely refused to step on the magma, even shaking off the effects of *Running Beast*. Silluka couldn't blame them.

She stayed near Cosquella, close to where Tamaya and Waskar helped out. Tamaya offered insights about how well she thought the sleds would run over earth and sand. It turned out her mother had worked with the Allwiya in building the sleds. Waskar's parents were both jakua trainers, which was why he'd been targeted to help them in the first place.

Silluka chatted quietly with Cosquella about life as they worked. Silluka could sense the missing parts in Cosquella's story as much as she knew the other girl could sense hers. Some things were still too raw, such as her parents' death, and Cosquella and her family fleeing her farm. She did gather they had been running for more than a week, from far up the coast.

"I wonder where the Eztli Mecatl who taught me ended up, I do. Are they in Chimor?"

The question came from nowhere, as Silluka worked with Cosquella and others to shift supplies to the back of the first sled, reducing weight on the front.

"The stone warriors seem to know about them, so I suspect at least a few made it, if they weren't killed by crazed Allwiya." Silluka braced her whole arm with her stump, helping to lift a bag of maize. She'd found even just barely touching her arms made lifting heavy objects easier, as if her stump was a support for her full arm. She could tuck a lighter object under her stump, pressed to her body, but couldn't carry nearly as much as Cosquella, who was taller than Ichu and built like a boulder. She lifted sacks and furniture that were heavier than Silluka. She pushed away the thought of being cradled in those arms. Maybe when they weren't in danger from all sides.

"I wonder if old Coaxoch made it to the city," Cosquella mused. "She was the oldest of them, she was, but strong as stone. If any survived, she might have, the old rock."

One of the stone warriors in front of the sled—the woman Akamu had called Kiqema—gestured with one hand and a circle of cooled lava in front of the lead sled crumbled to dust. Soon a puddle of water bubbled up, steaming and hissing.

"She did that with no chayu." Silluka set down the sack she was carrying to watch. The woman made the same gesture three more times, then traded off with another of the stone warriors, though the way wasn't cleared yet. They had done that all afternoon—removing the forming stone in some way. "They must be using stored chayu. But why do they stop? Did they run out of energy?" She needed to practice more, to find out how the chayus really worked.

"You ask a lot of questions." Cosquella lifted three bags of nuts weighing more than Silluka in one hand. "Right now, we should be clearing the sled to move quicker, I think."

"You sound like Ichu," Silluka complained, until she saw the fear in Cosquella's dark eyes. Fear for her father and her cousin. "But you're right. We can learn later."

Still, she watched the stone warriors as she worked.

* * *

On the third day, the stone warriors pronounced the sleds were ready to move. The warriors had cooled the lava around the immediate portion of the river, crumbling the new rock to dust and getting the sleds unstuck. Surprisingly, water had bubbled up from under the lava, creating a shallow waterway. Not enough for the sleds to ride on, but enough to let them move to dry ground.

The elders had never demonstrated such abilities. Silluka wanted to know more of the physical and mental adepthood

Akamu spoke of, but the entire village had been occupied with digging out the sleds. Citizens and undesirables worked side by side, and the distinction was fast losing any value. Compared to the stone warriors, they were all children with the chayus. There were whispers among those who held citizen chits, and she wondered if the elders would even bother to give out new ones when they got to Chimor.

After building ramps, the whole village pitched in to tow the sleds up the ramp one by one. While the stone warriors had cleared the path in front, everyone else had been moving supplies and digging out the ash and rock pinning the sleds in on the sides.

The lava rock spread across the landscape was cooled enough the jakua agreed to walk on it, though they stepped gingerly, as if it would leap up and bite them, ears slanted back as if offended to stoop to such a level. The jakua handlers followed closely behind their charges, and Silluka saw they had new recruits helping—some of those who had been labeled undesirable before.

By the end of that day, all four sleds, the cobbled-together barge, and the Allwiya's smoking contraption towing the turtleman-sled moved slowly across the new rock, crossing to the left of the still-smoldering volcano's looming anger. What had been desert sand here was gone, flattened and buried under the lava. The merging islands would change weather cycles drastically. This area would have bushes and small trees in months, fed by the nutrient-rich volcanic rock and the water.

Their lookouts nervously eyed the desolation behind them, searching for more signs of turtlemen. There were none for now. Had they defeated the front runners, with the help of the stone warriors? It might be weeks or months before more came this far inland.

Cosquella was sitting with her father, watching him slowly decline, Tamaya and Waskar were off somewhere by themselves, and Silluka was staring out across the blackened landscape, when a voice startled her.

"Now the sleds are moving again, are you ready to attempt the morning ritual once more?"

Silluka jumped, finding Akamu standing right behind her. He could move as silently as a snake when he wanted.

She saw the anticipation in his eyes. A love of learning, of reaching for the next step. Her questions surged back from where she'd pushed them aside.

"Absolutely. Where is Ichu?"

"He practiced with me this morning, before we began today's work. We took some time together, and he told me you usually did not like to practice with him anyway."

Silluka hid a smile. So, practice was not the only reason Ichu wanted to be alone with Akamu. She looked around for Elder Quilqi, but she had been holed up with the other elders all day, discussing the best path to the stable desert with the older stone warrior, who was also their geologist.

"Just you and me then? Where should we—" Silluka broke off as the world went sideways. She blinked, looking up at Akamu from the floor of the sled.

"What was that?" She looked ahead to see mounds of sand in the distance. As she watched, one seemed to slide to the side with the quake.

"You see now why we call it the shaking domain." Akamu offered her a hand and she grasped it, the end of her stump supporting her whole arm. This wasn't like the testing, being frowned at by a room full of dried-up bodycasters, and her unable to even summon the ampuka. Akamu pulled her to her feet with a grin. He was incredibly handsome, and gracious. She could see why Ichu liked him.

"The shaking domain. So this happens often?"

"All through this area, and more as we enter the true desert." Akamu braced against another round of bumpy shaking. A jakua howled in protest, and rising noise of conversation floated over the sleds. "It's a transition area between the chaos of the coast and the stable ground of the interior. It will take a few days to pass through, but makes for a good challenge when practicing. The stone warriors use it as a testing ground, and we can do the same."

"Then I'm ready when you are." She set her feet wide to compensate both for the sled's movement and the ground itself shaking.

They ran through the morning ritual together. Silluka was still rusty—she hadn't practiced it every morning like Ichu. In fact, she might have only performed it five or six times before they evacuated the village. But the pieces came together in her mind, a pressure building that told her she was summoning the ampuka, connecting with the core of the world.

Minutes later, she performed the last move, *Pray*, and the energy surged through her.

"Capture it in your *sunqu*, quickly," Akamu commanded. She could hear the stress in his voice as he did the same. "Don't let the energy escape. This is the basis of being a physical adept."

Silluka strained, trying to pull the energy flowing through her to some central part of her being. Like last time, there was a small portion that seemed to stay with her, but most of it left her body, racing through her fingers.

"Again," Akamu commanded.

Silluka panted. She could barely stand up straight. "We only did it once the first day, and you stopped our practice."

"Now you know more." There was a snap to Akamu's voice, and for the first time, Silluka understood he was the *leader* of this band of stone warriors. He commanded them.

The second attempt, the ground shook the whole time she moved through the morning ritual, trembling like a quirra caught in a jakua's jaws. She stumbled. The feeling of connection fading.

"Keep going," Akamu growled, moving from Strength stance to Unmovable stance, arms passing through *Raven Spreads His Wings*.

Silluka regained her stance, but the shaking continued. She copied his motion as much as she could with one hand, though that barely mattered any longer, using her intent.

"How long will this go on?" she asked. The whole sled was trembling. The first forward flip was coming up, and she wasn't the best at it on stable ground.

"Sometimes the tremors go on for minutes. Sometimes it is hours. They seem to happen more in the afternoons."

"Which is why you wanted me to practice now." She braced, moving into Reflex stance, then flipping. She landed on both feet. Barely.

"Your brother said you were weak in practice, even if you are strong in spirit. Those in Chimor have practiced connecting to the core since they were children. Nearly everyone is a competent physical adept by their teenage years, some much more than that. You and your village does not have that advantage, though they have others." They both made the second flip, and this time Silluka didn't stumble. She was getting used to the shaking. "Neither the crazed Allwiya, nor the Eztli Mecatl, nor the people of Chimor will give you a smidgeon of ground if you are not strong. They will eat you alive."

Silence reigned through the rest of the morning ritual, and at the end, Silluka pulled at the energy with every fiber of her being and her will, forcing it into her center. She felt like she was buzzing with energy, like she would catch fire from the inside. Silluka let her legs shift as the tremor finally ended.

Akamu came close, observing her, touching her shoulder to correct her posture. Finally, he stepped back, watching her.

"That was better."

Silluka relaxed.

"Again."

Another tremor began.

* * *

Ichu waited until Elder Quilqi was deep in conversation with the other village elders and Akamu before creeping along the side of the sled. He was aiming for the second one, where Lugopo was designing that contraption for Silluka. The little Allwiya held raw power. Ichu had kept watch on it ever since the elder hid it away in the village. It was a source of strength, a way for him to keep up with the others when his skills were failing.

He'd been tracking the measurements Lugopo liked to call out as they practiced. His own chayu for *Tortoise Shoulders His Load* was what the little creature had based his scale on. Now when Ichu practiced, he wasn't even generating a full "Tortoise" from that chayu. He was getting weaker.

Ichu paused at the end of the lead sled. Another tremor rippled through the encampment, starting the jakuas snarling and yipping. He was going to get caught. He shouldn't be here.

Akamu's face rose up in his mind, strong and moving with such grace. He was younger than Ichu, and so much more powerful. How could he ever hope to be worthy of the man?

He grimaced and began a chayu in Dexterity stance. *Quirra Hides in the Brush* was a demeaning chayu to most Huaca citizens, making the practitioner beneath notice. A scurrying creature.

The motions flowed through him. Even with this chayu—one he hadn't done more than twice in his life—the result felt weak. It wasn't in his head, was it? No. Lugopo had told him he was losing power. He had to catch back up to the others. To his sister.

This would be worth it. He probably wouldn't even use the vial. It was only a precaution.

Ichu snuck to where the Allwiya had their little enclave on the second sled. They were hard at work, crafting little pieces of wood and metal, affixing them to what looked like the figure of a Huaca. Ichu shook his head. They were always up to something.

He crept behind the little figures, *Quirra Hides in the Brush* keeping them from seeing him. There was a little pile of rubbish the Allwiya had collected on their travels, and from pieces of the sleds they'd fixed. Everything important to them was there.

Quickly, Ichu pawed through the scrap pile until his finger pushed a smooth surface to one side with a *clink*. He looked up, but the Allwiya were busy working. They hadn't heard. Some small part of him almost wished they had.

Ichu tucked the full Eztli Mecatl vial into a pocket sewn into his pants and snuck away.

CHAPTER EIGHTEEN

Desert Traps

"Great plans have finally come to fruition! We have devised a new construct for you, after weeks of inspiration from Crawling Dark of Squirming. Remember exacting measurements, in the Huaca? Other Allwiya have helped in this devious plan. Hard to build on moving, shaking sleds. Measurements are not precise, but will certainly cause death and destruction!" Lugopo swung to Silluka's stump, their tentacles feeling all around it. They had come to her shortly after Akamu finally let her go, shaking from exertion after their second day of practice and completely unable to connect with the ampuka or the core any longer.

Early that morning, Silluka and Cosquella had joined Akamu and Ichu for the morning ritual, looking over the sand dunes they now slid across, the jakua padding through the hot sand. The morning ritual had then turned into another extended practice. She had absorbed a little more power from the core, and Akamu had pronounced it "adequate" for the day. He'd made her promise to work with him every day the stone warriors traveled with them.

But as much as she'd improved, Akamu said it was still not enough to start working with storing chayus or learning about being a physical adept. Ichu's chayus were less effective, and he was barely able to contain the power. It shone out in a bright aura around him that faded over a short time. He grumbled, and his hands kept going to his hips, as if he had forgotten something.

Cosquella was the worst, and confused Akamu. No matter what precision or intent she used, she couldn't connect with the core, though she had more endurance for them than even Ichu. She'd barely broken a sweat, when Silluka was exhausted. So, when Lugopo asked her to come to the side of the second sled where the Allwiya congregated, Cosquella had made her excuses to visit her father again, on the same sled in the healing center. He still hadn't awoken. Ichu had stayed with Akamu.

"A construct?" Silluka stared down at the little Allwiya curled around her stump. Her mind went back to the village, in Lugopo's cramped shop. They had made all sorts of measurements on her, talking about the exact positioning of the chayus. She had forgotten about it completely, with the turtlemen driving them from the coast.

"Amplification of great powers! Think how you may crush your enemies!" They tapped the circlet. "Ahem, that is, how much more exactly you will be able to perform the chayus."

"Would it help with Akamu's lessons?" she asked. Lugopo swung around her stump, three tentacles feeling the little nubbin she used to grasp things.

"Perhaps? Certainly! If exactness is a measure of success that would be helpful."

"What exactly is this construct?" Silluka asked.

Lugopo tugged on her arm, though since they were also sitting on her arm, it didn't mean a lot. "This way, inside the valiant camp of Allwiya! I have more minions now, to aid my great weapons of destruction"—tap—"that is, instruments of torture"—tap—"of science!"

Silluka swayed with the land shaking around them as she made her way on rubbery legs inside a nest of what looked like discarded junk. The shaking stopped and started with no warning, sometimes making entire dunes shift or collapse, but she felt as if her legs had learned how to compensate. Now she simply wanted to sit down.

Once past the piles of debris, she was confronted with a person-sized outline of wood and metal slivers. Several other Allwiya peeked out from behind collections of spare parts and garbage. She thought she saw Muola with the others, and gave the sign for "hello," one of the few she'd learned.

"What is this?"

Lugopo swung away from her stump and onto the construction. "See here! It is adaptable for the strange, lumpy, hard, body you have. So rigid in some ways, so squishy in others." They passed a tentacle over their own squishy green and blue body, then moved a lever. It looked like the collection of parts waved. "This will constrain to the optimal paths for chayu!"

"And...*how* does it do that?" Silluka tried to lead the Allwiya through the logical steps they sometimes skipped over. The thing trembled as another quake went through the shaking domain. It looked fragile. Ahead, the jakuas pulling the sled stumbled to the right. They hadn't yet figured out how to compensate for the shaking.

Lugopo dangled between metal strips, then climbed into the middle of the outline. "It is worn! Like battle armor for Huaca or defensive bubble for Allwiya. Even like jeweled armor of the stone and storm warriors." They snuggled between hard wooden dowels. "So comfy!"

Silluka put her hand on her hip. She was tired and sweaty. "You want me to wear this, and you think it will make my chayu better?"

"Yes, yes, put it on now. We will adjust." Lugopo motioned, and five other Allwiya, Muola included, scuttled forward, signing to each other. Silluka picked up a few words, but she'd had little time to learn their language while they crossed the island, and she trained with Elder Quilqi and Akamu.

Tentacles wrapped around bars and poles, pulling and pushing in arcane manners until the person-shaped outline split into two.

"Yes! Here, here!" Lugopo directed, beckoning Silluka closer. She cautiously approached, reaching her hand inside the form. One foot inside, then the other. Lugopo retreated from her as she did.

It...fit. It was a very strange feeling, but Lugopo was right. It was almost...comfy. The wood and metal pressed against the lines of muscle in her legs and arms, bending where her joints bent, holding her like a comforting hug.

"There's an extra hand," Silluka observed, slipping her stump into the right "sleeve" of the construct. It extended to the same length as her other arm.

"Yes, to model the ideal form of the chayu," Lugopo said, swinging around the form and tightening or loosening connections. "Will let you complete the physical form with two-handed motion even while your intent summons destruction from the gods!"

They were busy with all eight tentacles and didn't bother to tap their translation circlet, but Silluka wondered how apt their words were. The power flowing through her when she performed *Flying Quirra* had been too much to handle safely, more than even that of the morning ritual. What would this let her do? Would it even matter, with Elder Quilqi's teaching of intent? But Akamu had admitted injured bodycasters couldn't cast as well as those who weren't. Maybe the same applied to those with differences of birth. She moved her stump and the construction followed with her.

The Allwiya finished strapping the construction to her and scrabbled down the sides like leaves falling from a tree. Silluka made an exploratory move with her stump.

She couldn't keep calling it "construct." Was it a mechanism? Armor? A suit? She settled on "suit."

The suit moved with her, both restraining and accentuating her movement. She had merely lifted her stump, but the outlines of an arm, hand, and fingers that weren't there unfolded. The outlines of fingers flexed open, as she moved her stump slightly. The false hand was hollow, and she could see through it.

"Amazing," Silluka breathed. It was strange to see herself with a second hand. It would be cumbersome to wear the suit all the time, though, and she had no problem with everyday actions as she was. Helpful for chayus, then. She imagined closing the fingers in and the suit responded, the fingers flexing inward.

"How does it do that?"

Lugopo swung back up on her shoulder, using the metal and wood as ladder rungs. "Your muscles know how to open your bony tentacles, even if you don't have them. Crawling Dark of Squirming breathes knowledge into our brains! Elder Quilqi spoke of intent. This is similar, maybe?" Looking closely, she saw the white and black-dotted aura shone around them. Were they communing with their strange gods right now?

She shivered, and the suit moved around her, both dampening and accentuating her movement. It was hooked around both her feet, and she moved to a Dexterity stance. There was pressure against her knee, and she automatically shifted slightly, her eyes widening. Her balance felt better. It was the same way Ichu always corrected her.

Silluka moved to a Strength stance and shifted again in response to a slight discomfort at her hip.

Without a word, she settled into the first moves of *Quirra Hides His Nuts*, in Reflex stance. Lugopo hopped down to watch. The suit pushed her subtly, correcting tiny things she would never have felt. The empty right hand unfolded like her left, real hand did. She saw the whole chayu from her own perspective, for the first time. Tears stung her eyes, but she blinked them away. Even the shaking of earth was dissipated in the suit. She barely felt the latest tremor starting.

The ampuka grew within her as she performed the grasping and holding motions of the chayu, mimicking the quirra as he went about collecting his nuts. From one Reflex stance to another, she moved in perfect balance, completely smooth, one flesh hand and one of wood and metal making the quirra's motions.

She planted the final movement, hands—real and constructed—curling, weight back, head up. The ampuka bloomed around her and for the first time, she *felt* what the chayu could do. This was not just intent, but perfection of form, too! She was as spry as the quirra, balanced and full of energy. She could move faster than the eye could see.

Scooping Lugopo up before they could protest, she effortlessly made a set of holds with her arms and hands as he swung around her. He was trying to get to her shoulder, but for once she was ahead of the tiny Allwiya. She could move her limbs faster than Lugopo could swing between them, making an endless stair for them to climb.

Silluka laughed, springing to the narrow vertical slat attached to the side of the sled originally to keep the water out, but which now held back endless sand. She stood on one foot, spun in a circle, then switched feet, all while keeping Lugopo in a never-ending climb.

She only stopped when she noticed villagers watching her with interest, and behind them, Cosquella approaching from the healing center farther down the sled.

As the other woman grew closer, eyes large, Silluka hopped down, with the suit accentuating her movements perfectly. She felt poised like she never had before. She had always accommodated for her stump. There was a slight difference in her weight and balance, side to side, which she'd never really noticed. This suit somehow felt heavier on that side, just enough to compensate. It made her movements...not better, but different.

"What *is* that?" Cosquella whispered—for her, still fairly loud—as she ran a hand down the metal and wood structured around Silluka.

"The Allwiya made it." Lugopo had climbed to her shoulder again and she turned her head to him. "Can you make another? Can you make it fit her? I want to show her how it works."

Lugopo rubbed the lower side of their head in an approximation of a human thinking. "Design is only for your body. Personal destruction only! Was crafted from measurements taken in the village. Now you want to make the armature modular, to fit multiple bodies?" They sounded put out.

"I'm...I'm sorry." Silluka slumped. "I didn't know you'd put so much time into it. It's just for me? Never mind then, I'll—"

Lugopo snapped two tentacles together. Silluka didn't know they could do that. "This challenge is worthy of Manylegs of Reaching. Out, out. The Allwiya bow to your ingenuity."

Within moments, the suit was crawling with Allwiya, tentacles plucking at her clothing, her skin, and the suit itself.

"Now step out," Lugopo commanded, and Silluka took one step. The whole thing crumpled into a pile behind her, and she couldn't hold back a gasp.

"Did I break it?" She needed to use that suit again. It was the perfection of chayu.

Lugopo waved three tentacles at her. "Later. Will be ready then. Go talk to tall muscly girl."

Silluka moved a ways off with Cosquella, until Lugopo stopped wiggling their tentacles at her. They dove back into a squirming mass of Allwiya, clambering around the suit and signing vigorously. The white and black of their aura grew as they plucked at the wood and metal.

"You were glowing with the ampuka. You still are," Cosquella squinted in the hot light of the sun reflecting off dunes as the other villagers went back to their work. There were barely any clouds here—a big change from the nearly always overcast coast.

She looked down to see a subtle orange glow about her. The chayu was one of Aunt Harvest's.

"You must try this, once the Allwiya fix it for you. It makes your movements...perfect. It was like floating through a chayu." Silluka tried to find a better way to describe, then shook her head at the impossibility.

"But Elder Quilqi said the intent was what mattered, didn't she?" Cosquella frowned. "Not that I can do either, it seems like."

"Yes, intent works, but so does doing the chayu perfectly," Silluka reminded her. "This will just make it easier to learn. Maybe then you can connect to the core. You'll see, once they fix it."

Cosquella cast an uncertain look at the suit. "It seems pretty flimsy, it does. Will it hold up to being in a fight?"

"I...don't know," Silluka admitted. It was flimsy, using her body for reinforcement. She'd felt the empty hand at the end of her stump wavering as she performed *Quirra Hides His Nuts*. Trust Cosquella to think of battle. "I think they just finished making it. Knowing Allwiya, they'll improve it soon."

She was trying to think of something more convincing when a warbling shout went up from the lead sled. Both their heads whipped around to see one of the Huaca standing at the fore of the sled, the glow of ampuka surrounding him, a silhouette against the stretch of sand rising in front of the sleds.

"*Coyote's Howl*," Silluka said.

"Up there." Cosquella pointed to a dune, rising to their left, far enough so Silluka could barely make out the line of creations on its crest. There was something waving, like hot air, but it was more solid. Tentacles. Long tentacles.

"Crazed Allwiya!" she said, just as the mass of things began rolling down the hill toward them. She ran back to Lugopo. "Can I get back in the suit?"

"You see our mighty cousins!" Three of Lugopo's tentacles signed, and the circlet translated while they hastily adjusted metal and wood. "They are ever guided by Whirling Abyss. They have chosen their timing well. We must complete the modifications now. Too late to turn back!"

Lugopo and the Allwiya continued to remove parts of the suit, reconfiguring and crafting. One scuttled over to Cosquella and measured her ankles.

"I guess this fight will be settled by our might, it will," Cosquella said. "The crazed Allwiya at the farm was unpredictable, and more powerful than expected."

"At least Akamu and the stone warriors are still with us." Akamu had said they would travel with them for this last day, though she sensed even this much was a stretch. Their glowing armor was already visible, near the front of the lead sled.

"Lugopo—how do we fight these crazed desert Allwiya?" Silluka shouted. The little Allwiya poked their head up from the mass of wood and metal.

"If they choose to fight, they must be destroyed! They will not rest. Grind them to dust and Crawling Dark of Squirming take their creations down to the pit!" They went back to rearranging sticks, their tentacles a blur.

"Yes, but that doesn't actually help me any," Silluka whispered to Cosquella.

The big girl slammed one fist into her other, open palm. "We hit them, yes? Until they stop moving."

"Good plan," Silluka said.

They ran, crossing between sleds to where the rest of the Huaca, citizens and non, were perched around the front of the lead sled. The jakuas had stopped pulling and their handlers had taken their harnesses off, ready to fight. They snarled and yowled as the handlers performed *Fighting Beast*. Those who didn't have citizen chits held poles, spears, and axes. The better bodycasters were busy with chayus like *Tortoise's Heavy Foot*, *Jakua's Claws*, and *Roots in Fitted Stone*.

Silluka found Ichu near the front, with Akamu. He was halfway through *Jakua's Claws*, though Akamu simply stood watching, amber armor glowing. Tamaya and Waskar were nearby, as were many of the elders. Elder Quilqi was pointing out places on the sleds and villagers were running there.

The desert Allwiya were eerily silent, save for the hissing sounds as five great mechanisms slid, rolled, and crawled down the slope of the massive dune toward them. One was a wheel with paddles, bigger than a sled, tilling the sand as it moved. A second had twenty or more segmented legs, like an insect, and they stabbed the sand quicker than thought. A third was a spinning disc, moving too fast to see detail, a fourth was a sled, almost as big as one of theirs, with canvas stretched across the top, and the last...was an Allwiya.

Those were the tentacles she had seen waving above the dune's top. It was a living Allwiya, larger than ten of the Huaca, with a cage of metal around its body. Its legs, big around as trees, and almost as long, stuck out of larger openings in the cage. Smaller Allwiya scampered around it, pouring water on things, tightening joints, and waving their tentacles at the sleds.

They had moments before the desert Allwiya would be in range. Something whistled, and an arrow plunked into the sand ten paces in front of the sled.

"Get back!" Akamu ordered, and the Huaca moved into the shelter on the lead sled. The stone warriors jumped down to the ground. They gestured as a group and a tide of sand thrust up and into the desert Allwiya's path, like a wave of the sea coming to crash on the coast.

The wheel with paddles bogged down in the tide of sand, tipping onto its side and spilling Allwiya out. These were thankfully normal-sized ones. The spinning wheel hit the wave as well, slowing to a halt, revealing Allwiya who stumbled drunkenly around its circumference. Had they been spinning with the wheel? They were starting to make Lugopo look reasonable.

The sled crested the sand, but was slowed, while the last two, the one with segmented legs and the giant Allwiya, crawled over the stone warrior's attack with little effort.

And then the fight came to them.

The jakua handlers let go of their charges first, and the dark beasts surged forward, all aiming toward the giant Allwiya. They must have sensed something unnatural about it. Each one was more massive than a grown Huaca, but next to the caged monstrosity, they were tiny. Black furred shapes leapt on the mesh cage, extended talons pulling them up easily. One snatched a desert Allwiya up in its teeth, flinging it to the side. Another thrust a paw through the cage, scraping bleeding strips from the giant thing within.

There was a screech like tearing metal and a tentacle like a tree trunk slammed down on the sled, scattering Huaca.

Silluka dove backward, turning the motion into a roll over her stump, tucked into her body. Cosquella merely stepped out of the way, then hacked at the limb with a hatchet she'd produced from somewhere. Muscles bunched under her shirt each time she raised her arms for another chop. A bellow—low enough Silluka felt it rather than heard it—made the entire sled vibrate.

She saw Ichu, hands like claws, swipe at an Allwiya that jumped at his face, slinging it to smash against the side of the sled. She screamed at a spike of pain in her leg, finding a yellow Allwiya, twice as big as Lugopo, with tentacles wrapped around her foot, hard beak buried in her ankle.

"Get off!" Silluka flailed, all thoughts of chayu leaving her head, and shook her leg vigorously. The thing stayed clamped on until she pried a splinter from the sled's rail to stab into the boneless thing.

Ichor spurted on her face and all its tentacles spasmed, flinging the splinter away from her. It writhed on the floor and Silluka kicked it away.

But there was no time. She couldn't summon her intent, or even think of a chayu to try. The Allwiya were everywhere, crawling over the railings, breaking into supplies, *making* things.

This wasn't like the turtlemen's attack—slow, steady, and unavoidable. This was vicious and chaotic. She couldn't tell how many of the tentacled creatures were on the sleds, but everywhere she looked, there was another. A jakua pounced in front of her, so close she could have petted it, and bore a mass of tentacles to the floor, biting at it. Silluka shuffled back as another Allwiya walked toward her on five legs, another three raised in the air. There was a lens driven into one of its eyes, and it blinked and flashed in the sun around the shriveled remains of the eyeball. Silluka stabbed at it with the sliver of wood, looking around for something larger.

There. A tent spike in a collection of supplies. But as she reached it, an Allwiya rose up from behind the pile with a shield held in three arms, obviously crafted from an old barrel. She dropped the wood and snatched the tent spike, stabbing at the shield until the creature fell off the side of the sled. Then she spun and pinned the first Allwiya to the deck through its body, grimacing at the squelch of fluids. She wasn't squeamish—she had grown up on the farm where wringing a chicken's neck was the way to get dinner—but this was different. These were thinking beings, but she had no doubt they would reduce her to ragged flesh if she didn't stop them.

A change in the air made her look up just in time to dive out of the way. A tree-trunk arm of the massive Allwiya slammed down on the sled beside her, throwing her off her feet and squashing several smaller of its kin beneath it. A jakua rode it, claws dug in deep, whiskers bristling, snarling. It ran back up the arm like a tree branch, leaping to the cage surrounding the head.

Cosquella and Ichu were both beside her suddenly, along with other villagers with axes and hatchets, trying to hit the same spot twice on the arm. It was covered with oozing sores, not all of which were from the weapons.

Another Allwiya flew at her head, tentacles outstretched, and Silluka pivoted on the balls of her feet, leaning back as she twisted the tent stake in an arc with her hand, stump coming up to help guide the path. The stake impacted the flying Allwiya with a satisfying *thud* and it flew off the side of the sled.

Where were the stone warriors? She scanned the battlefield until she saw them, working as a team to build a barrier of sand in front of the sled, wheel, and disc to keep the other Allwiya back. This attack was from only *two* of their vehicles? Granted, one vehicle was an Allwiya that looked like it had been dosed with fertilizer. Glints of amber shone around whirling limbs as the stone warriors kept the rest of the Allwiya away.

A tentacle pulled at her leg, and she stabbed down with the stake, only barely managing to stop as she recognized Lugopo's tiny green and blue body.

"Such destruction! My people truly have the blessing of Crawling Dark of Squirming, the whispers loud in their minds!" They crawled up Silluka's linen trousers and she tamped down a shudder. She would not feel their tentacles the same way after this.

"The construct. We have altered it so it may fit you or the large girl, with adjustment." Lugopo pulled at her arm, gesturing away from the fight.

Would the suit help? *Was* she helping at all? Cosquella at least could use a hatchet. Silluka felt useless.

"Take me to it," she said. Maybe then she would remember a chayu.

She ran back to the second sled, dodging crawling desert Allwiya when she could, stabbing when she couldn't. Lugopo seemed to have no resistance to slaughtering their species, even pointing out weak spots.

"There! Where the tentacle connects with the main body. Sever the link!"

They wiggled their tentacles when Silluka's strike went in.

"Through the eye! The eye!"

She grimaced, and stabbed, turning her head as she felt the stake hit. On her shoulder, Lugopo glowed white with black spots, listening to their gods.

"The construct. There!" They pointed to the only other Allwiya who weren't attacking, cowering behind stacks of supplies. "Use it to grind your enemies under your tentacles!"

It was near the edge of the second sled, but when she reached it, segmented legs burst from the sand, stabbing upward like the prongs of a hunter's snare. She couldn't comprehend it at first. They were coming *up* out of the sand. They looked like the same ones as on the Allwiya vehicle, but where was the body?

Then they wrapped around the side, arcing over her head, all attached to overlapping plates of metal. She understood. The insect-like vehicle had been missing from the battle, digging *underneath* the sleds. It had bypassed the lead sled entirely and was wrapping around the unprotected second one. She hadn't appreciated how long each leg was, before now.

"Off the sled!" Lugopo shrieked, and Silluka snatched at the collapsed suit as she slid past, diving over the edge of the sled. Allwiya tumbled past her, several clinging to the suit.

She rolled to a halt, spitting sand from her mouth. The tent stake was gone, dropped so she could grab the suit with her hand, her stump bracing against her fall.

It didn't seem to have been damaged, and Lugopo and Muola were poring over the wood and metal to check.

In front of her, the segmented legs curled over the second sled in a deadly hug, trapping Huaca, supplies, food, and the entire healing center. The lead sled was beyond it, the giant Allwiya locked in battle with most of the bodycasters. The insect-like contraption dragged the whole second sled beneath the sand with such speed it created a vortex, pulling Silluka in.

CHAPTER NINETEEN

The Price of Strength

Silluka scrabbled against the sliding pit pulling her under the desert. She had no purchase and still gripped the suit with her hand. Her stump windmilled against the sand, trying to find something to grab onto. The grit dug into the tender end.

"In the construct!" Lugopo clung to one of the suit's legs, tentacles a blur as they pulled on joints. Muola and two other Allwiya were on the other leg, waving tentacles and working just as fast.

Silluka slid over the suit, trying to get her legs inside without losing her hold on it. One of the Allwiya tugged at her foot, pulling it farther in, and she almost jerked away by instinct, but forced herself to keep climbing inside Lugopo's creation.

She could see the middle of the pit now. Parts of the sled were visible under the sand. The desert Allwiya's vehicle was under there too, legs curled around it. Occasionally one broke the surface of the sand, an upside-down appendage.

But the sand was draining down, as if there was a pit below them, or the insect vehicle had dug a space out below them. Silluka's waist was inside the suit now, and the Allwiya were crawling up her body, fastening joints as they went. As soon as her left, whole arm was inside, she dug it into the sand, slowing her descent. The suit aided her actions, giving her more power, though there was nothing to grasp. Only the resistance of the slipping sand held her back.

She felt Lugopo's small tentacles wrap around her stump, guiding it home. She didn't dare look, concentrating on the growing pit in front of her.

Finally, the last joints closed, and Silluka felt different, energized. The suit was whole again, and the adjustments

Lugopo made didn't seem to affect it for the worse. She faced the wall of sand and moved her stump, focusing her intent on the extension of wood and metal making up the false hand. The hand responded, dipping beneath the shifting sand so she had two hands slowing her down. Except there was no interior to the right hand. It was an outline of a hand, sturdy, but hollow. The sand passed through it, and it didn't hold as well as her real hand.

Belly down on the slope, she glanced over her left shoulder, into the giant funnel of the pit. The hole was bigger around than she was tall, sand rushing into it like warriors committed to battle. She could barely make out the lead sled and domed head of the giant Allwiya above the rim of the funnel. Everything else was blue sky.

Lugopo was on her right shoulder, Muola and the other Allwiya riding her back and legs. There was no way to get them out of this pit. The only way out was through.

"I'm going in!" she shouted, and the two Allwiya on her back signed something she didn't catch in response.

"For glory in battle, to crush our enemies!" Lugopo's tinny voice shouted in her ear.

Silluka pulled her hands free of the sand, turning to slide down the slope. The four Allwiya hung on to her clothing and the structure of the suit.

She screamed. Lugopo's circlet screamed. Muola and the other two waved their tentacles.

They fell.

Silluka thudded into a springy mass sooner than she expected. The pit was dark, and not as deep as she had thought.

Then the springy substance moved under her, curling, and she realized she was hanging on one of the vehicle's segmented legs. She almost let go, until she realized there was nothing else below her.

The leg shivered, but kept its hold on the sled. As her eyes adjusted, she realized it was upside-down, half of its legs pinned to the ceiling of the cavern they were in, scrabbling for purchase as it grasped the sled. The few conscious Huaca battled the legs, but couldn't get to the main vehicle itself. From here, Silluka could barely see around the curve of the sled, where more desert Allwiya were climbing up the legs.

No. *All* the remaining Allwiya were climbing up and around the sled, as if running from...

The insect vehicle lost its hold on the cavern wall and dropped, still holding the sled. She started counting seconds, as a scream ripped from her throat.

This distance was much greater, and Silluka was turned in the air, feeling the vehicle itself rotating somehow, until the sled was underneath it.

They landed with a crash like all the trees in the forest snapping in the blast from a volcano. Silluka would not have held on to the leg but for the suit, and Lugopo and the others desperately hung on to her.

Dust and sand filtered down in the ensuing silence. Then moans and screams drifted to her from the wreckage of the sled. She peered down in the slanted light filtering through the dust from the hole above them.

The sled would never move again. It was broken in multiple places, top side smashed into the cavern floor, the weight of the Allwiya's vehicle on top of it.

It had been the second sled. The one with the healing center. Cosquella's father and cousin had been there, along with other injured Huaca. She tried to glimpse any survivors, as desert Allwiya swarmed down the legs, most going to the wreckage. There were few figures moving.

The insect vehicle was still whole and struggled to its many feet.

"I'm getting down!" she shouted and dropped from the leg to fall more than her height to the floor. She landed ankle deep in sand, the suit letting her position perfectly, bending her knees, and absorbing the energy. Lugopo stayed on her shoulder, but the other three Allwiya hopped down, scuttling to help the Huaca.

Desert Allwiya were already back on board the vehicle with prizes clutched in their tentacles. She saw bags of rice and maize, tools, and even splinters of the sled disappearing up into the insect vehicle. It stamped across the sled, stabbing through the wood with pointed legs, burying the broken planks under the sand. It placed its frontmost legs against the wall, digging in. The cave they were in was barely wider than the vehicle was long.

It was starting to climb.

She tried to visually match up the pieces of buried and crushed sled. Surely no one could still be alive under there. Only a few Huaca had gotten out, and they were fighting with the Allwiya who still swarmed the wreckage.

"Lugopo, can that vehicle get out of here?" She ran alongside it. She didn't know how she'd lived without this suit before. Every step was precisely placed, sturdy even in the dark among slithering sand.

"Such majesty! A beauty of Crawling Dark of Squirming's whispered secrets. Such a grand creation will not be stopped by a simple cave!"

"So that's a yes," Silluka said. Once again, she looked between the sled and the vehicle. To the surely already dead, or the potential for more deaths. Cosquella's family. Sounds of fighting drifted down from above. If this insectoid thing got free of the pit, it would join the others again and kill even more of the villagers.

The strong survived in the Huaca. She sent a quick prayer to the Tiyus, Tiyas, and Tiyes that the few left fighting the Allwiya would prevail, and dig out survivors.

"I have to stop it from getting out."

"Us against the might of Crawling Dark of Squirming's ever-veering thoughts? Certainly, we are fated to die most horribly!" They tapped their circlet. "But yes, agree, we should definitely stop it."

When the desert Allwiya first attacked, Silluka hadn't had time to think of a chayu, or react in any way. Now, she was back in the suit and had several moments, running alongside the thing, to plan what she would do.

She planted her feet in Strength stance and began *Tortoise's Heavy Foot*, bringing in all the lessons she had learned. Intent, from Elder Quilqi. Connect to the core of the planet. Use both physical and mental ability. Here beneath the Earth, she was already in Tiyu Tiksimuyu's realm.

As she did with *Flying Quirra*, she visualized the chayu first, performing it quickly in her head, and the power from the core burned up from her feet to center on her *sunqu*. The physical moves came easily to her, after days of constant practice. Her focus was sharp as a spear. One foot planted, then the other. Her hips tucked under, shoulders rounding in. The false arm of the suit moved to her intent, matching what she did with her left arm.

The insect vehicle was halfway up the wall when Silluka brought both arms together in front of her, elbows nearly touching, shoulders pressed in as if resisting a great force. She shifted foot to foot, lowering her stance. She couldn't think of the sled or the people under it.

The ampuka bloomed around her and Uncle Earth's power flowed through her frame, nearly burning her from the inside. She gasped and ran for the vehicle, grasping a leg with two hands—her real one and the one made of wood and metal before it was out of reach. She pried it out of the wall with a shriek of metal, the leg cold to the touch, but as if metal had been given the properties of squishy wood.

The heat within her was building, her vision already narrowing. She had to *do* something with this power or it would burn her up.

She shook her hand out, grabbed another leg, and pulled it free too, then a third. Each leg weighed more than she did, but they were light as feathers with the power in her. She had to keep moving.

The insect vehicle wavered, slipping part of the way down the wall. There were Allwiya above, pointing tentacles at her.

The next leg jerked out of her grip as the vehicle made a low circle across the base of the wall, flowing around her until it faced her. There were three Allwiya sitting in what would have been the head, pulling levers.

It stamped toward her, each razor-sharp point of a leg trying to stab through her. Silluka danced back, feet punching divots in the sand, the suit stabilizing her. She winced as her belly burned. There was too much power in her. She dodged the legs, gauging their speed, then pounced, grabbing and wrenching. The leg had stabbed through the tree trunks of the sled, but splintered in her hands. The burning eased a little, then redoubled, and Silluka curled around her middle.

She grabbed another as it came past and twisted it off. It was as big around as she was, but she brought it above her head to smash into the thing's control center, flattening Allwiya.

"Your enemies are compressed by your glorious strength!" Lugopo crowed.

Another leg swung across, straight into her.

She flew back, impacting the wall, and something crunched behind her. When she stood, there was a lack of pressure on her back. She wasn't in a perfect position anymore. Silluka had been lazy, relying on the suit to correct her. She straightened into good posture. The power still burned in her belly, demanding release. She had to keep fighting or she would burn up as quickly as she had when she performed *Flying Quirra*.

"Lugopo, the suit!" She pointed to her back with her real hand and Lugopo swarmed down her shoulder, mumbling curses and reconnecting broken pieces.

Silluka stomped back to the vehicle, *Tortoise's Heavy Foot* making every step a powerful attack. She grabbed the next leg as it swung to her, and twisted that off, too. New desert Allwiya were in the head of the thing, waving tentacles at each other.

She swung the leg like a mace, but the vehicle brought up an arm to stop the strike, and the impact jarred through her body. She swung again and again, channeling the fire in her center into her swings. More legs crumpled and the pressure in her lessened for a moment.

"Fixed, for now..." Lugopo crawled back to her shoulder. "Try not to be crushed against the wall again."

"I'll do what I can," she ground out. The vehicle was down several legs, from the ones she'd torn off and others she'd hit. A few Huaca were still standing on the remains of the sled, fighting Allwiya, but there were more down than up.

They could do it, if they were lucky. They could keep this thing from climbing back up, let the warriors on the other sleds beat away the attack. She'd never felt this powerful before. But the power from the core kept filling her. She didn't know how to cut it off. Elder Quilqi hadn't taught her that.

She raised her left arm as a leg swung for her, trusting in Uncle Earth's strength to keep her whole. She was pushed back across the sand by the impact, wood crunching around her arm. Lugopo swung down to repair it, even as she turned her right side and stump to the vehicle. Her whole arm was occupied until Lugopo fixed the suit. She'd have to rely on her intent to control the construct arm, but she couldn't use as much of the core's power that way.

She caught a swinging leg with her right arm, tensing the end of her stump and forcing her intent into the suit. The construct hand clenched the leg hard, then twisted.

And shattered into a thousand pieces as the leg jerked away.

Silluka stumbled back as the tip of a leg stabbed down where she had been.

"No, no, no!" Lugopo swung across her body to her stump, six of his tentacles roving over the destruction.

"Is the left hand fixed?" Silluka asked. She was used to one hand and a stump. She could still take this thing.

"Fixed, but integrity is not good. Cannot take many more hits. Must listen to the whispers of Manylegs of Reaching to repair it later."

The vehicle surged forward. Desert Allwiya were scuttling back from the sled, bloody figures on the ground behind them. Were there any villagers left standing? She couldn't spare the time for a look. The Allwiya clambered on the insect vehicle as it pressed her against the wall.

Then *Tortoise's Heavy Foot* faded, as did the power in her *sunqu*. She gasped with relief as the burning within her died away. She'd performed the chayu with *two* hands and she was back to one. Her intent had changed. So that was a way to cut off the connection to the core. The power wouldn't burn her up, but strength drained from her body. She staggered to one side, suddenly tired.

The next blow she barely blocked, and only avoided slamming into the wall by digging her feet in the sand. Even though the desert Allwiya were crazed by their god, the ones driving this vehicle doubtless understood how Lugopo had crafted the suit by now, and what its weaknesses were. She didn't have much time.

The vehicle was moving faster, its drivers more certain. She parried strikes and slipped out of the way of spikes meant to skewer her. Uncle Earth's power was fading, and she could feel the suit failing. It no longer kept each step perfect, and she twisted her knee stepping out of the way, stumbling to the sand.

A leg raised, its gleaming spike aimed right at her head, and Silluka raised her arms. She'd done more than she ever thought she could, but it wasn't enough.

A blazing ball of glowing fury bashed the leg into the sand.

Her brother unfolded in front of her, seeming even bigger than usual. He gripped the leg he'd fallen on, and with a growl, stabbed the spike at the end into the guts of the vehicle.

Silluka scrambled to the side. How had he gotten down here? Ichu had always protected her, even here. But she'd grown, while they traveled. She had to be strong, or he'd go right back to being *over*protective. She stood straight, ignoring the pain in her knee.

"You're just in time! We can finish it off together." Her brother said nothing though, bashing the machine with the leg. Usually, he'd have some word of warning for her.

Silluka began *Tortoise's Heavy Foot* again. With one hand and a stump. As she'd been practicing. He wouldn't be rescuing her if she helped.

She didn't even try for the mental side of the chayu. It took only moments, and the result was nothing like before, but she felt the power of Tiyu Tiksimuyu fill her again. Enough to fight.

Ichu growled again, blocking another swipe from his opponent. Silluka let her anger bubble up into a yell and charged forward, Lugopo's circlet translating their waving tentacles into a roar of fury.

Running around to the other side of the vehicle, she attacked the legs with one hand and her stump. The squishy wood-like material was easy to grip, and deformed under her fingers, even if it didn't splinter like it had before.

Ichu roared like a jakua and slashed, fingers ripping through the strange, spongy metal of the insect legs. He still wasn't saying anything. Why not? Her eyes passed across his, away, then back. Were they...glowing?

It must have been the light. She recognized the fever of his movements as *Jakua's Fury*, a particularly complex chayu that turned the practitioner into a whirling ball of claws and teeth, at the expense of personal safety. Once again, he sacrificed himself to protect her.

Which meant she needed to do her part.

She wrestled with another leg, pulling the vehicle off balance and spilling Allwiya, while Ichu raked gashes across the main body. Muola and the other sane Allwiya appeared from somewhere, tentacles curled around splinters of wood, hunting the desert Allwiya.

Together, she and Ichu slowly drove the insect-like vehicle back to the wreckage of the sled, tearing pieces from it. It was missing half its legs, staggering, leaking a vile-smelling ooze from deep wounds. She saw no other villagers fighting, and there was nowhere else to push the vehicle. It took up most of the cavern. This was the place farthest away from the walls.

Silluka jerked another leg away, her stump propped on one side, bits of wood and steel dangling off it. The vehicle slipped on ooze and collapsed to the floor. Silluka was surprised to find it only came up to her waist. Most of its height was from the legs.

"Stab it together!" she shouted. Ichu looked straight at her for once, over the insect, and she wasn't sure he recognized her. His eyes were as red as if he'd rubbed itching weed in them. Then he seemed to gather himself and snatched up the last leg he'd torn off.

Together, they stabbed the spike ends through the body, pinning it to the sled. She winced at the impact, but there was no way anyone else was alive down there. This was a tomb for the Huaca and the Allwiya both.

The insect vehicle whirred and ground brokenly, before sighing to a halt.

There was quiet for a moment, before Lugopo leapt off her shoulder with a screech, brandishing a sliver of wood they'd gotten somewhere. They landed on top of a particularly large desert Allwiya, stabbing down into their main body.

The Allwiya flopped like a dead fish.

Silluka took in a deep breath and let it out. The second *Tortoise's Heavy Foot* was fading away again. She'd performed it fast and sloppily. She was drained, her *sunqu* feeling like it was clenched into a ball. She wouldn't be doing any more chayu today.

The only sound was the steady hissing of sand falling into the underground chamber.

"How did you get away from the fight?" she asked Ichu, but broke off. He was swaying on his feet.

"Anything. To protect—"

Ichu slumped to the ground, unconscious.

CHAPTER TWENTY

The Vial

Silluka bent over her brother, checking his breath, his forehead. He was hot, but breathing. She'd seen him fight before, in the bodycasting tournaments and then for his life with the invading turtleman. He'd never collapsed like this. What had happened?

He'd seemed almost out of control, barely hearing what she said to him. Lugopo and the other three Allwiya came up to them quietly, tiptoeing on many tentacles.

"The mighty warrior is fallen?" Lugopo's circlet chirped.

"He's alive, but unconscious. Is there anything you can do? We need to get away from here." Sounds of fighting drifted down from above, but it was fainter than it had been. Were the Huaca winning, or the Allwiya? Surely it must be her side, with the stone warriors helping? And what about Elder Quilqi? She'd single-handedly killed a turtleman when even Ichu couldn't. If she had been down here, she could have saved them. She could have prevented the deaths of many villagers, and Cosquella's family.

Lugopo traded signs with their compatriots. Muola and the other Allwiya took off, climbing the rounded wall with relative ease.

"They will bring help, if our god-burdened cousins haven't decimated everyone."

Silluka waited for them to tap their circlet, but they didn't. She pressed a hand to her belly. Her stomach hurt—no—her *sunqu* hurt. She'd done too much, channeled too much of the core.

"Then we do what we can down here to make him comfortable, and anyone else still alive." Sand trickled down through the hole with a steady hiss, but it was slowing. The pile was building up around them. The broken sled was almost completely covered, and even the insect-like vehicle, now it was still, had sand partway up the main body. She'd need to stay near Ichu and keep him on top of the growing dune.

She checked over his body to make sure nothing was broken, with Lugopo's help. Ichu's eyes were bloodshot when she pulled a lid back. No, not bloodshot exactly. It was as if he actually had blood behind the whites of his eyes, but she didn't think he did.

"What is this? Do you know?"

"A strange weakness." Lugopo rubbed beneath their eyes with a tentacle. It seemed to be the Allwiya's sign they were thinking. "But then, you Huaca are strange. Perhaps he's broken the hard things in his eyes?"

"We don't have bones in our eyes." Silluka stared at him. "What made you think that?"

Lugopo raised four tentacles in a complex shrug. "You have them everywhere else!"

Silluka shook the comment away and patted down his linen shirt and pants, trying to find some explanation for his condition. Finally, tucked into one of the pockets sewn to his pants, she found an empty vial, cork loosened and replaced. There was a single drop of a viscous purple substance left in it.

"The Eztli Mecatl's vial!" Lugopo's circlet made the exclamation almost a shriek. "Ooooh no. No, no!" They clutched at their body with their tentacles. "Elder Quilqi will turn me into dried squid." They snatched the vial away, turning it over and over in their tentacles.

"What vial—" but then Silluka remembered. Back in the village, before they left. Elder Quilqi examining the last vial left on the turtleman attacker with Lugopo, trying to decide what to do with it. Ichu's eyes drawn to it.

"It disappeared two days ago. I thought it had rolled into the sand when Crawling Dark of Squirming whispered to me of the construct."

"But Elder Quilqi said it was how the turtlemen connected to their god. Would that even work for one of the Huaca?" She remembered Ichu's eyes, almost glowing when he dropped into the pit. Now they were blood-colored with no blood. What had he done?

"Gods can grant power to whom they please. But how it is done, and staying sane in taking that power is another thing." Lugopo rubbed two tentacles together nervously in the dim, sandy light that filtered into the cavern. "You hard-bodied squishy things connect with your Aunties, Uncles, and Entles by the chayus. The Eztli Mecatl drink this substance. We are made to channel the swirling thoughts of our dark gods." Lugopo passed tentacles down their body. "Would Manylegs of Reaching answer your call if you entered the fugue? Maybe. Would you survive their secrets? Unknown."

Silluka sat next to her brother, her hand resting on his brow. The torn and twisted suit Lugopo made her dangled around her, a hindrance more than a help now, but she dared not take it off, in hopes Lugopo could fix it again. She wanted that feeling again, of being invincible in her perfection. It would come with time, once Elder Quilqi or Akamu taught her of physical and mental adepthood, but the suit was a shortcut to that power now, though a dangerous one. She'd almost burnt herself out, and she could feel it in her guts. She had to find a way to control the power from the core.

Ichu's last words came back. He said he'd do anything to protect her.

"Was it worth it, Ichu?" she whispered.

* * *

It was some time before a rope was fed down through the hole in the top of the cavern. Silluka moved Ichu's body three times while waiting, to keep the sand from covering him over. The rest of her and Lugopo's time was occupied with digging through the sand to reach the buried sled and the insect vehicle. They never reached the sled, with the accumulating sand, but they also heard nothing. No breathing, no cries for help, not even any sand shifted beneath them. The Allwiya had murdered the rest of the Huaca who had fallen in the pit, and the Huaca in turn had killed almost all the crazed desert-dwellers. Now both conveyances were completely covered, save for the pointed ends of two legs poking out of the pile of sand. She tried not to think of the dead Huaca down there. Of the healing center. Cosquella's father and cousin. What could Silluka tell her? That she chose not to save them? Did she make the right choice?

Akamu was the first one down on the rope and watching him climb down instead of blasting through the rock with a saved chayu told her a lot about what happened in the fight.

"How is he?" Akamu asked as soon as he touched down. Others, stone warriors and Huaca, followed him down. Some started digging out the sled and insect vehicle, making more progress in minutes than Silluka had made in the whole time she had waited. Silluka raised her hand to tell them not to bother, then let it fall into her lap. Maybe they would find something she hadn't.

"The warrior took into himself another god!" Lugopo blurted through their circlet, and Akamu frowned at both of them. Someone else brought a torch closer and it highlighted the hard planes of his face.

"We think he drank one of the vials the turtlemen used," Silluka translated.

Akamu's normally bronzed face paled in the torchlight. "This is very bad. We must take him up to the healing—" he broke off, looking toward where others dug through the pile of sand.

"Can you help him?" Silluka asked. She couldn't bring herself to talk about the healing center. Had Elder Sinchi been in there with them? Silluka hadn't seen her come out.

"We'll do what we can." Akamu squatted and easily picked up her brother, though he likely weighed as much as the stone warrior. "Help me tie him to the rope. We'll be able to examine him closer in the light."

They met Elder Quilqi standing at the very rim of the pit of sand, hands on her hips, looking very much like an angry grandmother. Little rivers of sand trailed down into the hole, mainly when Huaca entered or left by rope. Silluka guessed it would be filled in as soon as the wind shifted. Maybe within a few days. How many other pits and caverns were under this expanse of sand?

"Well? Desert Dunes! Is anyone going to tell me what happened? An old lady like me can't go jumping into every pit in the desert."

"Ichu has communed with the god of the Eztli Mecatl," Akamu said, raising the vial between them. Lugopo placed tentacles over their large eyes, as if not seeing the evidence made it disappear.

Silluka thought Elder Quilqi's lips might completely disappear into her mouth. Her jaw tightened, muscles standing out on her cheeks.

"Uncles, Aunts, and Entles curse that man! Flaming skies and thundering depths! Does he have a death wish?" She looked around as if for someone to throttle, then pointed to the flat open area on the third sled where they'd practiced a few days before. "There. Take him there. Someone find stores of the primitive unguents these villagers have. Anything will help."

She stared around at the Huaca milling around her, then back to Silluka. "You. What are you wearing?"

She glanced down at herself, realizing again that the remains of the suit were hanging in tatters around her. It looked like she'd fallen into a pile of wood scraps.

"A great invention! The Whirling Abyss has shown a way to improve the chayus. It is perfection, made solid." Lugopo stood on three tentacles on her shoulder, the rest raised to the sky.

"Hmpf. It will help I suppose. It's nearly the same as what this little village was doing out in the hinterlands. You won't need that crutch soon, girl, not with your connection to the core. Now, did you see Elder Sinchi practicing *Tree Sap Flows*? Where is that woman?"

Silluka glanced down to the hole, and Elder Quilqi followed her gaze.

"Well. That is unfortunate. I've seen what these desert Allwiya do. Could you do the chayu in her place?" The elder looked back to her, narrowing her eyes as if she was staring through Silluka. "You've connected to the core again. I told you not to do that without my leave. I'll have to open your *sunqu* again before you do anything. I don't like doing that, girl. Well?"

Silluka had a thousand questions, but the elder was waiting for an answer. She had seen some of the chayu's moves, but it wasn't a popular one, as it had limited uses.

"I...I think I could follow along with it if you show me," she hazarded. Open her *sunqu*? What did that mean? "Will it help Ichu?"

"It might keep him from dying today. Tomorrow, I can't say," the elder allowed. "And you, stone warrior? Can you spare anyone to perform the *Life Tree* with us? Does anyone have some saved?"

That chayu Silluka had not heard of. Something so general couldn't be useful, could it? Just *Life Tree*? What function did it have?

"We've used everything we have against the Allwiya, ancient one. We would have to recreate our stores, and a full rendition of *Life Tree* can take a full day." Akamu bowed over the vial in apology.

"Burning earth! Just the girl then. Back, back. Make some space. And move him to a flat surface!" Elder Quilqi pointed at the open area of the sled, and two other Stone Warriors quickly laid Ichu out, hands open to his sides.

Elder Quilqi meanwhile stared around as if she would pounce on anyone nearby like a hungry jakua. Huaca quickly made themselves scarce, and even the stone warriors, even Akamu, faded away.

"Hmpf. Better." She turned her gaze to Silluka, who almost fell back. The...intent...in those eyes was like a knife to her mind. She felt Lugopo tremble against her.

So that was what the elder meant.

Then Elder Quilqi blinked, and the pressure in her skull faded.

"Sorry girl, leaned a bit too hard on that." She clasped her hands together, rubbing them, as if deciding what to say. Was the elder actually nervous?

"I'll need your help with this. There needs to be two of us, one on each side, to balance the body's flows. It won't be easy. In fact, it will be quite dangerous, but you've progressed farther in these few weeks than I ever expected. You have a strong spirit, and it will be tested in the next few minutes, or hours. But you've tangled your *sunqu* like a quirra caught in a trap. This is going to hurt. Are you ready?"

Silluka didn't know what the elder meant. Untangle her *sunqu*? Was that why her middle felt like she'd eaten rotten seaweed? But Ichu would not survive without her help. She swallowed.

"I'm ready."

Elder Quilqi approached, her hands already describing arcs in front of her. It was a hypnotic pattern, and the elder's eyes blazed again, the pressure driving Silluka back a step.

"Don't move, girl," the elder grated. "This is hard enough as it is."

Silluka froze, transfixed by the wizened, whirling hands, moving as if they were tying—or untying—rope after rope.

Elder Quilqi passed her right hand over her left and her first two fingers pressed into Silluka's belly, right below her navel.

There was a flash of light and Silluka staggered back, gasping. It was as if a fishhook was caught in her middle, pulling her guts out. Had she screamed? She couldn't tell. She doubled over, but the elder pushed her upright.

"Fight it, girl. I need a few moments to undo what you've done. Straighten now, only for another moment."

Silluka slowly straightened her back, tears running down her face at the pain. She hurt too much to even cry out.

Elder Quilqi made a few more quick gestures, then pulled both hands into fists, and opened them at her sides.

The wash of relief made Silluka gasp a grating breath. The fishhooks were gone, and so was the twisted feeling in her belly. She put a hand to her stomach, then opened her palm in front of her face, certain she would see blood. But there was nothing.

Her breathing hitched in and out until finally Silluka let out a long sigh. The elder watched her.

"I said I didn't like doing it." She nodded once. "It's done. You'll be sore for a few days, but nothing for it. You're going to have to power through it to keep your brother alive. Believe it or not, the stone warriors are even more tired than you are."

"But wouldn't Akamu still be a better choice than me?" Silluka couldn't believe she could help her brother in the slightest, especially in this state. He looked smaller, laying there between them. He'd always seemed like a titan to her. An elder brother, a friend, and a protector.

"There is something to be said for family, and familiarity. If I say you're a better choice than the leader of the stone warriors to heal your brother, then you are." The elder stared down Silluka until she swallowed and nodded her agreement. "Now, take the memory of what you did in the pit. The same feeling as when you performed *Flying Quirra*. You're going to need that again."

Silluka's stomach dropped. The elder meant for her to use a mental chayu again. The first time she'd been the one out for three days. This time she'd only broken off the power by accident, and the pain in her belly told her what a mistake that was. And she was going to have to do it *again*.

"Focus, girl." Silluka snapped back to the elder's face. "You must have absolute focus to do this thing. Any less and you'll end up worse than him." Elder Quilqi flipped a hand toward Ichu's limp body.

"You're talking about intent," she said.

"Of course I am. It's the first real step on your journey." The elder frowned. "Though that...contraption will aid minorly. It makes you act as though you are already a physical adept, in some ways."

"Minorly? My brilliant concept! Crawling Dark of Squirming and Manylegs of Reaching put their pseudopods into my *mind* for this." Lugopo shook two tentacles at the elder.

"And it will give the girl a needed boost. Now, off her shoulder and fix what you can in the next few moments, or do I use you for fish food when we reach Chimor?"

Lugopo scuttled over Silluka's shoulder and down her back, stopping to fix the worst few connections in the suit while their circlet muttered dark prevarications about the elder.

"It is as ready as it may be with no tools to aid my handiwork," they gestured after a minute, the circlet translating their words.

"Now, girl. Silluka." The elder bent over, reducing her height to Silluka's. "You'll have to mirror my movements through the motions of *Tree Sap Flows* once. Let that fancy collection of splinters and nails guide you if you wish, but set it in your brain. Then we're going to do it again, but that time, we are going to connect our intent to the core, as you did with *Flying Quirra*. Do you think you can manage that?"

Silluka stared back. This was not the time to look away. Just as when she'd been forced in front of the elders the first time, she was committed, whether she liked it or not. "I can."

"Good. Then follow me. Remember, the mirror of my actions."

The moves of *Tree Sap Flows* were willowy, starting from Dexterity stance, changing to Speed stance halfway through while the arms moved through a complex dance in the air, as if directing the branching limbs of a tree where to grow.

Arms. Both of them. The right forearm and hand of the suit had been crushed by the insect vehicle. There was nothing left, and though the rest of the suit helped perfect her movement, that arm pulled and caught as she moved her stump. She wiggled it back and forth, loosening the joints up. It at least wouldn't hinder her.

Her stump hadn't mattered when she performed *Flying Quirra*, had it?

They finished the chayu facing each other, on either side of Ichu, the elder's right foot lifted, and Silluka's left, as she did the mirror image of the elder's chayu. Both the elder's hands were raised, palm up, above her head. Silluka's stump only went slightly higher than the crown of her head.

"Well, that may have helped him slightly or done nothing against the power of a god flowing through his veins," Elder Quilqi said. "This time, we do the chayu with *intent*. Perform it first with your mind, applying each move. Your body will follow. Do *not* let your focus waver. This is the realm of the mental adept. No one in your village can do this but you. We must be in tandem for this to work. Are you ready?"

Silluka nodded timidly. "Yes, elder."

The elder's eyes blazed and Silluka felt the spike in her mind again. "Blood and mountains! I don't want maybes, child. Are you ready, or not?"

Silluka looked down to her brother, unconscious and pale. She lifted her chin. "I'm ready, Elder Quilqi."

"That's better. Now, think it through in your mind first. We'll start in ten heartbeats."

Silluka closed her eyes and settled her mind, just as she'd done with *Flying Quirra*. She moved to the Mental stance, left leg to her right calf, creating a circle of energy. Three heartbeats. This time the Mental stance was more complex. *Flying Quirra* was meant to be done in the Mental stance. *Tree Sap Flows* was not. Five heartbeats.

She visualized how her limbs would move, where her right hand would be if it existed. Seven heartbeats. She would need her physical *and* mental body for this. The ampuka began to rise in her like liquid. Like sap. Nine heartbeats.

"Begin." The word was a command, too soon, but she would never be more ready.

Silluka flowed into the movements, her mind leading her body. A heat rose, as if the sun were beneath her feet instead of above her head.

That heat was outshone by Elder Quilqi, who felt like the sun itself across Ichu's body. For a moment, Silluka wasn't certain if she was connecting to the core, or Elder Quilqi herself.

Then a mental line of force guided her connection back to the core, as if it was a hand redirecting a stream of water. Had that been the elder?

But there was no time to think. Silluka tightened her control on the connection. By performing the morning ritual with Akamu, by battling with the insect vehicle, she knew where that energy should go, and she directed it into her *sunqu*, from the planet's core to hers. It twinged with pain—residue from the elder's correction, but the power flowed into it. Only from there would it fuel the mental side of the chayu, lending it strength far beyond what mere flesh and blood could do. When she had performed *Flying Quirra* she hadn't directed the energy, but let it rage through her, and it had almost killed her. When she fought the Allwiya's machine, she had used the power as fast as it entered her. Now she directed it consciously to save her brother.

She lost herself in the chayu, matching Elder Quilqi move for move, mirrored on the other side of Ichu's body. It was as if their mental selves danced a half-move ahead, showing them where to go.

A haze grew around Ichu—an ugly, purple, bruised haze. It came from his fingers, his toes, and his eyes, collecting into a pool above his body.

As they came to the end of the chayu, Silluka raised both of her hands above her head, one flesh, one mental. She couldn't see it, but that didn't mean it wasn't there.

Elder Quilqi flung her arms away, and Silluka mirrored her. The pool of purple spun away from Ichu to splash against the side of the sled. It dissipated into mist, then to nothing, as if evaporated by the sun.

Silluka's knees buckled, and she dropped to the floor, her *sunqu* spasming again. She was enervated by the chayu, but not like at the end of *Flying Quirra*. This she could do again, if she practiced.

"Amazing! Such measured power!" Bleary, she looked to Lugopo, who was holding one of their measuring tools toward her. "At least four and a half Tortoises. You will rain destruction down upon your enemies!"

Like lifting a bucket of lead with her chin, she raised her head to look at the elder.

Elder Quilqi smiled down at her.

"Good job, girl. I think he'll live. And you, you've just progressed farther than anyone in your village. When we get to Chimor you'll be able to train as a mental adept."

CHAPTER TWENTY-ONE

Leavings

Silluka stayed with Ichu while he slept. He was still as limp as when he had fallen next to her, but his eyes were clearer now, and he felt cleaner to some strange sense in the back of her head. Maybe it was left over from *Tree Sap Flows*.

Before Elder Quilqi had left her with her brother, Silluka asked if they needed to repeat the chayu, as that was what healers usually did.

"Repeat it? Whatever for? Did you put everything you had into it the first time?"

Silluka replied that she had.

"Then it doesn't need to be repeated."

The elder had brought a salve rescued from Elder Sinchi's private store on the lead sled—as the woman herself had perished with the healing center—with the instructions that it would bring down any residual fever and help his body release the last dregs of the foreign god's power. Silluka smeared the vile stuff over Ichu's chest. If he didn't wake from the smell, he was well and truly out of it.

Elder Quilqi left soon after, with words they would "talk soon," and Silluka was left with her thoughts, and Ichu.

That was how Cosquella found her, the big woman bending down to sit next to her. Silluka looked up at the motion. It was almost dark now, and it had been a long day.

"I thought you wouldn't want to see me," Silluka said.

"Me? Why wouldn't I want to see you?" Cosquella's strangely solid hair was a shield around her head, and there were tears in her eyes.

Silluka hadn't had time to search her out. She hadn't told Cosquella that her father and cousin were dead. Silluka hadn't been able to protect them. Everyone had been busy after the fight, fixing sleds, tending to people, and counting injuries.

"Because I failed your father, and your cousin. If I had been stronger, I might have—"

"You might have what?" Cosquella interrupted. "Gotten yourself killed, yes? You were the only one who went after that thing, you were, and the desert Allwiya driving it. The rest of the villagers held back. I was trapped up front, I was, with your brother, fighting that giant Allwiya, trying to keep it from squashing me in its tentacles. I saw the whole sled go down, but *you* went in there. You tried to help my family when no one else did. You didn't fail, no."

Silluka stared at her.

"He called out for you, you know." She pointed down to Ichu's still form. "Took all his restraint to keep fighting until we had the advantage, and he could leave. Kept fiddling with his pocket when he thought no one was looking, he did."

Emotions flitted through Silluka's mind, but she couldn't identify them. She *hadn't* gone after just Cosquella's family. That had been a side realization. Except she *had* gone after the Allwiya construct when no one else had. Cosquella was right about that. She just assumed everyone else was caught up in the fight, but of course everyone would have seen the sled taken down by the giant insect vehicle. Why had *no one* else but Ichu come down to fight? He'd taken a concoction he had to know would harm him, to protect her. If more had come quicker, maybe they could have rescued the sled. Maybe Ichu wouldn't have drunk the vial. She stared into Cosquella's deep, dark, eyes, wondering what she saw in her. They were both broken, in different ways.

"I couldn't help them," she protested weakly. As if to prove she wasn't actually worthy of Cosquella's praise.

"It would have taken the whole village to help them, yes?" the big girl responded. She took Silluka's hand in both of hers, her large thumbs rubbing the back of her hand. "Elder Sinchi said it was the grace of Aunt Healing that either of them were still alive. *She* didn't even survive, and she was an elder, she was! They would never have made it across the rest of the desert, hunted by Allwiya. It was a mercy I didn't give them, couldn't, to keep them from the pain they were in. Father hadn't woken up in days. He wasn't going to, ever." She looked down at Silluka's hand, then back up. "But you tried, you did."

Silluka's mind raced, trying to think of anything to take the focus away from her. She was used to hiding in the shadows of the village, not fighting giant insects and healing infections from gods. What was she becoming? Elder Quilqi said she'd gone farther than anyone else in the village, but that was preposterous. She'd been an undesirable with one arm. What could she do?

She looked to the front of the sleds. Cosquella still held her hand, but she didn't pull away. The other woman's tough hands were surprisingly gentle. Silluka had seen the slumped form of the giant Allwiya when she came up from the pit, but hadn't paid much attention to it. The wheel, the disc, and the sled were all broken too, dashed to pieces, presumably by the stone warriors.

"And you?" she finally asked. "How did you survive?"

Cosquella grinned, and her smile was like a night full of stars. "You know me. Big, dumb, and stubborn, I am. I didn't let that giant Allwiya squish me. Chopped through its tentacle with my hatchets, then jumped up to its head and went for the eye!" She lifted a hand to mime a strike with a hatchet.

Silluka wrinkled her nose. "Eww. It was bad enough with the little ones. Is that why you smell?"

Now the big woman laughed. "Sure is, yeah! I had to go all the way in to get to its brain." She swiped the air again. "Hacked through it until it was mush, then had a good roll in the sand afterward, I did, to get all the goo off."

"Oh, that's *horrible*." Silluka brought her stump to her mouth, as if to cover it, since Cosquella still had her hand, and she wasn't about to move it.

Cosquella's eyes followed her motion. "Well, you know, one good thing about my hair and skin is that it's easy to get grime off. Can't get anything stuck in my hair if I try!"

But her eyes went to Silluka's dark hair. She didn't do a whole lot with it, except to tie it back and out of the way. She didn't pay much attention to it.

"May I?" Cosquella lifted one hand to Silluka's hair.

"Yes," Silluka breathed, then closed her eyes as Cosquella's large, warm hand brushed her cheek and slid down her hair. Her skin was hard and uneven, but not rough, as if it were coated with rocks that had been polished to a hard shine.

"May I touch...yours?"

Cosquella gave a quick nod, and Silluka took her hand back for a moment, already missing the heat of Cosquella's hand.

Her hair was softer than Silluka thought. It almost felt silky, without individual hairs, as if the whole thing had grown in one piece.

"It feels smooth," she said.

"So does yours."

Their heads were close, sharing breath, and Silluka swallowed, her eyes pouring over Cosquella's face. That skin was hard too, but not nearly as much as on her arms. It softened around her eyes, nose, and mouth, almost like she had little scales there. Her lips especially were just as pliant and moist as anyone from the Huaca. More so, even. Silluka had never been this close to someone else. She'd had a few dalliances with others before her parents died, but never in this way.

Cosquella leaned even closer, stopping just before they would touch. It was an invitation, leaving room to pull away. Silluka thought about what she had learned since leaving the coast, about Ichu lying beside her, about Cosquella's father and cousin. She *had* been the only one to go after them and fight the Allwiya on her own. She'd come a long way from a girl scared to perform a chayu. She'd survived where Hufi had died, saved half the village on her own. She had performed *Flying Quirra* and learned of the mental adepts. Even with Elder Quilqi and Lugopo's guidance, that had been *her* power, *her* strength. Why was a finger-width of distance between their lips as hard to cross as that?

It wasn't.

She leaned in.

Cosquella tasted of salt and wind, but her lips were as smooth and as warm as water, heated for a bath.

They parted after a moment and sat, foreheads touching. Cosquella found her hand again and held it, large hands like a small bonfire around hers, warding off the cooling air as night began to descend. Hesitantly, Silluka placed her stump on top, allowing it to have the same comfort.

Together, they watched over Ichu.

* * *

The next day, Ichu was still asleep. Silluka had bundled up with Cosquella for warmth in the cold desert night, and barely needed the thin blanket she wrapped around them. Cosquella was hot like a bed of coals when she wrapped her arms around Silluka. It felt like home.

But there was always more to do.

Akamu found them shortly after they scrounged a breakfast of dried fruit and nuts from the stores on the third sled. Thankfully not all their supplies had been sucked down with the second sled, but they would barely need to ration to reach Chimor. They had lost many villagers to the Allwiya.

"The stone warriors are leaving today," Akamu said without preamble. "The" stone warriors, Silluka noticed, not "his" stone warriors. Always humble, Akamu. His bronze skin looked pale in the morning light. The fight had taken a lot out of all of them.

"And what of our wounded and dead?" Cosquella bristled, and Silluka wrapped her stump around the other girl's arm. There was a lot of rage in her too, thankfully not directed at Silluka, though she certainly deserved it. "We've lost provisions, we have, an entire sled, and there could be more desert Allwiya waiting over the next dune."

Not long ago, Cosquella had been an outsider. Now she was a part of their community. Of Silluka's community.

"Kiqema, my second, has been gathering information about the desert Allwiya. She thinks the only reason they were this close to the shaking lands was they had determined the Eztli Mecatl were on their way. They were planning to meet them in war."

"And instead, they met us," Silluka guessed.

"As you say. Which means there is no one to slow down a second Eztli Mecatl push from the coast. We have stayed longer than many of the stone warriors wished already." Akamu's eyes flicked to where Ichu lay, not far away. Silluka could guess what his vote had been. "Your village is but a tiny community, and though it deserves our protection, there are many more in Chimor who might suffer if we don't continue our patrols for the Eztli Mecatl. More are coming, and they will track you down if we do not stop them. They will track *him* down now he has drunk of their power." His hand opened toward Ichu.

"Then we aren't safe whatever we do, we aren't," Consquella argued. "Can't you guide us a little longer?"

Akamu shook his head. "You are nearly to the stable desert and this"—he gestured to the wreckage of the Allwiya devices—"was a much larger attack than we could have anticipated. It was good we were here, but the stone warrior scouts think this has broken the Allwiya's numbers for now. They will be quiet while you pass, save for maybe token resistance. You will arrive in Chimor soon."

"And we can't do anything to convince you? Not even one of your number might stay with us?" Silluka raised an eyebrow, and she thought he caught what she was hinting at. He glanced at Ichu again, longer this time.

"I'm sorry. Kiqema agrees with me, but the others insist we return to our duties. We must meet with the surviving storm warriors from the coast and regroup to form a solid defense inland. If we don't...well, the one who gives us direction will be displeased."

"You don't serve Tiyu Tiksimuyu directly?" The question popped out of Silluka's mouth before she could stop it. This was the first hint of someone mortal above the stone warriors. And the storm warriors, she supposed.

Akamu laughed, though it was a spare sound. "Uncle Earth is farther above me than the...one...who directs me is above you. We dedicate our service to him, but I have never met a god, nor spoken to one." He seemed to be about to say something, then changed his mind. "Ask the ancient one. I'm sure she'll be happy to tell you stories."

"I sincerely doubt that."

Akamu laughed again at her grumbling. "You will learn much more about the world in Chimor. I will meet you there later, for certain. After all, you'll need a supporter when you take your test for mental adepthood, won't you? The ancient one told me what you accomplished. Not a simple feat, for one with so little training. It has truly been a pleasure to meet your people, and you. Now, I must make one more goodbye."

He left Silluka and Cosquella exchanging wide-eyed glances and went to Ichu. Cosquella pulled her stump to go after, but Silluka held her back. This wasn't the time to eavesdrop.

"Let him go," she said. It was obvious they weren't getting anything else out of the stone warrior, and that their time with them was over, though not forever, it seemed. They would have to help prepare the remaining sleds on their own, and brave any future attacks by the Allwiya, if there were any left. She hoped their village really had broken their numbers. They'd lost enough people.

Silluka held tight to Cosquella and watched Akamu from a distance. He knelt above Ichu's head, hands clasping his jaw upside down. His mouth was moving, though Silluka couldn't hear anything. Akamu's amber armor wasn't glowing today, though the entire village had observed the warriors moving through long chayus this morning, restoring their spent power.

Finally, Akamu leant forward and kissed Ichu's forehead, then his lips.

He stood, jumped off the side of the sled, and joined his stone warriors.

CHAPTER TWENTY-TWO

The Stable Desert

Ichu awoke to the rocking of the sled. He tried to sit up, then clutched his head and fell back. It felt like his skull was slowly being squeezed by the giant Allwiya. But he had seen Cosquella kill it, hadn't he? Right through one of its gigantic eyes. The young woman was a monster with those hatchets, nearly as powerful as he was, *after* he had performed *Tortoise's Heavy Foot*. Whatever sickness her mother had passed on to her—because her father certainly hadn't—had also made her a mountain of a warrior.

So no, the giant Allwiya was dead, and he had seen Silluka and an entire sled sucked down beneath the sand by the giant millipede and then...and then.

His eyes widened when he remembered opening the tiny pocket sewn into his linen pants, the one where he'd stashed the vial the little Allwiya and the elder had kept him from taking. Its presence had gnawed at him over the past few days, calling to him until he finally used it.

Everyone had outpaced him over the last few days and weeks. First Elder Quilqi revealed she was more than she seemed, full of prevarications about their village. Then Silluka made some sort of mental connection he still didn't understand. The elder taught them of intent, and Akamu was showing them how to store the power from the center of the world in their *sunqu*. Even Cosquella, who couldn't summon the ampuka, had achieved more than him. He had been the most powerful bodycaster in the Huaca. Had been. Now he didn't even know if their village *was* a Huaca. Were they really blessed by the gods? It didn't seem so.

So, he had stolen the vial. It had power in it, that much he knew from fighting the turtleman on the farm. Each one of them was far more powerful than one of the Huaca. Who was their god? Kallpa had never found out from those who came to this island early. It certainly wasn't one of the Allwiya's slimy gods. More like the Huaca's gods, with their open displays of power and strength.

But he'd taken the vial for extreme situations only. After all, they'd been warned of the crazed Allwiya, and Akamu had told him the others in his band were itching to leave the stunted coast-dwellers. They had only stayed this long out of respect for their leader. He'd prepared, as he always did. Had the attack only been an excuse to use the vial? No. It had been to save Silluka. To prove that he still could.

Had he?

"You're awake. Well? Caverns and fire! Do you think it was worth it?"

Ichu blinked up. Elder Quilqi couldn't read his thoughts, could she? No. Certainly not. She had simply seen his eyes were open.

"Is Silluka safe?" he asked.

"Hmpf. No thanks to you." That stung. The elder's face relaxed a little, likely seeing the shame on his. "Well, perhaps *some* thanks to you. The girl *says* you saved her, but she was also instrumental in saving *you*. She's a rare treasure. I haven't seen one leap past the physical adept stage and reach for the mental like that in a long time."

Ichu tried to sit up again, and barely managed it this time, eyes squinting in the desert sun. He realized it hadn't rained in days. Ever since the volcano, there hadn't even been strong winds. Were even the tiny sand quakes gone now as well?

"Where are we?"

"In the stable desert. Far from any coast. It occupies a large part of what you call your island. Continent, more like it, especially with the Eztli Mecatl's island joining us. Chimor is not many days travel away."

"And the desert Allwiya?"

Elder Quilqi shook her head, then handed him a cup of water, which he downed greedily. "They've been quiet. We encountered a group of five yesterday who were interested in taking our sleds apart for scrap. They weren't violent.

The stone warriors think the first force had been gathering all the homicidal members for some time, to face down the coming Eztli Mecatl. Except they weren't expecting us and the stone warriors to stray into their territory. They haven't in some while. Haven't had any reason to." She trailed off, leaving the implication to speak for itself.

Ichu raised his chin to look around and regretted it.

"Speaking of which, Akamu is gone, with his group, four days ago. He says to remember his words to you. Something to eat?"

The elder produced a tray of nuts, fruits and dried meats and Ichu's stomach tried to claw its way through his spine. He grabbed a handful.

"Careful now. You haven't eaten in days."

He let the elder's words sink in while he chewed. So Akamu was gone. He'd promised he'd leave before they entered the stable desert, and Ichu had seen the other stone warriors sneaking glances at them when they thought Ichu wasn't looking. They didn't like their leader falling for a country bumpkin. Ichu hadn't felt that was true when they first met the stone warriors, but he knew it for a fact now. A country bumpkin losing his ability.

"He'll find me in Chimor," Ichu said after he swallowed. They'd shared the few nights together they could, and that had been enough, for now. There had been no commitment on either of their parts, no promises, but Ichu knew Akamu would find him. He was an honorable man. If he found another before they were reunited, Ichu wouldn't be bothered. He would gladly have the man even as just a friend, if it came to that. They worked well together, much more than anyone he'd been with in the past fifteen years.

Elder Quilqi was watching him, and Ichu grabbed another handful of fruits and nuts to give him a reason to look away.

"Speaking of Chimor, that brings me to another point." Her eyes panned over his head and around, quick as a quirra. "Your sister is fortunately on the first sled with her strange girlfriend, working with Lugopo on that contraption of theirs. I haven't quite figured Cosquella out yet. But it's lucky you woke when you did."

Or had the elder made sure of the timing to speak with him privately?

The old woman leaned closer until her nose was almost touching his.

"You used the vial. You brought the god of another people into your body. Speeding islands, what were you thinking, boy? Would you commune with the many-legged horrors of the Allwiya? The aloof matriarchs of the...well, never mind that." The elder brushed the comment away with one hand. "There are consequences for this, you know. Silluka and I purged the poison from your body, but that is only the physical effect. You'll find the mental effect is much different, and worse."

"Mental effect?" Ichu realized he had a handful of dried fruit held in front of him like an offering. He remembered the power, the speed, the *energy* the vial had given him. But he remembered it in a haze. Had Silluka been trying to tell him something? He only knew the pleasure of ripping the millipede vehicle limb from limb, the visceral happiness he felt as he beat it with its own legs. He had felt *strong* again. As strong as the turtleman he'd taken the vial from.

"You remember what Lugopo said? The elixir contained parts of Eztli Mecatl in it. It might have opened a link to their god, but it also connected you to its people. Permanently."

Ichu swallowed. None of this sounded good, but he still wasn't sure what the elder was getting at. "I admit my mind was clouded, but it's clear now."

"It's clear now," the elder repeated, "because we've driven the link deep into your center to give your body a chance to heal. But it's connected to your *sunqu* for good. And it's going to try to build that link up again, on its own. You'll feel the urge soon. Whenever you perform a chayu, you will feel tearing within you. That's your *sunqu* not knowing how to process the energy from the gods. You will want more. And you may even *need* more to be able to bodycast correctly. I don't know. I haven't seen this before, in all my days. It's been a very long time since so many islands, and gods, were clustered together like this. We'll find a lot more crossings of power in the coming days. It complicates everything unnecessarily."

Ichu slumped back, food forgotten. He didn't much understand the elder's last comments, but he did the first ones. "The one thing I was good at." He had felt his body growing weaker, had strived for some way to bring back the strength of his youth. And he'd gone for the first poison he found, just because it let him feel good for a few moments. There were plants around the Huaca, which if boiled and prepared correctly, brought on a feeling of invincibility, but it was just that, a feeling. Those that used them were looked down on for their failure. The strong survived in the Huaca. And he was weak.

"What must I do?" There had to be some remedy.

Elder Quilqi raised an eyebrow. "You think I know? Blood and bile, I just said I hadn't seen this before."

Ichu closed his eyes. He'd failed at the one thing he was good at.

"But it's never a bad idea to keep practicing," the elder continued. He cracked one eye open, and she nodded at him. "I'll work with both of you. I'm not planning on going anywhere. Your sister—and her girlfriend—are both most interesting. But *you'll* have to work even harder than you did in your competition days, just to stay at your level. You may have been a physical adept, at least in all but name, since your village has strange ways, but you'll take much longer to find the way to mental adept now. Take direction from your sister, if I can't help. She has a good head on her shoulders, though she doesn't need to hear you tell her that. Her pride's swollen quite enough for now, and everything will change when we get to Chimor."

Ichu's hand crushed the dried fruit in it. Set *below* his sister, who he'd protected his whole life. Having to work harder, merely to keep the skills he had.

It was what he deserved. He looked back up, meeting Elder Quilqi's eyes.

"I will practice harder than ever to make up for this. I *will* find out how to reverse it."

"I have no doubt you will." The elder rose to her feet and dusted her hands off. "Now eat some more and get your strength up. This is the last time we'll have time to relax. Chimor is not for the faint of heart."

* * *

The elder, and, he learned, Akamu, were correct in their predictions. Both thought the most violent members of the desert Allwiya had been building forces for some time, whether to control the shaking domain or to invade Chimor, they didn't know. But they had directed that force against the first wave of the turtlemen, and the sleds had been caught in the middle. It had been fortuitous the stone warriors were accompanying them. It would be a long time before the crazed Allwiya had enough new converts to make another army.

Whatever the real reason, it meant their travel into the stable desert had been relatively calm for the four days Ichu had been asleep and for the week afterward. There were marked oases which Elder Quilqi, of course, knew of. They carried stores of supplies—restocked yearly by officials in Chimor—so those crossing the desert would survive the journey.

There was little else here. Even the desert sand was in short supply. Mostly the landscape was sculpted bluffs, with yellows and oranges and reds dancing across them. It was beautiful, but deserted. Aside from scorpions, beetles, and the occasional bird or cactus, not much moved, especially during the heat of the day.

They changed their travel schedule as well, only letting the jakua run from late evening to just past midnight, then from early to late morning. It cooled off and heated up quickly in the desert.

They had all become refugees together. The three remaining sleds held everyone left from the village, elder, bodycaster, or undesirable. First with Silluka's revelation, then the introduction of the stone warriors, few bothered to mark the difference any longer. The cobbled-together sleds had been taken apart for repairs, all except the Allwiya's steam-powered one, stored on the last sled with other spare parts. They had lost too many in the fight with the turtlemen, with the volcano, hazards on the river, and finally the Allwiya. A citizen's chit meant nothing out here, and everyone helped out, directed by the knowledge of the remaining elders.

The jakuas pulled them, and people took turns joining a group chayu called *Wing of the Crow* that ensured a favorable breeze behind them. Several sheets acted as sails to keep the jakuas from tiring too quickly, and the breeze helped in the hottest parts of the day. The chayu had been going for days, undesirables and citizens both participating. Another barrier Silluka had broken down. If Akamu's hints about Chimor were correct, no one would make any differentiation between the most proficient elder and an undesirable child once they arrived.

In the meantime, Ichu practiced with Silluka and Cosquella. Elder Quilqi came as often as she could, correcting their style and lecturing them on intent, and on how to use their *sunqu*. Elder Papaki, Tamaya and Waskar, and a few others came to watch as well, but none were able to grasp the things Silluka did—with only one hand. Cosquella was even worse than Silluka had been before they left the village, but it wasn't for lack of trying. She just didn't seem to be able to connect to the ampuka.

Ichu couldn't blame her. He was nearly as confused. He continued to strive for the perfection of form that would bring the ampuka. It was what every elder looked for when conferring citizenship on a member of the Huaca. Akamu had called it part of being a physical adept. But Silluka didn't try for that perfection. She couldn't with her right arm, but even with the rest of her body, she shifted stances if she thought it fit the chayu better, or moved the placement of an arm or a leg. It was connected to a concept past the physical adept. The realm of the mental adept was one he could not grasp. Yet his sister shone with the ampuka the moment she started a chayu.

"What is the difference," Ichu asked Elder Quilqi on the third day, "between the ampuka and the energy from the core? Akamu said we connect to the core through the morning ritual, and I have been trying, but that doesn't explain the ampuka."

He had noticed the drop in his skill immediately. The afternoon after he awakened—since they largely traveled in evening now—he attempted Akamu's exercise of trapping the god's energy from the morning ritual in his *sunqu*. The elder was right. It was like there was a stake through his middle, tearing him in two. He hid his pain as best he could and was starting to get used to it. Visions of the viscous fluid in the vial rose up when he rested, exhausted, from practicing. There was no physical effect from the pain either. It was as if part of his being was dark and silent now, and he could only barely push the core's energy into the undamaged part of his *sunqu*.

"Think of the ampuka as...excess energy," Elder Quilqi told him. "It's showing how inefficient you are. That excess could be used if you tapped it fully." She pointed to Silluka, who was blazing like the sun after performing *Quirra Hides His Nuts*, one of her favorites.

"Generating two and a half Tortoises of power!" Lugopo crowed from nearby, where they fiddled with one of their tools.

"So, she's wasting energy?"

The elder twisted a hand in the air, moderating her words. "Not exactly. The girl has a strong connection, originally just with her mind, but now with her body too. She started on the path to mental adept before that of the physical adept. She cannot use that much energy without danger, so it shows as a bright ampuka. She will learn over time, and her ampuka will dim as she uses more of it. A few children in Chimor go through that stage when they learn." She turned back to him. "You, on the other hand, need to truly grasp your intent behind the chayu to overcome the weakness you've brought on yourself. Your ampuka is dim because you are pulling in much less energy from the core than you used to. What is your purpose? What do *you* want to do with that power?"

She turned away, heading back to Silluka to give her more instruction. "Keep practicing," she said over her shoulder.

Ichu sat back, staring out into the desert. What *was* his purpose? He'd been the best bodycaster in the village. No longer. He'd had a farm. Gone. He was a protector to his sister, but she barely needed him, especially now she had Cosquella. So, what did he *want*? He didn't know.

Once again, he was a failure.

CHAPTER TWENTY-THREE

Chimor

Silluka stared out from the first sled, her arm around Cosquella, Lugopo on her shoulder, and Ichu not far behind. He'd been quiet lately, deferential after recovering. She thought Elder Quilqi said something to him, but it would have to wait for at least another day. The sun was just peeking over the horizon, and many of the travelers had gathered on the sleds, once the towers of Chimor appeared.

The city was *immense*. Silluka's village could have fit in the front gates. The distance from the village to her parents' farm—likely buried in the face of a mountain after the last few weeks—was less than the distance from the gates to the center of the city. Spires rose higher than all the sleds put together, standing on end. She could see bridges connecting at different heights, and tiny figures walking the walls. She wouldn't have believed it was real if she wasn't seeing it for herself, even though Elder Quilqi told them about it.

A patrol on a steaming sled, much like the one Lugopo had crafted, but far larger, rode out to meet their sleds. Elder Quilqi, of course, was the one to step out in front to greet them, once the jakua had been persuaded to stop with strips of meat and the handlers performing *Sleeping Beast*. Elder Papaki and Elder Kuchiki—who had taken over most of Elder Sinchi's duties—were with her, but the rest stayed back with the other villagers, obviously intimidated. The elders had faded into the background over their travels, and the old men and women she thought were so powerful, ruling over their village, held almost no true power in the wider world.

As they got closer, Silluka saw the little Allwiya perched at the head of the steam sled, pulling lever after lever with their many arms.

"Such potential!" Lugopo crooned in her ear. They had been hard at work the whole trip, repairing and adjusting the suit, and making a second one for Cosquella. They had drafted all the other Allwiya on the sled to help them. "See the design Crawling Dark of Squirming sends to their most trusted acolyte! I have received such power as only those of Chimor might have!" They chuckled and rubbed their tentacles together. Silluka refrained from reminding them of the giant vehicles of the desert Allwiya, crazed though they were.

"Do you think they'll let us in?" Cosquella's voice wavered, just slightly.

"Look at the size of their city." Silluka pointed. "We could all live there without anyone even noticing. I bet there's entire populations that stay in hiding their whole life." She thought of the alleys in their village which she'd mapped out in her head, finding the quickest route between stealing food and returning to her latest nest. She'd need a much bigger map for Chimor.

"Then we're going hide in there, are we? I wonder if they need a gardener."

Silluka took a closer look at her girlfriend. Both hands were in front of her, clasped together, tough hands working over each other. "I'm sure they just hand out wealth. They don't even have to worry about storms or volcanoes! This is the stable desert, remember? Look at all they have. We'll be fine until we figure out how to get food and shelter here, and we can start training to be physical and mental adepts." The winds and rain that had plagued their travels had dried up in the desert. Aside from the occasional dust storm there had been no hurricanes, no tidal waves, not even any rain. No wonder Chimor was so big, if the residents didn't have to move all the time. How long had it been here? A hundred years? More?

Elder Quilqi was making hand gestures to the leader of the patrol, a man even larger than her brother. Now Silluka looked closer, she could see the person next to him had pointed ears, high on their head and...whiskers?

"Ichu, look." She pointed, making space as her brother approached.

"They look like a jakua, they do," Cosquella said. "And look there. That one has spines."

As another of the patrol turned, scanning the horizon, she saw quills on their back.

"Huaca, Allwiya, and turtlemen," Ichu said. "What's to say there aren't other people, from other islands? Elder Quilqi said this place was bigger than we thought."

Just then the elder turned, pointing to them, then down next to her. Silluka exchanged uncertain glances with Cosquella and Ichu.

"Onward, to your mighty destiny!" Lugopo called from her shoulder.

They jumped off the sled and went to the elder.

"Sunrise and dewdrops! Taking your time," she gruffed as they came up beside her. "I can't handle everything, you know." She turned back to the leader of the patrol.

"Lieutenant Ati, these are the ones I was telling you about. They have news from the coast and carry the favor of Akamu's storm warriors." She turned back to them. "The lieutenant has a place for us to stay—all of us—but I have a question for you four specifically."

She turned fully toward them.

"You have a chance to learn more than you ever dreamed here. Are you ready to take it? You've all begun the training. Here you can truly start on that journey."

"All four of us?" Ichu sounded hesitant.

"Yes, all of you. You reach for more, fight with honor, and want to understand the gods. Its more than I can say for the rest of your village, hiding like barnacles on the coast for hundreds of years."

Silluka looked back to the sleds, where faces she had known her whole life, if from a distance, stared back. Waskar and Tamaya watched her. They had practiced with Elder Quilqi at the beginning, but once they were called away to help organize the migration, their interest had dropped off. She'd barely talked to them after the fight with the Allwiya. They hadn't trained with her since. Elder Quilqi was right. Silluka had figured out how to fly through the air, even if it had almost killed her. She had fought one of the desert Allwiya's creations mostly on her own.

She was different.

"Will you be with us?" she asked the elder.

"I have some matters to attend to in Chimor, as I've been gone for a while, but I'm not abandoning you, girl. I wouldn't have put this much effort into you if I didn't mean to stick around, would I?"

Lieutenant Ati was watching them with bored interest, waiting. Elder Quilqi obviously knew much more than she claimed. Silluka could clearly see now the jakua-looking person and the spiny-backed person on the sled. If their village was to survive in Chimor, they would need all the help they could get.

"I'm ready," she said.

"I have nowhere else to go, me." Cosquella snaked a rough arm around Silluka's stump.

"I shall devise great and powerful weapons of destruction!" Lugopo tapped his circlet. "That is, great new inventions!"

"I will find a cure," Ichu said quietly. Silluka cast a quick glance at him. She really needed to learn what the elder told him.

Elder Quilqi nodded at them. "Then it's settled. Lieutenant, please lead the sleds to the refugee center. I'll be taking these four to report to the head of the warrior patrols."

"Yes, ancient one." Lieutenant Ati leapt off the sled, two others with him. One went to each remaining sled with a line of rope, tying them to the lieutenant's steam contraption.

* * *

The sleds were pulled through the gates of Chimor together, tied to the one small steam sled driven by

Lieutenant Ati's team. It generated as much power as all their jakua by itself, towing three sleds ten times its size with ease.

Silluka stared, her mouth agape, as the massive iron doors, each as thick as she was tall, passed by either side of the sled. There was plenty of room for the rest of the traffic coming into the city, and a creation with many legs, reminding her of the Allwiya's construct, passed them, leaving the city.

The walls soared above their heads, and as they traveled underneath, Silluka could see slits above, with eyes watching their every move.

Then they entered the city proper.

Lieutenant Ati turned sharply, and the train of sleds followed him to the left, sliding between the base of two buildings rising like mountains above her. They were made of stone, but all of one piece. She'd seen Akamu manipulate earth like that. Had stone warriors built these?

There were *so many* people. They passed all kinds on the streets, some of whom watched the train of sleds passing by, but not all. Most here were Huaca, like her, but Allwiya swung along on poles attached to the wall or sped by on steaming sleds or walkers. The jakua-like people seemed to be next in number, then the spiny people, with other ever stranger ones mixed in. A thing sort of like an Allwiya, but with many more arms, seemingly lighter than air and with no visible eyes, was running a stall selling unusual fruits and vegetables. She even thought she saw a turtleman passing through an alley.

They stopped not far from the gates, in what looked like a city within the city. Low stone and wood buildings, with no coherent theme, popped up like mushrooms behind a short wall, three blocks high. A fountain bubbled in the middle of the buildings. In fact, it looked a lot like the village back on the coast.

Lieutenant Ati went to a small hut near the entrance, and came out with a rotund Huaca, who eyed the sleds with professional disinterest. They began talking, and Silluka jumped at Elder Quilqi's hand on her shoulder.

"Let Elders Papaki and Kuchiki bargain for their place here. That's what's they're good for, after all. Get your brother, the big girl, and the squid, and I'll show you the real Chimor. Stones and iron! It's good to be back."

"Will they be safe here?" Silluka wanted to go exploring, but she had at least a little loyalty to the people she'd grown up with.

"This is the refugee camp of Chimor," the elder said. "They could continue their lives here just as they did on the coast. The'll have better access to resources, in fact. Any who decide to stop pretending the rest of the world doesn't exist are welcome to train to be adepts at one of the schools in the city. It's only a question of whether they will."

Whatever happened, Silluka decided she would keep track of the village and how it incorporated into Chimor.

She soon followed Elder Quilqi, Lugopo in their usual place on her shoulder, and Cosquella and Ichu close by her. She felt comforted by their bulk. The two of them could probably fight off anyone in the city much better than a girl with only one full arm, no matter what new chayus she could perform.

They'd entered the city in early morning, but the streets here were still dark, the buildings so tall they obscured the sun. Elder Quilqi led them fearlessly through twisting alleys, her white bun bobbing behind her as she strode between hulking buildings. They walked until the sun began to peek through buildings ahead, striping the cobblestone street with morning light.

"Where are we going?" Ichu finally asked.

"Glaring light! Don't you listen?" The elder didn't even turn around. "I'm taking you to the one who sends the warriors out across the land. We need to tell her about what you experienced at the coast."

"But...wouldn't Akamu tell her when he gets back?" Silluka asked. She trusted the elder, but something seemed off about her story.

"Yes, yes, but even better to hear it now, when the news is fresh. Hurry up. It's right here." Elder Quilqi turned suddenly and pushed open a door to a large building. It was many stories tall, like the ones at the gate, but this one had a veneer of a shiny rock polished to perfection. The doors were of a dark wood she'd never seen before. The elder waggled a hand at them to go through. Was she...nervous?

Inside, the sounds of the city fell away, leaving them in unnatural quiet. It reminded Silluka of the elder's testing hall, back in the village. Elder Quilqi marched up to a desk in the center of the entrance hall, addressing the woman behind it. She wore armor twinkling with points of light, like little blue jewels, and with a start, Silluka recognized it. It was the same as the storm warrior who had died outside their village.

She should have realized the similarities by now. It also reminded her of the cut of Akamu's armor, though his glowed amber instead of blue.

"I bring news of Loma Tika's death, though you likely know of that already," the elder said without preamble. "Is Nina available?"

"She is, if you will wait—" the storm warrior at the desk looked up, then did a double take. "Ancient one! Yes, she's always in for you. Go right up."

Silluka stared at Ichu as they followed the elder. Her brother's face was closed in thought. Akamu had also called her "ancient one," as had Lieutenant Ati at the gate. Was it a name? A title? An honorific?

There were two flights of stairs leading to the office Elder Quilqi aimed for. She knocked briefly, then pushed inside, waving them in behind her.

Inside sat the biggest woman Silluka had ever seen, even with Cosquella right beside her. This woman was head and shoulders taller than Ichu, wearing armor like both the storm warrior and Akamu's stone warriors, but distinct, layered with night-black jewels.

"Nina. Tell me you know how far the Eztli Mecatl have pushed into the interior," the elder said.

The woman, Nina—the one who commanded the storm warriors and the stone warriors?—looked up placidly.

"Mother. Couldn't even be bothered to send a message ahead, as usual." Her voice was lower than Ichu's.

Silluka stared, the words catching up to her. That didn't sound like a term of respect. In fact, there was very little respect in her words at all.

"Mother?"

"Hm, yes. And as ungrateful as they come." Elder Quilqi folded her thin arms.

"We already have the problem in hand. You've wasted your time coming here, and bringing—" Nina's gaze swept over them and Silluka blinked at the intent behind those eyes. Nearly as much as she'd felt from Elder Quilqi, not long ago. "Who are these, anyway?"

"New students," the elder snapped. "Well, not the Allwiya. They're an associate, of sorts."

"And why did you bring them here, Mother?"

"We bring news of the turtle—the Eztli Mecatl attack on the coastal village..." Ichu broke in. He trailed off as Nina pinned him with a glare.

"Correction. Why did you bring this *broken* collection of individuals here? None of them looks like they've even touched the core before, much less tested for adepthood. Are you dealing with children in your dotage?"

"Give it time." Elder Quilqi looked off balance for the first time since Silluka had known her. "We have important news."

"But the stone warriors and the storm warriors already know about the Eztli Mecatl, they do," Cosquella suddenly put in. "That's why they were there in the first place. The storm warriors have been out at the wall of storms for years. Surely them, they know more than we do about the new island."

Silluka blinked. Cosquella was right. Nina, and Chimor by extension, must know all about the turtlemen already. She'd even seen one here, and Cosquella had told them about the small enclave fleeing their new god.

"Why did you bring us here?" she asked, staring at Elder Quilqi.

"Ah, so you've picked another clever one," Nina commented, leaning back in a large chair that creaked ominously under her bulk. "Want to tell them or should I? You obviously want to share some secrets, or you wouldn't have waltzed back here for the first time in over a decade. Mother."

Elder Quilqi paced two more steps, then sighed. The sun was just peeking through a window behind the massive woman.

When she turned, her eyes were serious. "I didn't have anywhere else to go, Nina."

Nina lifted both hands, palms up, inviting more explanation. One of her hands could have fit around Silluka's middle.

"You all know I'm not an elder from your village."

"That much was obvious from the start." Ichu had positioned himself near Silluka, still protecting her unconsciously.

"Yes, well, I'm not from Chimor originally either." She waved an old hand. "Doesn't matter where for now. You've never heard of it. But I've been traveling this island for longer than you or your parents have been alive. The Eztli Mecatl are only the most recent to join us here. Before them were the Allwiya. The *point* is, many of the islands roaming the seas are coming together again, something that hasn't happened for hundreds or even thousands of years. You've seen what destruction it caused near the coast. Too many collisions and even the stable desert will be threatened."

"My sea warriors tell me there are another two islands within six years of colliding, and ten more ranging farther out." Nina was studying Cosquella, who swallowed visibly, then she turned her gaze to Ichu. Silluka saw her brother's back stiffen.

"How did they get past the wall of storms?" Silluka asked.

Nina actually laughed, a loud, deep guffaw. "Wall of storms? That's what you yokels call it?"

Ichu took one step forward, but Nina leaned across her desk, dark armor glinting in the morning sun. "Your 'wall of storms' is what my storm warriors *create* to hold back the winds and rain lashing the coast of the island. It cuts down on the destruction of the collision. It was only there because *we* decided to save your little village from being completely wiped out when the Eztli Mecatl's island aimed itself directly toward you. Ridiculous perfectionists, going off on their own."

Perfectionists? Silluka wanted to know more, but it seemed like a bad time to open her mouth. Cosquella gripped Silluka's hand in hers, almost to the point of pain. Silluka bumped her girlfriend with her shoulder.

"If we can get back to the point at hand, Nina." Elder Quilqi faced what could only be her daughter. That was another story Silluka needed to hear.

"And I suppose you think you've found the next champion of the gods here?" Nina snorted. She pointed her chin toward Cosquella. "That one at least looks well put together. Not a whiff of the gods on her, though."

"Champion? What's she talking about?" Ichu naturally had perked up at the mention of any sort of prowess.

"If you're really planning to train these bumpkins, after what happened last time, you've got a long way to go." Nina was shaking her head.

"Can someone please explain in small words for us *bumpkins*?" Cosquella's voice rang out like an iron axe ringing from a cut.

"The islands are coming together." Elder Quilqi's words were flat. "It is something the world has not seen in most people's lifetimes." She stamped a foot on the polished wood floor. "This place, Chimor, is in the middle of a very large island. So large it could be considered something bigger than that. A continent in the world ocean. The Huaca are the people with the most gods. Eight of them. You remember I said the gods are tied to their islands?"

She seemed to be waiting for a response, so Silluka said, "But if an island merges with this one, then what happens?"

Nina pointed a finger. "Clever. I thought so."

"When the gods come together, all magic is in the same place. Conflict ensues between them," Elder Quilqi said. "You've already felt the effects. Uncle Earth could barely protect you from the volcano while the islands collided."

"And Uncle Smith and Entle Love have barely been answering prayers at all." Ichu looked worried. "The Aunts, Uncles, and Entles are going to fight?"

"How does that even work? Don't the chayus come from Uncle Earth, or Aunt Sea, or one of the others? Would chayus just stop working?" Silluka was getting more confused by the moment.

Elder Quilqi gave them a rueful smile. "Not conflict *between* the gods of the Huaca—well, maybe some—but conflict between the *factions* of gods." She pointed to Lugopo. "Their creepy crawly gods will be rooting for their people. So will the Eztli Mecatl's."

"A fiery death with whirling knives! I will design new tortures from the abyss!" Lugopo raised two tentacles in triumph, then used another to tap their circlet. "All in good fun, naturally."

"They speak?" Nina raised a bushy eyebrow. "I think I prefer signing."

"Lugopo is quite inventive," Elder Quilqi said.

Silluka was suddenly aware of Lugopo's weight on her shoulder. "So...are you going to be fighting us now? Like the desert Allwiya?" She didn't want to brush them off, but their many exultations of destruction and chaos didn't seem as lighthearted, now.

"Tangling tentacles! Don't go estranging your friends, girl." The elder paced between them and Nina. "Gods will come into contention, yes. But they don't want to destroy their followers either. Even gods have limits, and the core is stronger than us all. Most likely, we will hear of contests and tournaments soon. Ways to find the new ranking of the islands."

"There's already a match between Misini and Huaca, scheduled for next week," Nina offered. "The Misini claim their magic is stronger, of course."

Silluka didn't know what that name meant, but something else had grabbed her attention. "Wait. *Who* is deciding contests between gods?"

"Who has something at stake?" Elder Quilqi fixed her with a stare.

"The gods themselves," Ichu breathed. "This is why the Eztli Mecatl are pushing inland so fast. Their god has changed somehow, pushing the original turtlemen away. They want to cement control, with them in charge."

"Hmm." Nina sat back with a thump. "Hadn't thought of that."

"I told you I had a reason for picking these four," Elder Quilqi grinned.

"Then these contests must only be decided when the gods are near each other, in the core, and under their islands," Nina confirmed. "Though I still don't know why you think *these* people will be worthy champions, Mother."

"Wait, *that's* why you brought us here, you did? Making us fight against the gods?" Cosquella stood up to her full height. Silluka frowned at the elder. Was that all she saw in them? Pawns for a fight?

"Shifting lands, girl, I'm not tying you a sled and dragging you through the desert. You did that on your own. There are big events coming, once in a lifetime events. You can be a part of them, or you can watch them change the world around you." She looked at all of them, in turn. Ichu flinched back almost immediately, Cosquella hunched her wide shoulders forward, and Lugopo went rigid on her shoulder. Then it was Silluka's turn. Even braced for what was coming, Elder Quilqi's eyes were a physical weight in her head, bearing down on her. Her eyes started watering, but she held the old woman's gaze as long as she could, then broke, panting.

"Are you in, or out?" There was a feeling of finality to the statement.

Silluka pulled in a long breath. There was no question. "I'm in."

"I shall rain destruction on my enemies!" She assumed Lugopo meant that as a "yes."

"I go where my sister goes," Ichu said quietly.

"And I have nowhere else to go," Cosquella said, "but I have friends here, I do." She clasped Silluka's hand.

Nina gave a low whistle from behind her desk. Silluka, somehow, had half-forgotten the giant woman.

"You've done it again, Mother. I don't know how, but you have." She turned a baleful glare on their little group.

"You have no idea what you're in for."

Adversary

Akamu entered the hut perched on top of a stone outcrop looking over a small oasis. The sun was shading into night, and the bluff was polished to a smooth surface. Only a fortunate dip in the sandstone here, a hundred paces across or more, gave shelter from the wind that blew across this barren part of the stable desert. It allowed the small oasis here to flourish, complete with scrubby plants, a few stunted trees, and even a few fish. Farmed carefully, it was enough to keep maybe one person alive.

"Coaxoch," he said by greeting. "You have something for me?" He was away from his patrol. He had just enough time to tunnel through the sand back to them with *Quirra Digs a Hole* before he was missed. If he was quick.

The ancient Eztli Mecatl looked up from the vial she was studying. She was old enough that the gray skin around her scaly beak was shading to stone white. Beside her bubbled a noxious substance in a rough bowl. Herbs and fish guts were strewn about the table. She'd been here long before the island was close enough to cause danger, one of the first to flee the oppressive regime of the invaders, and the odd change in their god. But her beak could still crush iron, and her clear blue eyes regarded him for a long moment with keen intelligence before she picked up the vial and gestured with it.

"I do. Confirmation. But I suspect you already know, you do, what I'm going to say. Otherwise, you wouldn't have brought this to me. So tell me, Akamu of the stone warriors: what would happen if the worst came to pass? If the confrontation when the islands' assembly is tainted? Do you know what it means?"

Akamu sighed, wiping a hand across his face. Then he stood tall and formed both hands into a ball, releasing a portion of *Tortoise's Growth* from where he'd stored it in his core earlier. *Tortoise's Hard Shell* was a good shield against inquisitive ears. Even powerful ones.

"I do. The confrontation of the gods is in danger. And Uncle Smith is a traitor."

THE END OF BOOK 1 OF THE SHIFTING LANDS

ACKNOWLEDGEMENTS

This is a story I've had bumping around in my brain since (checks notes) 2012. It was originally about a society that migrated south to a new island, and practiced martial arts magic, sort of combining the moves of Tai Chi in different sequences.

I got about twelve chapters in, and realized I wasn't good enough to write the story, so I put it on hold. In the meantime, I continued my own martial arts practice in Wado-Ryu Karate, and recently tested to San-Dan in that system.

At the beginning of 2023 I read through an amazing book written in 2000 called *Origins: The Evolution of Continents, Oceans and Life*, by Rod Redfern. It details how the continental plates move, and how that affected life on Earth over millions and billions of years.

At the same time, I was beginning to read the developing genre of progression fantasy, where the heroes continue to get more powerful across a whole series. They often travel to new lands and learn the world is much bigger than they thought. This book is definitely a bit of an homage to *Cradle*, by Will Wight, one of the most enjoyable series I've read in a long time.

These three things—the original story, tectonic plate movement, and progression fantasy—sparked a crazy collection of ideas in my brain. I would start a multi-book series, where tectonic plates moved 400+ times faster than on our world. That would of course cause devastating weather, and the world would be uninhabitable. So, the gods would protect their worshipers from the worst effects.

This is what I came up with. Silluka, Ichu, Lugopo, Elder Quilqi, and Cosquella are only at the beginning of a wild journey. I anticipate running about eight books in total. We'll see how that goes.

As always, this book wouldn't have come about without a lot of help. Thanks and much love first go to my wife Heather for supporting (and dealing with) me for 20 years of marriage this year. She's also an excellent copy editor.

Go check out Serene Chia's art. She created a fantastic cover, and I look forward to more from her. Thanks also to the intrepid READ group for their ideas, feedback, and help as I run this still-growing publishing company.

Finally, thank you to everyone who backed the Space Wizard Science Fantasy Year 3 campaign! You're all awesome.

ABOUT THE AUTHOR

William C. Tracy writes and publishes queer science fiction and fantasy through his indie press Space Wizard Science Fantasy (spacewizardsciencefantasy.com).

His largest work is the Dissolutionverse: a space opera with music-based magic, including ten books and an RPG. He also has a standalone epic fantasy with seasonal fruit-based magic, a nonfiction book about body mechanics and correct posture, and a hard sci-fi trilogy with generational colony ships and a planet covered by a sentient fungal entity.

William is an NC native and a lifelong fan of science fiction and fantasy. He has a master's degree in mechanical engineering, and has both designed and operated heavy construction machinery. He has also trained in Wado-Ryu karate since 2003 and runs his own dojo in Raleigh, NC. He is an avid video and board gamer, a beekeeper, a reader, and of course, a writer.

You can get a free Dissolutionverse novelette by signing up for William's mailing list at spacewizardsciencefantasy.com

Follow him on Bluesky at wctracy.bsky.social, Threads at threads.net/@tracywc, and Twitter at @wctracy for writing updates, cat and bee pictures, and thoughts on martial arts.

Please take a moment to review this book at your favorite retailer's website, Goodreads, or simply tell your friends!